Praise for the
RI██████
WA██KINS

"*Definitely looking forward to reading more from this author.*"
– K. Warren

"*Omg, the intensity of this book is incredible.*"
–Holly Epperson

"*I did not want to put it down once I started reading it.*"
– Gladys Harrison

"*I thought this was a darn good story! I highly recommend it to anyone who likes a strong female character. Lots of action.*"
– TJ

"*Great book full of twists. Loved the ending. Totally unexpected. Can't wait for a sequel. Was a great read. Wow!*"
– Sonia Brumfield

"*Grabbed me from the first chapter and was a wild ride with lots of action! Enjoyed the whole story, looking forward to reading more from Richter Watkins. Don't pass up the chance to read Cool Heat!*"
– Betty Jane

"*Very intense from beginning to end. I couldn't go to sleep until I finished reading…I'll definitely be reading more books by Richter Watkins.*"
– Mary Beth

RICHTER WATKINS

COOL HEAT

Pryde Multimedia, LLC

Cool Heat

Copyright © 2013 by Richter Watkins
Published by Pryde Multimedia, LLC

Dear Reader,

For a writer, some projects are just a lot more fun than others. This was one of those stories where the characters on both sides were so colorful and engaging for me that I may have to see them again in some future project.

Richter

Acknowledgments

Thanks to the kind folks at the Lahonton Fish Hatchery and the best reporter at the Tahoe Daily Tribune.

COOL HEAT

For Aaron, Richard and Jocelyn and those great trips to Lake Tahoe.

1

A door? Or did something fall?
Alone that Sunday afternoon in the closed fish hatchery, Sydney Jesup, holding a tiny cutthroat fingerling trout in one gloved hand, a syringe in the other, paused when she heard a noise that might have been a door in the other building. She ignored the hum of generators, focusing only on the noise.

Finally, deciding it was her overwrought imagination, Sydney just shook her head and laughed at herself. All the damn stress had built to the point where she found herself hearing boogie men and talking to fish. She wiped sweat off her forehead with her arm. It was a lot cooler in the cavernous hatchery than out in the boiling sun, but she had on rubber boots and jeans, and that didn't help.

But then something made her stop again to listen.

Her weapon, a snub Colt—her backup piece when she was with the sheriff's department and, later, chief investigator for the DA in South Lake—was in her shoulder bag fifty feet away in the clean room. She suddenly felt naked.

C'mon, ease down. Damn. It's probably Dave.

I'm getting paranoid, she thought. The fish hatchery in Lahonton, managed by her cousin, was the safest place for her anywhere around Lake Tahoe these days, she figured, mostly because it was government property.

She went back to work, shaking off the lingering feeling of caution. What she needed to do was concentrate on the problem at hand. They were dealing with an outbreak of Ich and Furunculosis that had nearly destroyed the cutthroat trout. They'd been using UV disinfection after having had to euthanize something like a quarter-million production fish that had been targeted for release by the Pyramid Lake Paiute Tribe. Only about two hundred thousand were saved and released into Walker Lake.

"You think you have it bad…" she said as she inserted a syringe with red dye into the fins of the tiny fingerling. She held the tiny body firmly yet carefully between the fingers of her left gloved hand, while the flow of negative thoughts swirled angrily in her mind about the disastrous investigation and the deaths of her two witnesses.

She struggled to stay focused on this welcomed temporary job. Her cousin, and about everyone else she knew, had advised her in no uncertain terms to get the hell out of the area, take a long vacation. Move. Let it go. And she knew they were right. She couldn't win, but she couldn't let go, either. *I'm nuts,* she thought. *Maybe I'm getting OCD. Or is it obsessive stupidity disorder.* She chuckled to herself.

Lost in bleak thoughts, it took a moment to realize that she was definitely hearing something. The clean-room door opened. She was no longer alone in the "wet" building with the fish tanks.

"Dave, that you?" she called out, knowing even as she spoke that she shouldn't have, not without knowing for certain who it was. *Christ, I'm getting rusty.*

A man stood in the doorway.

"The hatchery is closed to the public," she said. "And this building is in quarantine."

He stepped forward from the clean room, a dark cutout beneath the dull ceiling lights of the cavernous interior of the hatchery's main floor.

Ah, shit.

She saw the gun. This was no tourist. The short, heavyset guy moved gingerly and awkwardly down the center aisle, his gun hand shaking a bit, like he was nervous or even a little drunk.

Thorp sent a drunk to get me on government property?

He was in enough light now that Sydney could see the weapon he carried was most likely a Glock fitted with a suppressor as long as the weapon's barrel. Extending from the trigger housing like a goiter was a TLR-1 light, an utterly useless bit of additional apparatus.

He was now about twenty feet away. A real pro would never have come down the center aisle. Or, for that matter, come in from the clean room. The side door would have been the preferred entrance. He was giving her the fish tanks for cover and the side door for an escape attempt.

Unless he had a partner waiting out there.

The intruder stopped. "The man says hello," he said as his other hand came up to steady the one with the weapon, and then he turned, as if mimicking a TV-show detective.

Sydney ducked and bolted between the tanks for the side door, holding the fish bucket up by her head as a shield. The gunman fired multiple times, the *crack crack crack* amplified in the metal building like cannon blasts.

Bullets ricocheted off fish tanks, generators, the walls. She felt a sharp sting on one side and as she crossed the side aisle, another sting on the inside of her leg.

Sydney dropped the bucket as she slammed out the side door, hoping like hell the shooter was alone, that she wasn't going to run into his backup as she emerged into the brutally harsh sunlight. More bullets clanged the door behind her as she sprinted between the outside mesh-enclosed fish reservoirs, glancing left and right and looking for a potential ambusher.

In her visual search, she spotted a black Ford pickup truck parked over by the visitor's kiosk near the front entrance, where no vehicle was supposed to be. She believed her wounds were superficial, probably just grazes. Otherwise, she figured she wouldn't be able to sprint all out. She ran in the one-hundred-ten-degree heat under a blazing sun toward the open field.

The hatchery was isolated between the rise of the Sierras, a quarter-mile west, and a steep hill leading up to the highway on the other side. She headed toward the old farm buildings a hundred fifty yards north of the hatchery.

Sydney was in great physical condition, but the rubber goulashes were like dead weights on her feet, and she had to get them off. When she glanced back, she saw the shooter getting into the pickup. At the barn, she paused to get her breath and looked back to see the bastard driving across the field. She ran to the street, stopping there just long enough to yank off the goulashes, her socks coming with them.

Glancing back, she saw the pickup having some trouble getting through a rough patch, slowed now to a crawl for a brief moment before lunging forward. With no time to put the socks on, Sydney took off running again, the sizzling tarmac quickly scorching the bottoms of her feet. She headed for the closest housing development, cursing herself again for not having her weapon on her.

You really didn't think they'd come after you there? You idiot! Damn, girl!

The only thing she did have was her cell phone. But, given that the local sheriff was best friends with her worst enemy, she had no intention of calling law enforcement.

She heard the truck gunning up the bank by the barn a hundred yards behind her. Her right leg was starting to give out from the stress of the wound and the intense heat, reducing her run to a limp as her left side wound also flared. And, adding insult to injury, the boiling tarmac was burning her bare feet. Ahead, the housing development looked abandoned.

Where the hell are you people? Church or the goddamn mall?

That's when she heard the deep-throated purr of a big engine. She turned and saw a red Mustang convertible swing onto the road coming from the highway, heading her way about two or three times the legal speed.

The backup?

She figured, given his speed and her location, she had nowhere to go.

I'm dead. You had to leave your fucking weapon in the clean room. Get yourself killed. Jesus!

Caught in the middle of the street, Sydney had nowhere to run, nowhere to hide. She turned toward the onrushing car. Definitely a Mustang, but when it barreled closer, she recognized the macho front grill. A Shelby, no less. A beautiful death machine.

That bastard Thorp got me like he said he would.

She faced the onrushing Mustang. Her only regret at the moment was that she didn't have any way to fight back.

The Mustang's engine backed down into a lower gear, giving off a powerful guttural grumble. The guy in it looked Mexican—black curly hair, music blasting on his radio—for him, a fun day for an easy kill. Would he shoot her or run her over? She decided he'd shoot her to avoid damaging his beautiful machine.

Sydney Jesup faced death with the same attitude she'd faced a lot of things in her life lately: she gave the finger to the Mexican killer in the bright red Shelby Mustang convertible and prepared for a bad end…

Fuck you and the horse you're riding in on.

2

What the hell do we have here?

Marco Cruz pondered the question as New Amsterdam's "Turn Out the Lights" boomed on his radio. The lady on this hot Sunday afternoon stood in the middle of the street in a bloody, sweaty T-shirt, bloody jeans, no shoes, no socks, bare feet on boiling hot macadam, flipping him the bird as his music blasted. He expected, when he got close enough to see, she'd be some haggy, worn-out drug addict on her last legs.

He turned off the radio.

This is my welcome-home committee? I didn't do it, whatever it is.

He eased down the Shelby's big 660 engine into first gear. The smart voice in his head, the one that's supposed to protect a person, told him to wave *hey, have a nice day,* and get the hell out of there. But that was a voice he never did listen to. Coming to the rescue of some distressed female was such a quaint, old-fashioned notion, but instincts are what they are.

It had been, until now, such a great ride coming back to Tahoe after what he'd been through. He had been just one more former border-patrol agent who'd spent two miserable years in a Mexican prison and was now, after services rendered to Uncle Sam, "free and sanitized," as the Homeland agent told him on their last meeting.

"Free, free at last," he'd yelled more than once as he hit speeds equal to the one-hundred-ten-degree temperature across the desert up 395, laughing and singing, his curly black hair popping and dancing in the wind, his life back on track and big things ahead. He'd done his time in hell, now he wanted a little taste of heaven and, to him, Tahoe was heaven.

Don't stop, you fool.

He downshifted the magnificent beast to a crawl and drifted up to the woman.

He leaned toward her and said, "You okay?" About as pathetic a question as he could muster.

She looked shocked, as if he wasn't what she'd expected. Her offending hand dropped to her side, the angry finger holstered.

He saw her turn, as if whatever was chasing her might be catching up. He turned and, indeed, there was a pickup heading toward them a quarter-mile back. Without an invite, the lady opened the passenger door, slid in all bloody, sweaty, and—now up close, he realized—she reeked of a rank, fishy smell.

"Get the hell out of here fast!" she commanded. "That moron is aiming to kill me and he'll kill you as well."

As if to amplify the truth, the guy in the pickup was now leaning out the window and started pumping lead in their direction, the Shelby taking at least two pings.

Marco jumped on the gas and the rocket of an engine threw them back in their seats as it shot forward. He weaved violently to throw off the shooter and put some fast distance between them, then made a hard turn at the intersection and headed south.

"You coming from church?" he asked her.

In spite of her situation and condition, she actually emitted a dry chuckle. "No. Actually, I was injecting cutthroat trout."

"The hatchery?"

"Yeah."

In an instant, he liked this woman's hardcore attitude. "I take it the blood is from gunshot wounds?"

"Yes."

"You take any deep penetration?"

"Not lately. These are superficial."

Didn't look all that superficial to him. He figured she was no regular civilian.

He shot down the road shifting gears and hitting sixty, seventy, eighty, ninety.

Glancing at her, he saw her looking back at their pursuer but saw no panic, no terrible fear on her face. Good-looking woman with a street-hard disposition. Her reddish hair snapped like flames in the hot wind.

"You want the nearest hospital, once we lose this guy?"

"No."

"Sheriff's station?"

A more definitive, "No!"

He swore softly to himself, then shook his head. He had a real live one here. He turned up the 207 toward Daggett Pass and headed for his uncle's place high above Lake Tahoe.

"That an ex who shot up you and my car?"

"No. I don't date short, fat guys," she said. "He can't shoot worth a shit. I think he's high or drunk. Maybe he'll drive off the road and kill himself."

On the border, the men he'd worked with before all his troubles called good-looking, kick-ass female agents *cool heat*. He figured he had one sitting next to him and, at this stage of his life, getting caught up in some chick's mess was the last thing he needed.

Why couldn't she at least be ugly, toothless, and fat?

He wondered if, in some past life, he'd really pissed off the gods.

3

Sydney Jesup struggled to regroup. Moments ago, she'd been facing death and now found herself sitting in a very fast Shelby convertible driven by a wild-haired guy blowing through the Sierras.

"Thanks for picking me up," she said.

"My pleasure. You don't like hospitals or cops, and somebody wants you dead. I can't wait to hear what's going on."

"Sorry about that."

Sydney Jesup figured her good fortune was not merely being picked up by this guy, rather than being run over or shot by him. It was a certainly a bonus that he had a very fast car and knew how to drive—all nice qualities, for sure—but she suspected he was more than just a guy on a nice Sunday drive. She watched him as he kept tracking their pursuer in the car's mirrors without missing a beat on the squirrely road, yet could carry on conversation. *He's used to bad situations,* she thought. It didn't hurt he was nice looking in a rugged, unfinished sort of way.

How lucky can a should-be-dead girl get?

"You don't date short, fat guys?"

"No."

He grinned with a head shake. "Maybe that's why he wants to kill you."

"Maybe. Fortunately, he was a lousy shot."

"Good enough to get my car. And you look like he wasn't totally off the mark with you."

"You shoot a whole clip at thirty feet and you don't get a kill, you're in the wrong profession."

"You have any idea who he is?"

"No. I have plenty of enemies. I'd have to check my Rolodex."

Sydney tried to look behind them, holding her side, but it hurt too much and she turned back to using the side mirror...no sign of their pursuer.

"You don't by any chance have a gun?" she asked.

"No." He gave her a raised-eyebrow glance. "Not at the moment. Don't worry—he won't catch up. Who are you that somebody is trying so hard to take you out? I kinda need to know that while were together, even if it's a short time. He knows my car. Red Shelby convertibles aren't all that common."

"Slow down a little," she said. "Getting stopped by a sheriff or CHP won't be a good scenario, and this area is something of a speed trap."

"You have a background in law, the military, or crime?" he asked as he backed off the accelerator.

"Sheriff and DA's office in South Lake," she said. "Past tense. You from around the Tahoe area?"

"Reno. I have relatives up here. I haven't been back in about seven years or so."

"Military?"

"That and border, but now I'm a free multimillionaire in the making."

"Unemployed."

"Temporarily," he said. "Actually, I was on my way"—he took a sharp turn with race-car finesse—"to a job interview. You're an unexpected diversion."

"Sorry 'bout that. It's a risk when you pick up random chicks on the road."

"I'll try and remember that."

They sailed up through the curves that led to the top of the mountain.

"I'm Marco Cruz," he said, breaking the silence.

"Sydney Jesup. Thanks again. Listen, I know a place on the other side of the lake where you can drop me."

"I'll make a stop first," he said. "I have a safe place where you can get your wounds cleaned and secured."

"I really need to get across the lake. I have a doc friend who'll deal with them."

"Sorry," he continued, "but I'm not running around the lake in daylight in this car with a shooter tracking me. Maybe he's in contact with friends who are waiting on the lake side."

She thought of arguing, but he was right to worry about that. If the source of the botched hit was coming from Incline Village, there could be five guys out there looking for them. This guy had all the qualities of the macho alpha-male types she usually bumped heads with, but in this case it was exactly what she needed.

Don't look a gift horse in the mouth, as her father liked to say. She put her head back. She knew Thorp wanted her dead, but he was too smart to pull a dumb stunt like this. She had the feeling she knew who the shooter was but just couldn't place him.

"You have water? I'm really thirsty."

"No. I finished the bottle I had. I'll get more in a minute. When I get to my uncle's, we'll get you rehydrated. Runnin' around in that dry heat will take down anything short of a two-hump camel."

Just over Daggett Pass, he turned off on a side road, then again on another feeder dirt road back along the mountain. He slowed to a crawl and put the top up.

"Where is this place?" she asked, not feeling very comfortable getting bumped around on a dirt road, Mustangs not being off-road vehicles.

"The last place your shooter wants to show up. And it's hard to find. End of this old logging road. Not far. Close to the top of the mountain above Kingsbury Village. I haven't been there in nearly a decade but spent a lot of time there as a kid. It's a great place. View of the whole valley."

"I'm sure it's nice," she said. Small talk at this point wasn't appealing to her. But the man had saved her life, and she needed him to get her to a place that would work as a safe house, so she indulged him.

"You didn't like border work?" she asked.

"I did. For awhile." He didn't elaborate.

"I'll get out of your curly locks quick as I can," she assured him. "Who owns this house?"

Before he could answer that, his cell phone rang. He touched the synced phone button on the steering wheel. "Hey."

"Marco, when you getting here?"

"Be there in about two minutes."

"Great. Can't wait to see you."

Marco hung up. "You'll love my uncle. He's like an old-fashioned mountain man. I loved coming up here."

She was quickly losing any desire to further engage in conversation, and she wondered just how much bleed-out there was.

She put a hand under her belt, and it didn't feel very good.

He must have noticed her movement, because he tried to ease along, but now she was too miserable to appreciate it. She had her eyes closed, felt her face muscles tighten. No hiding the pain any longer. Sometimes the pain of a wound didn't show up until the adrenalin subsided. She was feeling the burn now, especially in her side.

She had to call her cousin to get over the hatchery, but she didn't want him going over there right now. She opened her eyes again and stared out the windshield as they turned toward the lake. It appeared like a mirage through the big lodgepole pines and outcrops of boulders.

Ahead, perched high above Kingsbury Village and Zephyr Cove, the approaching stone and wood house indeed had a world-class view. The sun was suspended on the mountains across the lake. It would be down in half an hour. Already, shadows were sliding off the western slopes toward Tahoe City and Meeks Bay.

She said, "Your uncle's?"

"Yes. Eagle's view of nearly the entire twenty-two miles of Lake Tahoe, the 'big water.' He and I once walked around the entire shoreline, the *Da'aw 'a:go'a*, as the Washo Indians called it. Did it in one day."

He eased to a crawl to avoid jolting her along the last stretch of rutted dirt road.

"He's got this *temescal* sweat hut and rock pool. Do you a world of good once you get those wounds dealt with. We used to sit out there at night. Nothing like it. The sky and the lake are—"

"Sounds nice, but I don't think I'll have time," she said, cutting him off.

They lost sight of the house for a moment, then passed some trees, and it came back into view. And with it, a dozen or more cars parked near the house. Looked like a lot of people up on the deck.

"You couldn't be safer," Marco said, as though anticipating her next comment. "Nobody in their right mind would mess with my uncle and his friends, even if they could find this place."

"Exactly who is your uncle?" she asked.

He parked behind a white Lexus. "That man coming to meet us. I'll be right back."

No way. Not happening. "Your uncle is Tony Cillo?"

"Yes. Why?"

"I think you should get me the hell out of here, if you don't mind."

"Marco! Welcome home, boy!" the big voice of Tony Cillo boomed as he bounded down the steps of the porch.

Marco, half out of the car, glanced at her and then turned to his uncle. "Let me talk to him and tell him I'll be back."

Sydney tried to protest, but he was already walking toward Cillo. Up on the porch stood half the illegal bookies and crooks in Lake Tahoe.

Had she the capacity at the moment to laugh, she would have. Her hero, her savior, was the nephew of Tony "Macaroni" Cillo!

Are you fucking kidding me?

Then, seeing the key still in the ignition, Sydney figured she could very easily slide over behind the wheel, steal the guy's Shelby, and get the hell out of there. It was manual, and she was right at home with a stick…

4

Marco's uncle bounded down the steps, looking all thrilled to see Marco. There were at least a dozen people behind him up on the deck and a *WELCOME HOME* sign on the porch railing. He came up toward the car with a big smile, saying, "I didn't believe it when you said you were coming back here."

"Yeah." Marco got out, glancing at his passenger.

Marco's uncle gave him a bear hug, a slap on his arm, then stepped back. "Good to see you, boy. Been a long time."

"You didn't need to throw a party for me," Marco said.

"Hell, yes, I did."

"You're looking good," Marco said, thinking his uncle looked like he'd put on about thirty pounds. Fat and happy.

"For an old, flea-bitten dog," Cillo said with a wide grin. "Damn, it's been way too long."

Cillo, now seeing Marco had a passenger, lowered his voice. "Heard some about all your troubles south of the border from your mom, but you don't look any worse for wear. Gonna get you fixed up. Big things happening." His eyes shifted to the car. "You got yourself a real serious ride. Damn fine car. You're gonna have to give me a tour in that, but first an intro to your lady."

"She's not exactly my lady," Marco said. "Look, it's great to be back, but I have something I need to deal with." Marco glanced up on the porch, where the party had slowed and attention was on him.

Under the porch, Cillo's old wolf-dog, Cujo, watched with yellow-eyed suspicion. That the dog was still alive was amazing. Had to be twenty years old, he thought. A real survivor. Like his master.

On the deck, and no doubt up the hill behind the house at the sweat hut and pool, he heard the shrill giggles of liquored-up females.

"Sure, sure. Whatever it is, we'll deal with it." Cillo waved his arm to embrace the Tahoe basin. "Things have changed. Something I want to get you involved in on the ground floor…if you're of a mind to get rich, and I'm sure you are."

Marco grabbed his uncle's arm and said, "I got a little problem here." Marco realized his uncle was a little high. "Something I need to deal with now. I didn't think there would be so many people."

"Hell, those are friends and associates of mine and soon to be of yours," Cillo said. He stooped to get a better look at the female in the passenger seat of the Mustang.

"There's a problem," Marco said again.

"With women, there always is. Nothin' can't be fixed," Cillo said. "What's the deal? She angry at you?"

"No. She's been shot."

Cillo's expression darkened after he took another look. Did he recognize her? Now Marco had his full attention.

"Shot!" Cillo moved forward and peered again into the Mustang. "What the hell's going on? Christ, you know who—?"

"Somebody tried to kill her…at the hatchery. I picked her up running down the road in her bare feet. She needs somewhere—"

"Hell, no," Cillo said. "No-no-no. Can't be. Damn, boy, why would you bring that woman, of all people, here? You shoulda dropped her off at the Carson Valley medical half a mile up the road from the hatchery."

"We had a bit of a chase. And she's not interested in hospitals or cops right now. She didn't explain. She needs her wounds cleaned."

His uncle gave him a cold, hard look. "This isn't good, Marco. That woman ain't welcome up here under any circumstances. She's a goddamn pariah around the lake."

Behind them, the party seemed to slow as if sensing collectively something was wrong.

"I don't know anything about that," Marco said. "All I know is I found her running from the hatchery over in Gardnerville. Some guy chased us in a pickup but I lost him. Bastard put a couple bullets in her and in my car. She needs help."

Cillo turned as a couple men came down the steps from the porch, drinks in hand, celebrating, calling to Marco.

"I'm dealing with something here, boys," Cillo said. "We'll be up in a minute. Go on back to the party."

The men stopped but didn't go back up on the porch. They were staring at the car.

Marco said, "I need some painkillers. You have Vicodin or anything? And if you have a medical kit—"

"Boy, you don't understand nothin'. You picked up the wrong goddamn woman to bring up here on my property." Tony Cillo's face muscles tightened. "You get that bitch outta here fast. Drop her wherever. In the fucking lake if you have to. Just away from here."

"Hey, the lady's got wounds that need to be cleaned. And there's a fucking shooter—"

"Get her outta here now, Marco. Call me when you don't have her anywhere near you. She's poison. Go. I'd as soon nobody knows she's with you. Call me when you're rid of her. Move before these guys see her. She might end up with more than two bullets in her. I'll explain about that crazy bitch later when you're rid of her. Go!"

Marco, enraged by his uncle's attitude but seeing the gathering of his friends, knew he had to leave. They looked like they had already recognized her. *Something going on here in paradise that can't be good,* he thought. *I stumbled into a real mess.*

Marco said, "I'm going, but I got a shooter out there looking for her. You have a piece on you?"

"Sorry, can't help you there," Cillo said. "You need to get rid of her and get rid of her fast. Go, and don't be thinking of coming back here until she's out of your hands. And don't get into her shit, Marco. You've had enough trouble in your life. Time to know when to fold 'em, as the song says."

Marco turned and went back to the car. He slid in behind the wheel, turned the key, and backed around, glancing one last time at his uncle, then pulled out.

"You aren't winning any popularity contests up here," Marco said. "What'd you do, kill all the babies?"

She had her arms wrapped around her stomach, her face pale, and it seemed to him her side had new blood. Then he saw blood on the steering wheel. "What's this?"

"I was going to take the car and go. Didn't work out so well. Couldn't get over the damn console."

He shook his head. *I left Mexico and the border to get away from this kind of crap.* He needed to deal with her real quick, and he had no desire to be out on the road, especially in daylight. He was going to have to pull over and deal with the wounds whether she liked it or not.

He was very pissed at his uncle's attitude, but maybe, once he understood what was going on, he'd have a change of mind. But first he had to deal with this woman, then get her off his hands fast.

"If I'd stopped for that cup of coffee at Starbucks…"

Sydney Jesup grimaced and nodded. "I'd be dead and you'd be seven dollars poorer."

5

Sydney knew Cillo and the men who'd come down to greet Marco. They ran the loan-sharking business among other things. "I wish you had told me who your uncle was," she said as they drove down the dirt road through the heavy lodgepole pines.

"I had no reason to think it mattered."

"I said I was with the DA and sheriff's department. Nobody there I saw is a normal, law-abiding citizen. Maybe two plus two?"

"Yeah, well, I haven't been up here in over seven years. And you weren't interested in bringing in the law, so I figured you were on a different path."

Realizing the magnitude of the impact this was going to have on both of them, Sydney said, "This isn't good. You need to drop me off and get out of this."

"Maybe you need to tell me what the hell is going on."

"Maybe the best thing for you is not to know anything from me. Sooner you're free of me, the better."

"Yeah, well, first things first. You have bullet wounds. You need medical attention, and I'm not free of you until I know you're not going to die on me. Been through that kind of mess. I don't need a repeat."

She didn't ask what that was about. Her little fantasy relationship in her mind was now over. "The wounds are minor, and I'm not going to be your problem."

"What the hell did you do you have so many enemies?" Marco asked.

"It's what they think I can do that's the problem."

"Who are they?"

"Everybody who stands to profit from the biggest, most corrupt deal this lake has ever seen."

The car bounced in a rut and she made a painful grunt. Marco slowed and found a spot where he could pull off the road. He backed in between some pines and stopped.

"What are you doing?" Sydney asked.

"We'll wait a bit. I don't want to be running around in this car while there's still some twilight, not with a shooter out there. We need to get those wounds wrapped. You die on me with your blood and DNA all over my car…won't look good."

Sydney had no desire to hang around anywhere near the Cillo crowd. Her sense of good fortune at getting picked up by Marco took a bit of a hit. She trusted none of them. As far as she knew, they could well be the ones who sent the shooter.

"I'm not bleeding that much. Just get me across the lake. There's a house there that isn't occupied—"

"I will, just not yet," he said. "In daylight, this car stands out like a Roman candle." He glanced at the seat and the floor mat.

"Sorry I'm messing up your car. And your homecoming."

"Yeah, well, it is what it is," he said. "Let me get something to wrap those wounds."

He popped the trunk, then got out. She saw him check the bullet holes on his way to the back. When he returned, he had a T-shirt and neat little stack of boxer shorts. At least they looked clean. In fact, new.

He opened her door and she reached out for them. "I can stick these to the wounds. That should contain any further bleed-out. I have this doctor friend in Tahoe City. It'll be dark soon. And I'll pay for cleaning and repairing your car."

"Let me take a look at the wounds. See how bad they are. I can wrap a T-shirt around and use the shorts to put enough pressure—"

"Not necessary. I can just stuff them against the wounds. I don't think they're all that bad."

His eyebrows arched. "Relax. I'm not operating. Just trying to see how bad you're hit. I've had plenty of field first aid, and I've seen about every kind of wound there is."

"My doctor friend—"

"Right now, I'm your field medic, so stop arguing. Scoot your legs out so I can reach you better."

After she'd complied, he gently pulled her shirt up to look at the side wound. She peeked, and it looked nasty. At least a three-inch cut.

He said, "It may have nicked a rib. You're lucky. You turned just a little and something vital would have taken the bullet."

He put a folded pair of his shorts on the wound and told her to hold it against it. Then he pulled out a pocketknife and made a cut in the T-shirt so he could rip it to make a long strip. He wrapped it around her torso and reached around to tie it, their faces close, making her look off at the trees.

She mocked herself for reacting to this guy like she was some teenybopper, feeling her cheeks get hot and her pulse quicken, wondering if her breath was as foul as it tasted.

"No major terrible with that one," he said, pulling back and checking his handiwork. "You'll probably need stitches. Or some QuikClot would work. Let's see the leg."

No way. "I don't think that's anything. I'll just put something there and we can get out of here," she said, feeling a lot more defensive about the location of that wound and the guy all over her, with her smelling from the sweat and working all morning with fish. The thing about him was his easy cockiness.

He paused and leveled dark-chocolate eyes at her. Not hostile so much as irritated. "Look, when somebody jumps into whatever swamp you're in, pulls you out, and wants to make sure you don't continue to bleed all over his new Shelby, maybe just let him tie up your wounds, all right? That too much to ask?"

"No, I guess not."

"And get over being sensitive or whatever. Believe me, I'm only interested in saving my car, not in seeing if you're put together different from every other female on this suffering planet. Okay?"

Fuck you, she thought. "Yes, okay."

"Unzip and I'll help you pull the jeans down."

For want of something better to come at him with, she said, "I figured you for Jockey briefs."

"I don't like confinement. Of any kind."

She hated that he could get a smile out of her so easily. She blamed her ridiculous reaction and lack of willpower on being dehydrated and the loss of blood. He did have a good sense of humor and, no doubt, had a long, sad trail of broken hearts behind him.

Then he said, as if to mollify her, "Believe me, if getting close to your crotch excites me, I'll have no choice but to shoot myself."

She let out a sardonic chuckle. *You win,* she thought, then said, trying to be as nonchalant about it as he was, "Fine. I guess there'll be no foreplay."

"You're in a Shelby. What more foreplay do you need?"

She smiled and shook her head. *I hate this guy,* she thought. *He's way too smooth.* She focused a moment on the woods. The rustle of squirrels chasing each other. Tahoe, sub-alpine, had not escaped the heat wave scorching the West or her own personal heat wave from this guy examining her up close and personal.

She surrendered, pulled down the zipper, and tried to help with the pants, lifting her behind up off the seat as he tugged. Once her jeans were down around her ankles, he gently pulled her knees apart to see the wound on her inner thigh. It wasn't as big as the one on her left side, but it still stung.

Even more than she hated that she smelled, was being all sweaty and bloody. At least she had on nice underwear. The thought made her eyes roll, and she shook her head at how ridiculous this was.

"What's short, fat boy shooting?" he asked, showing no interest in her discomforts, not sensing her embarrassment.

"A Glock fitted with a suppressor. And a TLR light."

He pressed against the wound with his boxer shorts. "You need to get these wounds cleaned up and professionally wrapped, but for now, this'll have to—" He stopped as a car came down the road from his uncle's place. It came fast. A Lexus. They watched it shoot past. The driver never looked in their direction. From what she could see, it wasn't his uncle.

She sat there, legs apart, smelling terrible, looking like shit, blood everywhere, this guy hovering over her, both of them staring out at the road. She hated feeling helpless, and now she was starting to think that at any moment, she could fall unconscious from lack of fluids and blood.

"I'm uncomfortable," she said. "Really uncomfortable."

"Let's get you wrapped and out of here."

He folded the blue boxers up against the cut, then wrapped another T-shirt strip around her leg and tied it snug. "That'll hold you."

He helped get her pants back up and zipped, then moved back and said, "This doc in Tahoe City somebody you can trust?"

"Yes. First I want to go to this house on the lake. It's really secluded, and I know the people who own it. I check on the place from time to time when they're gone. Get me there. It's a mile south of Tahoe City, where he lives. We can switch out vehicles there if you want."

He nodded. His expression of dark humor gave way to edginess now as he looked carefully down the road both ways before he closed her door, walked around to the driver's side, and got in. He started the engine, and that deep, powerful rumble was unlike anything she'd been riding lately.

"Is there a sweeter sound than that?" he said.

"It's nice."

You were really going to steal my car?"

"Just borrow it."

"You're looking a little pale. Sit back and relax."

"Don't go toward Incline," she said. "You've been away a long time. There's a new parkway around the main drag."

"Wouldn't Incline be faster?"

"It might be better if you go around South Lake and up the 89. Most of my problems emanate from Incline Village."

She thought, *I'm a wreck, somebody's trying to kill me, and this guy's uncle is embedded with Tahoe's underworld.* Could it get any better?

If she wasn't in so much pain at the moment, she would have laughed at the insanity of it all.

***

Marco Cruz had to get rid of this woman and her problems, but he was stuck with her right now. He couldn't just leave her out there knowing somebody wanted her dead. And him. And now he was getting interested in whatever the real issue was, given how his uncle had reacted.

"Answer me one question," he said as he curled down to the main road at Zephyr Cove and headed toward the State Line casinos. He was surprised at the amount of traffic. "Is whatever you're involved in something that's more than a personal vendetta or a revenge situation?"

"It's all of the above. Just drop me off and your uncle will explain the situation. I don't have the energy right now."

"You can't leave me in the dark," he said. "You're going to have to talk to me at some point."

"Not right now. I don't have the energy."

He nodded. The dehydration and loss of blood were taking her down. He had to get over to that house she wanted to go to and get some fluids in her. Then he had to find out what this was all about.

But he also had an urge to get her situated and just get on out of here. Head for San Diego or Phoenix. Tahoe wasn't looking so good any more.

6

When they were halfway between Zephyr Cove and the State Line casinos, Marco's cell rang. He looked at it, but didn't answer.

"Your uncle?" Sydney asked.

Marco nodded. "Look, I don't know what's going on, but I'm not thinking you should hang around Tahoe. After this doc friend of yours fixes you up, and you still don't want police involvement, is there a safe place for you to hide out until you fully recover? You have friends or relatives somewhere away from Tahoe where you can recuperate?"

"I'll figure it out. Once you drop me off, you're home free. Not your problem." She figured he was worried about what it might mean for him. "As long as you don't know where I went, or who I contacted, you can get away from this. Just get me across the lake."

"No problem. Unless, that is, somebody spots the car. I tried to get a piece from my uncle, but he wouldn't give me one. That makes me unhappy."

She wondered what his real reason for coming to Tahoe was and what he'd actually done in Mexico. There was a lot about Marco Cruz she was curious about.

Feeling like shit, thinking being hit by a couple of bullets—even only ricochets—wasn't a good thing, she looked over at this guy who'd saved her and said, with both sincerity and a bit of sarcasm, "Well, whatever else happens…on this day, you're my hero."

He glanced askance at her, eyes tight, and said, "Everybody's a hero on a good day, but nobody's a hero every day. Don't get used to it."

She smiled. Hard not to like this guy, whatever he was.

As they approached the half-dozen casinos on the South Shore, Sydney said, "You should take the Lake Parkway loop. It probably didn't exist when you were here last. It'll get you past the slow traffic at the casinos."

They went around back of the Montbleu, the newest of the hotels. Then she had him get off on the Pioneer Trail, avoiding Lake Tahoe Boulevard traffic altogether. It was longer but safer, the road most used by locals.

He asked, "This house you're going to safe?"

"The owners are very private. I come over now and then to check to see it's not been messed with. I don't broadcast it."

"How far?"

"A mile or so before you get to Tahoe City," she said. "It's past The Pines."

"Neighbors who might pay a visit?"

Babysitting her a little. But she was thankful. "The house sits back in the trees by the lake. No close neighbors. It's very secluded."

As they headed down a back road behind the State Line casinos, he said, "How deep is my uncle involved in whatever this is?"

"Half the people in Tahoe are knee deep in it one way or another," she said.

She watched him as he checked every truck and car, rode the mirrors constantly, and tried to keep from getting bottled up. When they approached the busy intersection of 89 and the 50, he slowed, pulled off, and waited a bit until the lights were turning in their favor, then he shot through and headed up the western side of the lake toward Camp Richardson.

Sydney had been so isolated since getting let go from the DA's office that appreciating somebody who might understand what she faced was hard to resist. But she couldn't drag him any further into this, much as she might want to. What the future would be, once he hooked back up with his uncle, was another story.

They headed north up 89, past Camp Richardson and past Emerald Bay, the traffic not nearly as heavy as around the South Shore. But there was little room to run if somebody was parked along the road waiting for a red Mustang convertible. Then, past Emerald Bay, it thinned out.

"We close?" Marco asked.

"Just up ahead."

"It has a feeder road?"

"Yes. You can go down with lights out. I'll tell you when we're close"

7

S haun Corbin couldn't believe his bad luck. He'd shot at least fifteen goddamn bullets at the woman and she still got away.

You goddamn fool. You botched it. She got away. Thorp will have you killed for this! Now he was in the crisis of his life. He'd made a big, big mistake. His whole thing was that he would get her before his cousin brought in a pro. It'd make him a hero. This greatest of all ideas he'd ever had—killing Sydney Jesup so his cousin would finally accept him as worthy—now looked like the stupidest idea he, or anyone, had ever had. Hitting the steering wheel and dash with his fist, he knew he'd made the biggest screwup of his miserable life.

"I didn't kill her!" he yelled to a deaf universe. "She was right there! Right there and she got away!"

I'm a fucking dead man.

He was horrified, astounded. "I had her right there, right in front of me, and I missed." His stomach—a swamp polluted with an acidic compound of alcohol, speed, and fear—felt as if it would eat through the walls.

Corbin sat numb in his truck in the Barton Memorial Hospital parking lot looking at his laptop for all the damn medical centers around the lake. There had to be twenty of them or more. And medical-care places all over South Lake. More in Incline. Urgent cares and a Kings Beach Wellness Center. *Jesus!* She could be anywhere. And no sign of that red Mustang.

He felt sick to his stomach. Why in hell had he thought this was the greatest move ever? He would have to check them all and do it fast. She wouldn't go to her condo. She wasn't stupid. And who the hell was the guy who picked her up? A boyfriend? Or some random asshole? At least the fool drove a car you couldn't hide.

I need to find that damn car, Corbin thought.

How bad had she been hit? He'd seen her limp. He hoped she died but doubted she would. Not with his stinking luck. He knew, to keep up the search, he'd have to take a hit of speed, but he was still too drunk.

Out loud, in a self-hating voice, he said, "You don't get her, you're a dead man. You moron. You were drunk. Jesus, what's the matter with you?"

He put his head back on the headrest for a moment. He'd actually attempted to kill her, to jump in and make himself a hero to his damn cousin. The king of kings. Now it seemed like the stupidest decision he'd ever made in his life. He hated his obsession with trying to please his cousin. He hated the man yet couldn't escape the need to get his acknowledgment.

And Oggie, as his asshole, big-shot buddies called Ogden Thorp, would not react well to this. Thorp was the most powerful man in the Sierra Nevada, and the man had always had a very low opinion of him. Even when Shaun had gotten his PI license, nothing really changed. He was still the gofer. The pimp for the big parties, bringing in high-class pussy.

Killing Sydney Jesup had seemed like such a great idea. It all started when that lowlife bastard Gary Gatts, the supplier of party drugs, the guy who had the skinny on everything and everybody, told Corbin what was in the works. A pro was coming in to take care of the former investigator because she was still causing problems and had sullied the name of the Thorps. It was literally an historic kind of deal, Gatts had said. The Thorps had been killing their enemies since the Gold Rush and Indian days.

It came up in some casual conversation when Corbin was up to Gatts' Mountain View Restaurant to get himself resupplied with his medications of choice. Gatts was the Grand Central terminal for drugs coming up from Mexico.

They'd sampled a little, gotten high together. Then Gatts had started running his mouth.

Corbin couldn't remember how, exactly, but the Jesup woman had come up. "Don't worry about that bitch," Gatts had said. When Corbin pressed, Gatts went off on how it was already a done deal. They were bringing in some guy from New York. A guy Vegas used from time to time. Gatts didn't say how he knew, but Corbin had learned long ago that when Gatts said something, it came from the horse's mouth.

They were both pretty baked that night when Corbin got his

biggest idea ever. He'd save his cousin the money and get the job done. And the more he'd thought about it over the next few days, the more brilliant the idea sounded to him. Finally, he'd be taken seriously.

How many times had he imagined walking into his cousin's Incline Village estate, saying, "Got the bitch!" and Thorp would be shocked, surprised, and finally have no choice but to acknowledge him.

Now, as the last remnants of the miserable day slipped away, night covering the lake, he went over the shooting again and again in his mind. *She was twenty feet away! He'd unloaded a whole clip!* Then he thought maybe Gatts was just setting him up and knew it would get *him* killed. He tried to think of something he'd done to Gatts.

"Jesus, you fucking drunk asshole," Shaun Corbin said of himself. At times, he despised himself more than anybody on the stinking planet.

He took a sip from his whiskey flask, lit a cigarette with a shaky hand, and thought of what to do next. Failure wasn't an option. Failure was a death sentence.

And he knew he didn't have much time. His cousin was down in Vegas making some huge deal. Big boys. Silicon Valley types and Chinks all looking to put money in Tahoe. And his uncle was busy buying, stealing, grabbing properties all around the lake. And next weekend was the big party of the year, the Great Gatsby Gala.

Then he thought about the pro they were bringing in.

I gotta find out when. Or it'll be me the bastard comes for.

First thing he needed to know was when his cousin was coming home from Vegas. The only other person who might know was the top girl on the string Corbin ran, Kora North. Thorp had a thing for her. She was to be his Miss Daisy at the big Gatsby gala.

He took out his phone. Tried to think straight, get his brain into the moment. He felt lethargic and took another hit followed by a pull on the flask, then lit another cigarette with shaky hands. Lately he found his hands shook a lot. He managed to press in Kora's number.

When she answered, Corbin said, "Kora, it's me. Look, I'm in something of jam. A big damn problem."

"You're a big problem," Kora said. "I'm busy."

"Don't hang up. This is serious. This is life or death, Kora. You got to help me out here. I got enough on you to send you up for five life sentences, bitch, so listen to me."

"Shaun," Kora said, "piss off." The bitch hung up.

Enraged, Corbin smashed his cell on the dash again and again. When he calmed down, he knew one thing for certain: He had to find Jesup, to kill her and that bastard who picked her up.

And he had to do it tonight.

8

Sydney told Marco where to pull off. He turned down toward the lake, lights out, and then stopped in front of a padlocked gate. "You have a key?"

"Yes. I'll get it," she said, starting to get out, but he stopped her. "I'll get it. Sit tight."

"The post on the right. The cap unscrews. It's underneath. Old technology."

Marco found the key and opened the padlock. He swung the gate open, then slid back behind the wheel.

She said, "You don't need to come in. I can handle things from here."

He didn't respond, just drove on in, got out, and went back to lock the gate behind them. When he came back, she had gotten herself out of the car but was feeling a little wobbly. He grabbed her. "Easy. You need water. There a house key?"

"Beneath the second bird feeder."

"Whatever works," Marco said.

The Shaw house was secreted in the trees along the water, well hidden from the highway, guarded by thick stands of trees on both sides shielding the place from any neighbors. There was a boathouse, a small dock, and a detached garage.

He came back with the key. "Alarms?"

"Yes. Inside the door. Five, five, six, one, one."

He opened the door and turned off the alarm as she waited, leaning against his car and feeling like she might pass out.

"Who's place is this?"

"Bernie and Meredith Shaw," Sydney said. "He's an Indie filmmaker. His wife's his producer. She acts in their films."

He helped her inside. "How do you know them?"

"I was an adviser on a small project they did when I was working with the sheriff's department in Sacramento."

"How'd the film do?"

"Straight to video."

He started to escort her to a chair, but she told him to get a towel from the kitchen. She didn't want to mess up the furniture. There was a nightlight in every room. It wasn't much but enough so they didn't have to turn any lights on.

He came back with a towel, spread it on the chair, then opened a bottle of water and gave it to her. While she sat and drank and tried to get herself together, he went and quickly checked other rooms downstairs, then up on the second floor.

"Where are the Shaws now?" he asked when he came back down.

"Some Greek Island…looking for a location." She was exhausted but already responding to the water. It was time for him to leave, if he was going to leave. "I'll be okay now," she said. "I have a car, and my friend is only a few minutes away in Tahoe City. You've gone way above and beyond, and I really appreciate it."

He gazed through the French doors to the porch that overlooked the lake. "You know if he's even home?"

"I'm sure he is, but I'll make sure."

She called, and when James answered she said, "You home alone?" He said he was. "I need to come over. Be there in a few minutes. Keep it to yourself." She hung up before he could ask questions.

Marco said, "Ready?"

"I don't need you to drive me over there."

"When you're in good hands, I'll leave. No guns in the house, are there?"

"There's a gun upstairs in the master bedroom. A Beretta. The bottom drawer of the nightstand next to the bed, in back of the socks. Should be two clips. And, if you would, bring a pair of slippers from the closet. My feet—I'm messing up the floor."

He came back down a couple minutes later with the Beretta and slippers.

"Great," she said, reaching for the slippers. He pulled them back. He had a wet towel over his shoulder. He cleaned her feet and then put the slippers on.

"You don't need to be moving around, bending down. At least not until your doc friend gets you fixed up," he said.

When he handed her the gun, she handed it right back. "You

have better mobility and speed in case it's needed. Until I'm, as you say, *fixed up*."

They went back outside and over to the garage. He pulled the Range Rover out and the Shelby in.

"They pay you for keeping everything in order here?" he asked as he helped her into the front seat.

"Because I consult on their films when they involve cops and robbers, and they like to have somebody reliable keep a watch, it's a quid pro quo. It's nice to come over and sit quiet and away from my life."

"Doc's the only one knows?"

"Yes. He's a good friend. I dated him for a while, but we proved much better as friends."

He nodded and walked around to get into the driver's seat. When they were on the highway heading for Tahoe City, Marco suggested any doctor treating a bullet wound was obligated to report it.

"He'll deal with it in the best way to protect me. He can write a report, if he's so inclined, and neglect to submit it."

After a few moments of silence, Sydney decided to ask a question that had been bothering her. She turned to him and said, "You aren't on the run, are you, by any chance?"

"I had problems, but I paid my debt. I'm clean."

"You do time?"

Marco nodded. "Nearly two years in a really nasty system below the border. Then I got rescued and did some work for Uncle Sam. In turn, I got my records sanitized, so now I'm a free man with no record."

"What'd you do?"

"A colleague on the border, and a good friend, was ambushed and killed. The killers escaped back into Mexico. I took a leave, hunted them, and brought them to justice. Unfortunately, I didn't get away clean."

"But you are now."

"I am now."

She was seeing this guy from an angle she would never have even considered a short time ago. He was one of those guys living in that gray world, that no man's land, the lawless underbelly, and she was becoming more and more comfortable with that. And hers was a story not all that far removed from his. It was a definite connection.

And nobody does favors for Homeland or the feds and gets his record washed after he's killed people and spent time in a Mexican prison unless he's really good at something they want. She wondered just what it was and whether that skill set might be of use to her. But she was a major threat to his chances of a new life. He was Tony Cillo's nephew, and that made it a very complicated situation for both of them.

"Your uncle's Italian. Cruz is Spanish."

"I'm half Italian, half Mexican on my father's side."

She glanced at him. He had a very heavy background. If she wanted help, she couldn't have ordered up anyone much better prepared for whatever she decided to do. All she knew was, she had no interest in running.

9

On the way into Tahoe City, Sydney replayed the shooting in her mind. She tried to fit the size and shape of the shooter to someone from her past. Who the hell was he?

The problem with running through her internal contact list was that she'd been involved in a lot of arrests, busts, and—later—prosecutions with the sheriff's department. Then there were her many investigations with the DA. She'd gathered more enemies than friends. It was a very difficult environment because South Lake was divided between California's jurisdiction and Nevada's, and further divided by counties.

One conclusion she had to face was that she couldn't believe Ogden Thorp, a man who really wanted her dead, would send somebody so incompetent to take her out. That complicated everything in her mind, because it was Thorp she wanted to bring down, and having some random fool out there looking to kill her was an unwanted complication.

"Your doc live right in town?" Marco asked.

"He lives a few blocks off the main drag. Go through town, and I'll show you where to turn."

When they crossed over the bridge on the Truckee River, Marco said, "I used to love boating down this river. One of the first things I learned from my uncle was that the Truckee River, instead of flowing west toward the Pacific, flows east into the lake, then continues on east to Pyramid Lake. He said the lake takes forever to drain. Supposedly, if you dropped a cup of coffee in Lake Tahoe, it wouldn't be gone from the lake for six hundred fifty years. You believe that?"

"I've heard that. Nobody has been able to test it yet."

He looked over at her. "How you doing?"

"Miserable. I'll be a lot better as soon as I get some pain pills and medical attention. And some food."

"Wanting food is always a good sign."

The center of the city was slow, a lot of foot traffic crossing every block. Marco said, "I don't remember it being this busy. Especially on a Sunday night."

"New restaurants, walkways, plus new, well-lit trails along the water," she told him.

Sydney directed him to the doctor's house on Fairway Drive on the north side of town, a green and white bungalow on a quiet, unpretentious street of mostly single-story houses. He put the Range Rover into reverse and parked few houses back. He told her to wait. He wanted to look around.

"This is a very safe neighborhood—"

"You called him. He knows you're coming. I just want to be sure he didn't call anybody."

"He wou—" she started to say, but he was already out and walking away.

He had the Beretta under his shirt, a button opened so he could get to it in a hurry. She watched him as he paused, studied the street, the houses, and then moved between the doc's place and the neighbor's, quiet and stealthy as a ghost.

When he came back a few minutes later, he nodded, and she got out and followed him around back. A patio door wasn't locked. She didn't ask if he'd done that or James had just neglected it.

The doc was sitting in his home office doing something on his computer when he looked up and saw Marco, then her. Then his gaze drifted to her blood-stained clothes and his eyes flashed alarm. "Sydney, what the hell is going on?"

"I'm sorry to come in on you like this, James. But I have no choice. I ran into a problem. I need you to take a look at some scratches."

The doc looked at Marco like he might be the source of the "scratches."

"I just need a quick patch-up. Maybe some of those new type of stitches. This is the guy who saved me or I'd be dead."

The doc nodded, not showing the shock she knew he felt. "Syd, what is going on?"

"No time for Q and A," Marco said. "Just fix her up and we'll be out of here."

Sydney nodded. "I have some problems. Do what you can for

me. And we need a few things. We were never here, and you don't know anything about anything."

"Be smart," Marco added. "This can be nothing to you, or it can end up being everything."

The doc didn't waste time. He went to work on Sydney's wounds.

Marco said he needed a few food items from the kitchen. He laid some money on the desk, but James said he didn't need any payment. Marco took the money back and left the room.

James Young, one of a dying breed of GPs, gave her questioning looks as he worked.

"Just do what you can and let us go. He's not my problem," she reassured him, nodding toward the kitchen. "I'm sorry I put this on you, but I needed a place to get cleaned up. And, obviously, you can't report this because it never happened."

Sydney apologized profusely for smelling of fish and sweat, but the doc didn't seem to care about that. He still seemed unsure of what Marco was really all about but went about the business of getting her fixed up.

After cleaning and sanitizing the wounds and using Dermabond, a kind of superglue liquid stitch, he wrapped the graze wounds. Then he went into the adjacent guest room and came back carrying a clean blouse and loose jogging pants. "My sister won't miss these. I'll buy her new stuff when she visits again."

Then he gently cleaned the bottoms of her feet. He didn't ask how that had happened. He put some ointment on them, bandages, and then got her some socks and slippers to wear.

When he was finished, he handed her some antibiotics and some cover bandages, then a bottle of ibuprofen.

Sydney said, "I was never here. This never happened."

"I understand."

"Thanks."

Marco returned holding two filled paper grocery bags. "We all on the same page?"

The doc nodded.

Marco smiled. "As they say in Mexico, stay smart, *mantenerse con vida*. Stay alive."

10

They left the doc's house out the front door. Walking back to the car, Sydney said, "The Spanish bit, that wasn't really a necessary touch."

"You lay the coffin nails out on the table, and it tends to get attention." They both got in the Range Rover and Marco eased away from the curb.

Just as they were about to turn into town to head back, Marco got a call from his uncle. He pulled into an empty strip mall lot and put Cillo on speaker.

"Marco, we need to meet now," Cillo said, sounding highly stressed. "This is way out of bounds."

"I'm not sure what 'this' is."

"Don't play around, Marco. The big boys at Incline know what's going on. Word is out. Was out before you got half a mile from my place. I can't talk on the damn phone. I got to meet with you. This has to get settled fast. Tonight. Where are you?"

"Just driving around thinking."

"Where's that damn Jesup woman?"

"I assume she's long gone. I dropped her on a back street behind the casinos and some friend picked her up. She's probably on her way to who knows where."

"Don't bullshit me. I know you too well. You got her stashed somewhere or you know damn well where she's headed. That's your nature and your problem. Marco, you and me need to talk, and right now. Not on the phone. Pick a place."

Marco glanced at Sydney as if wanting her opinion. She nodded in the affirmative.

"No problem," Marco said. "Go past Camp Richardson. Take that turnoff that puts you at the museum. I assume it's still there."

"Valhalla?"

"Yeah, that's it," Marco said. "Park back there. I'll meet you in an hour. Don't bring anybody else. We'll figure this out."

"It's bigger than you know. Don't even think about playing games."

Marco hung up and turned to Sydney "Well, this is where it ends. I'll deal with my uncle, make amends. You need to be long gone. You should be in Truckee on the 50 in about half an hour, and in Sac—"

He stopped as a black Ford 250 pickup truck shot past. The driver paid no attention to two people in a Range Rover. Besides, with tinted windows they were all but invisible in the night.

"You think that's him?" Marco asked.

"Could well be," Sydney said.

They watched the pickup disappear up the street heading to the north end of Tahoe City.

Sydney said, "I want to find out what's going on, what your uncle has to say. Maybe he has an idea who the shooter is, or who ordered it. Anything will help. I don't want to leave until I have some idea what's going on. I'm coming with you."

"That can't be a good idea," Marco said. "You get someplace safe, you call me, and I'll let you know what I find out."

"You might have a target on your back for rescuing me and then letting me get away."

"I'll deal with that."

"You go by car, you're vulnerable to getting trapped. The shooter is hunting right now, and maybe some other guys, too. You can't go meet him by car. Especially *your* car. And if you want me to take off, it's in this car. No, we'll take the Shaws' boat. I know how to get there and where to drop you off. You can see Cillo. Nobody will expect you to come in that way."

He stared off a moment, shook his head, but he didn't seem to have a counterargument.

She said, "You don't understand how things are up here, and I mean with your uncle as well. You need to have an easy escape if it comes to that. I'll sit in the boat. Let you off where you can hike through the woods to the museum parking lot. Talk to Cillo. Be real careful. He's not running things, and somebody could be using him right now. On the way, I'll explain some things you need to know about what's going on."

He stopped at the Shaw house drive, unlocked the gate, and

pulled in. "You sure about this?"

"As a cat on a hot tar roof. But I'm not ready to run just yet. I'm not happy somebody tried to kill me, and I need to know if it was some minor-league fool or somebody connected to the major players around here. Sometimes you run, nobody follows. Sometimes there's nowhere you can run they can't get to you."

He didn't argue with that.

**

Corbin hated the voice at the other end of the GPS. Stupid bitch. "That's not what I asked, goddamn you."

The robot said she didn't understand. If he knew how to hunt *her* down, he would have.

Mustangs were everywhere, but not many were red convertibles. He had never realized there were so goddamn many of them.

"Where are you, dammit?" he yelled as he headed for the next medical clinic on his GPS. "You can't hide. I'm gonna find you bastards!"

He felt a degree of sobriety coming on and he needed it. This was getting crazy. He wondered what he'd do if he found them in some damn clinic. Shoot them on the spot?

He drifted slowly now, looking at all the parking lots, all the tourist cars. So goddamn many stupid tourists. The GPS idiot robot lady telling him to go here, go there, West Lake, 505, now 531.

"Jesus, these aren't clinics."

"Take the next right and then take the first left on Christy Hill…"

"Jesus, how the hell many places are there?"

He couldn't stand the sound of her voice. "You stupid bitch!" he yelled. But she just cut him off or something. He sometimes felt she knew him and deliberately gave him a lot of shit. Goddamn robot.

Shaun reached the clinic's empty lot. He needed a drink at the moment more than he needed to be sober, so he took one, a strong one. His hand shook so bad, he had to hold the flask with both hands.

He called Kora North again and it went to voice mail. He left her a message. "You better start answering, Kora. You don't, I'll be coming over and paying you a visit. You hear me?"

Kora North was now exclusive to Thorp and his party scene.

She'd know when Thorp was coming back from Vegas. And if things went to hell, and he had to get out of Dodge, she always had a lot of cash, and he had plenty of things on her she'd trade for.

Corbin knew he was running out of time. His cousin found out what happened, every stinking hitman in Vegas would be heading up to Tahoe to find *him* first.

11

Sydney watched as Marco pulled the lock rod and opened the door of the boathouse so she could ease the Reinell 220 out into open water. She was already feeling much better. The doc had done good.

"Nice," Marco said, climbing on board and getting into the front passenger seat. "It fast?"

"Fast enough, but we won't be using speed unless something goes wrong. We'll be running with no lights along the shoreline, which the coast guard patrols. If there's one out tonight, they won't appreciate it. Their channel is on the boat's radio, so we'll know if there's any activity."

"Good," Marco said, removing the Beretta clip, reinserting it with a slap of the palm of his hand. "Are they still headquartered in Tahoe City?"

"Yes. They have new rules thanks to the regional planning agency. Like a no-wake zone six hundred feet from shore. The white buoys are the ones to watch for. They show where the rocks and other obstacles are. It's easier on this side of the lake. Mostly wilderness, and I can run it blind. You just have to know where the pilings from the old docks are, and the rocks. If we need to run, nobody will catch us in this baby."

He didn't say anything more. She eased the boat away from the Shaw house and headed down along the west side of the lake, riding a soft chop. It was all designated wilderness along most of the west side, and pitch black. As planned, they went lights-out, sliding along at a low purr.

Marco said, "Okay, be straight—what's going on?"

She said, "I've made plenty of enemies, but none as obsessed with me as Ogden Thorp."

"I don't know that name."

"He's the front man for some major casino and resort investors. He's from one of the big families who've been in the Sierra's since the beginning of the gold rush. He owns an estate at Incline, another at Fallen Lake, and is buying up every piece of stressed property and whatever else he can get. He's planning on building one of the biggest resorts on the planet. Your uncle is among the many who stand to profit from the land grab. There's a lot going on below the surface, and some of it isn't very pretty. When it comes to land, the territorial imperative kicks in big time."

Marco said," How'd you get in the middle of all of this?"

"I was dealing with two key witnesses—a girl and her boyfriend—in an investigation of one of Thorp's associates, and it spread to hookers and drugs. The key witnesses ended up dead."

"How'd they die?"

"They drowned in a supposed drunken post-party swim out at Fallen Leaf Lake. It's a long, sordid story. When I persisted in the investigation of the drowning of my witnesses, I got myself fired. I had no idea when I went into the questioning of various potential witnesses what we were getting into."

"And that's a problem when you're not backed by powers equal to the task. But you got lucky—whoever tried to take you out wasn't up to the job. You're alive. You should try and stay that way."

She looked at him but didn't respond to his suggestion. "It's like these guys have gotten control of much of the Tahoe Basin political power grid by intimidation, blackmail, and murder. There's nothing they won't do to get what they want. And what they want is to turn the North Shore into Las Vegas Boulevard. It would have been unthinkable a short time ago. But now, with state governments broke, city coffers near empty, they have a good chance of pulling it off—getting long-standing land-use rules changed."

"It sounds like you were way over your head and pay grade."

"When two people who were doing what you wanted them to do—forced them to do, in a sense—end up dead, you can't walk away."

"I understand the emotion of that," Marco said. "I've been there. But why are you still a threat? You don't work for law enforcement. You work in a fish hatchery part-time."

Sydney stared toward Incline Village. "Thorp blames me for dragging his name into the gutter. He's not a man who forgives and forgets, even when he wins. And they still think I'm running a clandestine investigation looking for something, or someone, who can help me get them."

"Are you?"

"If you can call it that. I don't have much to work with. A South Lake police reporter and I are friends, and he knows what I'm doing. He helps out. If I want somebody checked out, he'll run down whatever's in the public record. He's been warning me for a long time to back off, but I'm a little hard-headed."

"I knew a girl like you who lived in a border town on the Mexican side. Drug dealers overran the place. The police were either killed or went over to their side. Nobody would take on the job of police chief. She did. She was young and idealistic and, inevitably, ended up dead. The moral to that story, and maybe yours, is don't get in a war where you have no allies, no support base, and no chance of winning. Idealist motives, or revenge motives—or any kind of motives—aren't enough."

Sydney pulled as close as she could to the rocky shoreline near an old, now unused boat dock. Marco was laying down the law, and she realized he wasn't going to get involved in her problem. His white-knight moment was coming to an end. He was right, of course, but running was just so hard for her to think about, or do.

"No rocks to worry about here," Sydney said. "You're about a quarter-mile from where he'll drive in. There aren't any other access roads up this far, and they closed the one that used to come here. You won't have to worry about somebody coming in behind you. Careful"—she pointed at the dock—"that dock hasn't been used or repaired in years."

Marco checked Bluetooth communications with her in case something went bad, then checked the Beretta for the fourth or fifth time. Finally, he climbed out and headed into the woods.

Good luck, she thought, staring after him, the woods quickly swallowing him up. *This is where it ends,* she thought. If Cillo had people coming in to grab Marco, or if his uncle convinced him he was committing suicide, it could get nasty very fast. Now she couldn't do anything but sit and wait and hope it worked out in her favor.

What did she expect Marco to do? He had to protect himself. And he was right about her. So was her police-reporter friend. So was everybody who knew the situation.

She thought about the girl Marco had mentioned, the one in that town taken over by gangsters. Tahoe was on the verge of being taken over by a different form of gangster, and she knew she was a persistent, dangerous irritant that had to be removed simply because she was someone who knew the entire narrative of what was going on. And, to make matters worse, she had spit in their faces.

I'm a dead woman walking, she thought, *and Marco Cruz knows that.* It was too bad, though—she needed help. A lot of help to do what she'd always wanted to do, which was to find a way to break into Thorp's lawyer's palatial estate and see if, as rumored, he had an impenetrable office containing a vault with all the dirt gathered on everyone who might stand in his way. People didn't call lawyer Richard Rouse "Tricky Dick" for nothing.

12

Marco took his time moving through the pines, careful to avoid the dry limbs as he made his way toward the meeting place several hundred yards from where he'd come ashore. He wanted to see the parking areas near the museum first.

He found his uncle standing by a small outbuilding near the museum. Marco watched and waited for a time, reflecting how much his ability to move quietly and swiftly in the woods at night came from those many hikes and camping trips with his uncle. Some of his best times.

"You alone?" Marco asked quietly as he slipped up behind his uncle.

His uncle turned, an unlit cigarette suspended in his left hand. "I was beginning to worry. Yeah, I'm alone."

As Cillo snapped his lighter, his bloated face illuminated momentarily. He took a deep drag, the smoke drifting out as he spoke. "I'm going to level with you. Deal with this real fast, or it's going to be real bad."

"What's that mean?" Marco asked.

"It means, you don't do the smart thing, you don't just lose the deal here in Tahoe. It means you're a dead man, and maybe you'll be killing me, as well, if I fail to bring you to your senses."

"Maybe when I understand—"

"What you need to understand is you owe it to yourself and me...all I did for you and your family—"

"I know what you did for us, and I appreciate all of it," Marco said. "But that was then, and this is now. Let's deal with now."

"You have her somewhere, I know you do."

"Just get to what this is about. No games. I'm way beyond that, where I'm coming from."

"I understand you got involved accidentally," Cillo said. "Nobody faults you for that. But what you do from this point onward is no accident. You walked into something blind, but now your eyes are wide open—you need to get smart and walk back out fast."

"Are we talking about this Thorp character?"

"You don't mess with guys like Thorp," Cillo said, taking another drag. "No future and no purpose to it. Come on, Marco, you're a smart guy. You've been around the hard blocks, so wake up and smell the roses before you end up fertilizing them."

Marco turned and looked around, making sure they stayed alone, then said, "She told me about some girl and her boyfriend who got taken out to put an end to an investigation. Drowned, supposedly."

"Jesus." Cillo shook his head, snorting smoke. "You really buying into this? You can't stand staying out of the line of fire, or what? Don't play the stupid hero shit up here, my friend. You don't want any part of any of it, and you don't know squat about the truth of it. Whether they drowned on their drugged-out own or were helped, doesn't change anything. They were used by Jesup. She might as well have drowned them herself. What you have to do to clear this up is tell me where the hell she is, and then come on back and we'll get this party on track. It's not too late."

Marco said, "I can't hand her over if she's already gone, now can I?"

"Well, that's bullshit," Cillo shot back. "Girl's wounded. She ain't driving around by herself, and she's got no friends here. Wake up. You put me in a real bind I don't much appreciate. I invite you up here and you run me over because of some crazy woman you know nothing about. That doesn't play."

"Didn't mean to, but—"

"The girl tied up on the railroad tracks doesn't cut it."

His uncle lit another cigarette off the butt of the one he finished, before dropping that and crushing it in the dirt under the pine needles. "Where'd you leave her? You want out of this, then the only way is tell me where the hell she is. Listen, damnit, I got people on my neck."

Marco stared at the dark rise of the mountain across the lake. "These people you say are such big deals, how is it they sent some rank amateur to do her in a hatchery, on government property, no less?"

His uncle said, "That's the thing. Nobody knows who did this, but it happened at a bad time. She probably was gonna get hit, but not now and not there."

"Nobody has any idea who it was?"

"If they do, they aren't talking to me about it—you know nothing about what's going on. Some of the most powerful and richest people on the planet are coming to the big party next weekend, the Great Gatsby Gala Thorp's putting on. These people are the ones gonna invest a hundred million into this resort. What nobody wants right now is a scandal. People getting killed. And that woman, getting shot up, isn't good. She can do something to upset this whole thing. End up on fucking TV or something."

"She didn't call the police or the news, so it's obvious she isn't interested in this going public. Maybe if she agrees to stay away, she won't be a threat."

Cillo gave him a long, hard stare. "You don't understand anything. And you aren't listening to me."

"You aren't telling me much."

Cillo stared at him, his face angry and tight. He looked off. Then came back, saying, "You won't listen to me, then maybe you'll listen to an old buddy of yours. Someone who can tell you what the hell you need to know."

"Who might that be?"

"Gary Gatts. He's got a place up the mountain south of here. A restaurant. The Mountain View, I think. Go talk to him. He knows everything going on. He'll straighten you out. Go up there now and see the guy."

Cillo stopped and pulled out his buzzing cell phone. "Yeah. Yeah." He took some steps away from Marco and listened to whoever was on the other end. Then he put the phone back in his pocket and walked back to Marco. He had a tight look. Whatever the call was about, he didn't like it much.

"Well, your time frame to make the right decision just got shorter. Word went to Vegas. You know how things work in that world. They want this shut down real fast."

"Which means?"

"Which means they'll send somebody to shut it down. Marco, this woman has no future. The guy who shot her has no future. And you, you don't get smart, won't have a future either. And that puts me in a spot. I'm not asking you anymore. I'm telling you. You got to get smart fast. Go see Gatts, goddamnit. Maybe he can get you thinking straight."

"Why's Gary Gatts so important?"

"Don't worry about that. He's in the know. He's got his inside information chain all around the lake."

"Give me at least tonight," Marco said. "I'll talk to Gary. Then, when I understand things better, I'll work this out."

"Good. Now you're making sense. Damnit, I love having you back. I got big things in store for you, and you deserve something good after all you been involved in. Keep me updated. I can shield you for a short time. Do the right thing. It'll pay off big in the end. Marco, you've been down the wrong road, and you know what's that's all about."

Cillo crushed out the second cigarette with the toe of his shoe, then gave Marco a quick half-hug. "You and me will be sittin' pretty. Let's get this behind us."

He walked away, heading back through the trees to the museum parking lot.

13

Marco waited until he saw the car lights and heard the engine. Then he headed back to the boat, jogging past the Baldwin Beach picnic area and Taylor Creek. He saw the headlights of two cars swing from the highway toward the parking area. He got on the phone as he jogged and told Sydney to crank up the engine.

When he reached the old dock, he climbed down in the boat and she headed fast out into the lake, no longer hugging the shoreline.

"I take it that didn't go well," she said.

"Not real well," Marco said. We're going to have to talk. My uncle says the powers that be are aware of the situation, and that means they'll send somebody to clean it up. It could get ugly real fast. You need to get the hell out of here."

"He know who had the shaky trigger finger?"

"No. But he mentioned a guy I used to go camping and hiking with. One of the group. Says he's the guy who knows everything around here. Gary Gatts. You know him?"

She gave off a dark chuckle. "GG. He's the supplier of choice for party drugs. Works for the Mexican distributors. He wants you to talk to Gary—that sounds like a setup to me."

"He wouldn't do that. He really wants me to get clear of this. Big plans."

"You and Gatts buddies in the past?"

"Not exactly. We ran in the same hiking, camping group. I always knew Gatts would find his place in the world."

"Now what?" she asked.

"We'll talk about that back at the house. I'm getting into a really bad mood. I don't like being shot at, pushed around, and given ultimatums. Never works well with me. But then, I don't like going around deaf, dumb, and blind, either."

He glanced at her and saw a thin smile. "Don't think for a minute I'm a candidate looking to join your crusade to save the Tahoe Basin from evildoers. Not my thing. I'm way past that."

"What is your thing?" she challenged.

"I want that shooter who put bullet holes in my car, messed up my day, and put me on the run. Once I settle that, I'm done. And you need to get the hell out of here. I mean now. Tonight."

"No. I'm not going anywhere until I find out who shot me. I need to know that more than you do."

They stared at each other. On some level, he understood that if he took a step in that direction, his involvement was going to get sticky. But she was a big, added problem. Still, she had a point. If the shooter was some rummy, that might change things for her. She could maybe get out without being tracked down if she was no longer seen as a threat. Still, she wasn't in good shape and might be a drag. He liked to move fast.

"You know where we can find Gary Gatts? This Mountain View restaurant of his?" he asked.

"Yes. Up past Markleeville," she said. "I don't know where he actually lives. I just know that's the rumored transition point for party drugs. I also know he's got connections and would be hard to bring down."

"I like to move fast," Marco said. "Maybe you can stay at the Shaw house while I'll go up tonight, have a little talk."

"We'll discuss it when we get back. You have a trust in your uncle, and I understand that. But it's a trust built a long time ago. Things change. You uncle is probably not the man you thought you once knew."

"Maybe. That'll be my problem."

"No, it'll be our problem, at least until we find out who the shooter is. Look, I know this world better than you do. I've worked it for three years with the sheriff's department and two with the DA. I know every scumbag, every would-be mogul, and the current affairs. It's a very beautiful world until you pull up the covers and look beneath. We'll talk."

Marco sat back and she headed out deep into the lake, then north. He didn't know exactly how to react to her. She was pushy and authoritative and that was okay, but she had an agenda, and he had to steer very clear of that.

14

Sydney felt Marco had made some kind of decision and wasn't telling her about it. They drifted up the lake toward the Shaw house.

"Cillo knows what's going on, doesn't he?" she asked, really hoping for a different answer, and also hoping she could get to know this guy. If they were going to end up working together—and she had no idea if they would—she needed to understand him better. And part of her really wanted to, which surprised the hell out of her.

"Like I said, he's maintaining he's in the dark."

She wanted to know every detail of what Cillo had said, but she sensed Marco was struggling, in a dilemma. "Look, you can walk, but I need to know where I am in all this. Did Cillo really have no idea who the shooter was?"

"It seems to me you have something in mind or you wouldn't be here. We need to be straight with each other."

"Two-way street."

Marco nodded and said, "Tell me again why you're still hanging around in harm's way?"

"I already told you."

"Not really," Marco said. "You have some kind of plan. You aren't that naive, idealistic girl in Mexico. You're a hard-nosed investigator. You're shot up and still you're in a boat on the lake with somebody out there looking to finish the job. What's going on? What aren't you telling me?"

She looked off for a moment, then turned back to Marco. Time to come clean if she expected him to trust her at all. "You're right. I have something in mind."

"It involve me now?"

"I don't know yet and, right now, neither do you."

"Try me. Because this is going to deteriorate fast. I'm not a happy puppy."

Sydney took a deep breath and let it out. "Thorp and his lawyer, Richard Rouse, live next to each other on the waterfront at Incline Village. The lawyer—Tricky Dick is how he's better known—is rumored to be the power behind the throne. My witness, Karen Orland, the girl who drowned, she was in the party circuit for a time and one of his favorites. She knew a lot. All about the sex and drugs, the videotapes of important people having fun, the garbage. But those Incline estates are over the border on the Nevada side of the lake. I worked for the DA in South Lake, in California, and couldn't get any cooperation from Nevada where those guys were concerned."

"Get to where you are now, what you think you can do about this."

"Rouse has this office that's built to withstand anything short of an atomic bomb. Karen thought the way they manipulated people— got support for what they were doing—was because of the dirt Tricky Dick has on just about everybody who matters. And that he keeps it in that office in a safe. Since we could never get any Nevada authority interested, I wanted to get associates on the California side. Those parties that Thorp has are drug and sex festivals, but nobody's ever attempted to bust one of them. In fact, the local police and sheriff's departments on both sides of the lake provide much of the security."

"Sounds a little like Mexico. A place I left and am in no hurry to go back to. I see where you're headed, and I'm not interested."

"I know." She paused a moment, then said, "But while we're being open, I'm curious about what you did in Mexico that got your records sanitized."

"It won't matter."

"Satisfy my curiosity."

"I had a partner who got ambushed and killed. I went after the guys who did it. End of story."

"I hardly think that's the end of the story. I didn't ask about that. I asked about how you managed to get out of prison and then home free with a new lease on life."

"It's the end as far as I'm willing to talk about it. Look, I have a very good idea where you're headed, and there's no way in hell I'm getting into your crusade against these guys, justified as it may be. You're way over your head. Not happening. Here's where I am with all of this: I picked you up; the guy who shot you came after not just you, but me."

"Shot your Shelby," she added, with a touch of sarcasm.

"That's right. So I'm real unhappy about that. I'm not going to be happy until I settle it with him. I'm in this for that and that alone. And it doesn't sound like it's connected to your vendetta against Thorp. It sounds like some lone guy you pissed off. You accept where I'm at, we can work together. If not, we need to part ways."

"What if he didn't act on his own? What if he's part of a bigger thing, whether it's Thorp or someone else?"

She steered toward the Shaw house from deep out in the lake. They were cruising at a slow speed, lights still out. The moon was partially covered by some thin clouds.

Marco studied her a moment. "That isn't my problem. He wasn't coming after me, per se. He was after you, and I got in the way. I'll settle with him for that."

"How did you handle it in Mexico?"

"You don't give up." He shook his head, then said, "I had plenty of contacts. I took a leave. Slipped into Mexico. Part of my family is down there. I got some help, tracked the killers, settled the issue. The troubles I got into later weren't directly connected to that. I can tell you that I spent some very bad months in a prison near Mexico City. I wouldn't have survived if a relative hadn't made contact with friends in the prison. I got protection from a powerful clique. Then, well, I got out."

"That the part you can't talk about."

"Yes."

"Okay," she said. "I'm good with getting the shooter. I'll deal with the other part once I find out who he's connected to, or if he's on his own."

They pulled into the boathouse and were just starting to talk about going up to Markleeville, getting a room, and then seeing Gatts in the morning, when she fell—her leg buckled getting out, and she missed her step. She went down against the side of the boat and the ladder. Had he not grabbed her, she would have gone into the water. He helped her to her feet.

"Muscles cramped up," Sydney said. She massaged her leg and headed up to the house slowly, with Marco's hand on her arm for support.

"Hey," he said, "you need to rest everything for a while."

When she realized she wasn't really doing as well as she had thought, that the pain meds had fooled her a little, she acceded to the necessity of settling down, maybe getting a little sleep.

"I want to go with you to see Gatts," she said. "Let me get some rest for a couple hours."

He did a perimeter check, then, in the dark, they ate peanut butter sandwiches with blueberry spread and drank some milk with it, thanks to what he'd taken from the doc.

She grew very tired around midnight and took the guest room on the main floor. He chose a recliner in the living room. It gave him the best surveillance of the grounds and the house.

***

Marco was up every hour checking the grounds, worried that more people knew about her relationship with the Shaws than her doctor friend. For a time, he sat out on the deck and stared at the darkness of the lake, trying to get a clear understanding of the mess he was in and where it might go.

He could go up and try and find Gatts without her, but he didn't much like the idea of leaving her in the condition she was in. Plus, if she found him gone, what would she do? Then there was the issue of whether he would take the Shaws' vehicle. He didn't want to drive his around. Adding to it all was the problem of his uncle—if Marco couldn't respond positively, and soon, what would he do? Questions and no immediate answers.

We've got to talk to Gatts, he thought, getting up. He went into the bedroom to see how Sydney was doing, and she was in a deep sleep. Marco frowned. It was almost midnight. He went back outside to check the perimeter again. He started wondering if her fall had been faked.

But then he thought that was a stretch. She could have really hurt herself, hit her head, and that would have pretty much put her out of business. He knew she wouldn't have risked it.

15

That Sunday night, four hundred sixty miles southeast of Tahoe in a penthouse suite at the Desert Towers high above the Vegas Strip, Ogden Thorp ignored his lawyer, who was at the back of the room trying to get his attention.

Thorp was busy displaying his investment dream to a small gathering of wealthy investors, some of the richest and most powerful men in gaming and hotels. Two of them were CEOs of Silicon Valley tech behemoths. Also in the mix was a Chinese billionaire who claimed he had relatives who helped build the transcontinental railroad's western section, and that many who died had been dumped into Lake Tahoe.

Thorp stood before an eighty-two-inch screen that displayed the mockup of his vision. He was selling them on the grand Regal Tahoe and its venues. He led them with a toast to great dreams and grand designs. "Bad recessions provide great opportunities for those positioned to take advantage."

Never before had Vegas been hit this hard and the opportunities here, like Tahoe, were big.

"Lake Tahoe's North is the next big thing," Ogden Thorp said. "This is Tahoe now…" They stared at the big screen. The picture zoomed in on the Cal-Neva and the other old, ready-to-be-torn-down casinos. Then the picture moved around to the mountains on the east side of the lake, the undeveloped forty-two thousand acres that once belong to George Whittell.

For Thorp, this was his moment. He'd arrived. These men, the big movers and shakers whose money had helped build Macau into the gambling capital of the world, were looking to get into something new, and he had what he thought would entice them. It had been five long years in the planning. These were the men who were going to make him king of the Sierras.

"The new design…including the outlying ski resort and the main casino hotel that will replace everything on the Cal-Neva highlands…"

With a click, there it was in close-up detail. And it was beyond spectacular. He watched the expressions on the men as their eyes widened.

"This will be the eighth wonder of the world," Thorp said. "And it's just the beginning."

He moved the scene to the famous landmark, Thunderbird Lodge, on the Nevada side of the North Shore. "Here's the big prize. We're making some serious progress. We'll have the ban lifted on enough land for this. This was once the dream of George Whittell. He owned the forty-two thousand acres—you heard me right— forty-two thousand acres that are now wasted parkland. The entire eastern side of Tahoe is waiting for us."

He loved talking about George Whittell, his idol in many ways. "All that's there is his home, which is now the Thunderbird Lodge. Before he died in nineteen sixty-seven, George changed his mind about building his great resort. I'm not sure who or what got to him. But we're going to rectify that. Tahoe needs it and needs it now.

"George Whittell was the king of playboys in his day, and I admit to copying as much of him as my system can handle. He made Charlie Win Win look like a choirboy."

They laughed, knowing well that he meant the famous parties— right down to the tunnels, the lion's cage, the speedboat, and the girls. Thorp even had the stonework at his place fashioned by Paiute and Washo Indian masons and ironworkers just as Whittell had done at the Thunderbird Lodge. He didn't import any Venetian ironworkers as Whittell had but came close. Nor could he bring in honest-to-God Cornish miners to build the tunnels. But Mexicans, well supervised, did a very nice job.

"It true," one of the men asked, "that you have a lion in some underground cage under your house like Whittell had?"

"That will only be revealed to those who end up there. Back in Whittell's day—as it happened to Errol Flynn—they'd wake up after a drunk and find the fucking lion licking their faces. People heard that macho swashbuckler Flynn's scream clear across the lake."

The men roared. He went on regaling his audience with Whittell's life back in the day when he had those big parties, the gambling, Hollywood stars including Howard Hughes.

Thorp's smile filled his smug face. "Next weekend, I'll be hosting the party of the year, the Great Gatsby Gala, and I want all of you to be there. All expenses for all the pleasures will be free, of course. And if you aren't interested in talking to me, you'll have on hand movie stars, politicians, and, in the poker room—modeled after the famous one in Tombstone—the world's greatest poker players will be in the world's biggest cash game."

With all of the Vegas Strip glowing below them, the brightest lights in all the world, he toasted once again to the fruition of his grand dream.

He turned to the Chinese gentleman and his small entourage. "It must be very satisfying that a relative of those who labored to build the great railroads that opened the Sierras and linked the country are soon going to own them."

More laughter. Thorp was on.

"Show us this famous gun you have," one of the Silicon Valley investors said. "I heard it was the brother to the pistol that killed Lincoln."

He pulled out the Derringer, laid it in the palm of his hand, and then passed it around for the investors to see.

"A piece of history. This baby is the brother pistol to the one that killed Lincoln at Ford's Theatre. Man that made them, Henry Deringer, made them in pairs because they only shot one bullet. Each pair had a specific bullet mold." He retrieved the gun and held it up. "Black walnut stock, checkered grip."

"It authentic?"

"This is the real thing. Cost me a fortune to get hold of it. It's been going around. The original is kept by the U.S. Park Police in Ford's Theatre. They authenticated it about ten years ago as the second of the pair. I heard that it was out there three years ago, and I had some people run it down for me. Paid big."

"How can you be sure that's the one?"

"Forensics and science. You check the rifling pattern, tool marks, shading, the grain. The metal of these single-shot percussions is chemically browned iron, and you can check the age, which I did. Look at the barrel—see how it's flattened and slotted on top for the blade front sight. You have engraved German silver. Lock plate and barrel stamped with Derringer Philadelphia. His named was Deringer, with one R, but the gun was called a Derringer, using two

Rs. Made in pairs, the double-R makes sense."

"You ever shoot it?"

He put the gun in his pocket. "Not yet. But I'm sure that day will come."

That brought a big round of laughter. It was at that moment, as he was raising yet another toast, that he got a shoulder tap by his lawyer.

Thorp finished the toast, then followed Richard Rouse, his attorney, business partner, and life-long friend out onto the balcony.

16

"What's the problem?" Thorp demanded. He was quickly sorry he asked. And it got a lot worse when Rouse told him about the shooting at the hatchery, about Cillo's nephew saving Jesup, and how he was out there somewhere as well. Then the most distressing news of all.

"Looks like the fool who jumped the gun was Shaun."

"How do you know this?"

"I've been talking to everybody who knows anything. It really looks that way."

Thorp's incredulity turned instantly to anger. "That's…that's insane. That bastard. Jesus Christ."

Thorp stared down at the flow of lights on the Vegas Strip as he tried to process the idea that his moronic cousin, a lowlife piece of crap, would take it upon himself to do something like this. It was almost unfathomable.

"Media have this?"

"No. So far she hasn't reported anything. Probably to protect her cousin at the hatchery. This is potential disaster."

"What are we doing about it?"

"The guy I told you about, a plane will bring him in tomorrow."

"This guy from New York?"

Rouse nodded. "They say he's top of the line. I've been told his specialty is that he's a suicide expert. He doesn't whack people in the old Italian way. He's a new breed. Quiet, quick, and very effective in what he does. You won't even know he's in town."

"I want to know he's in town. I'd like to talk to him, make sure he understands that we can't afford any kind of negative publicity. How can I meet this guy?"

"I don't know that's a good idea."

"I didn't ask you that."

"Well, he did have a demand. He insists we get the Marilyn

Monroe Celebrity Cabin at the Cal Neva freed up for him. I'm taking care of it."

Thorp stared at Rouse. "He wants the Marilyn Monroe Celebrity cabin."

"That's what our contact said. He's some kind of movie buff."

Thorp was beside himself. "This can't be happening. If it was my idiot cousin, why? Is he deliberately trying to destroy me or what?"

"I don't know. Maybe he's trying to impress you."

"He's succeeded. If it was him, he's dead. I want him gone. I want this cleaned up fast. That guy comes in, I want to meet him. Have the Cal-Neva open the tunnel from the kitchen to the Celebrity cabin that JFK and Sinatra used when they went secretly to visit Marilyn."

17

The rather anonymous, inconspicuous young man smiled to himself, remembering what he had told the man he'd killed as he walked the night streets of New York City near Times Square late Sunday night:

"You're going to do the world a favor and commit suicide. I'm going to help you in that. It's what I do. I'm a suicide specialist. Your profession is bilking folks out of millions. Mine is getting them some justice. I love my profession."

It was the best of times…and Sunday night, when people were least aware, it was the killer's night. His profession was booming and he considered himself at the top, with his pick-and-choose of gigs. One of the reasons Leon had considered taking the job in Tahoe so soon after the Brooklyn job was Marilyn Monroe's cabin. He'd heard they were thinking of tearing it down, and he'd always wanted to spend some time there. Watch her movies on his Kindle Fire while lying back, reposing as it were, on her bed.

Henry Craven Lee, aka Leon, the man referred to by the code name Urbanwolf, had come to New York for a job in Brooklyn and was now enjoying a night off after another success. He thought about his recent target. How the man had stared at death more with acceptance than fear. How like Leon was maybe doing him a favor, doing what he'd wanted to do but didn't have the guts.

"It's not business and it's not personal, it's Mother Nature…the Italians notwithstanding."

He'd said those words as he'd looked into the widened eyes of the man, eyes more resigned than any Leon had ever seen. That thousand-yard stare, as they say. Something you see in war zones…and wasn't Wall Street the final war zone?

Post-kill was Leon's second favorite time. The long, slow comedown from the ultimate high the hunt gave him. Leon had taken his current name from the French version of one of his favorite old movies, *The Professional.* All the names he'd worked under over the years were lifted from favorite movies. *The Professional* was *Leon* in the French version, staring Natalie Portman and the hitman Jean Reno. It was one of Henry Craven Lee's all-time top flicks.

Leon strolled now down Fifth Avenue. He loved the night crowds. The anonymity, the knowing. He talked silently to people. He was never alone. The world was his playground, and he talked incessantly to people, imagining what he would do to some of them. Leon's mind never stopped except on the hunt. Then it calmed. Then it focused. Otherwise? It ran and ran and ran.

You don't care, do you? Life beat you. Nature has no sympathy.

Leon took great pride in the professionalism of his work. And though he'd learned much of it from watching movies and critiquing the killers, even mocking them, movies were his outlet. After the military denied him, which he was forever grateful for—*fuck them*—he'd studied his profession with zeal. Awarded himself a Ph.D. He didn't like taking orders anyway. He was a genius with an IQ near 160, but what he possessed above anyone he encountered was that he knew the fundamental truth of life. He was absolutely convinced he knew the nature of things and the "others" were just kidding themselves.

A limo was now waiting for him in front of his hotel to take him to a private airfield from which he'd be flown to Tahoe. But tonight, he'd especially enjoyed his time prowling aimlessly through Times Square, working off his restless energy, the man whose real name was Henry Craven Lee, so pleased with himself. Sure, he got physically lonely at times, sometimes wanted a hooker for release. But for the most part, he liked being a lone wolf.

Leon loved nature's laws. The true existence of life was the hunter. And he loved movies. He liked to think he looked a bit like De Niro in *Taxi*—his best role, in Leon's mind, though he was great in *Goodfellas* and *Casino*. He couldn't decide, when he thought about it, which of De Niro's movies was the best. But what about *The Deer Hunter* and—hold on—*Raging Bull?* You can't leave that out. And then what about *Cape Fear?* And—Christ, yes—don't forgot *The Godfather!*

But it was De Niro and Jean Reno in *The Professional* who were his greatest screen heroes. No contest.

Leon, carrying his travel bag, laughed out loud at the great movies De Niro had been in, all of which he'd seen almost as often as the Monroe movies. Laughing out caused people to glance at him.

Robert, my friend, you are the best. You are the man.

Back at his hotel, Leon got in the back seat of the limo with his bag, then pulled out his phone and checked in, listening to the message. He texted a simple message in a simple code. His contact numbers rotated with the calendar and various countries' holiday schedules. This month it was Scotland. June. Lanimer Day.

He smiled at the thought of his next night being in MM's bed in the Celebrity Cabin, where she had been nailed by Kennedy, Sinatra, and Giancana.

The truth of it was, killings for Leon weren't murders. They were purges, cleansings of the rot and corruptions of civilization. People were, by and large, scum. Stupid and petty. Most. There were exceptions, to be sure. Still, the world needed more than a bunch of Leons to clean it up. He was a firm believer in the real need for a major pandemic or global war. It would be fine with him to get rid of about half the world's population.

18

Sydney woke at noon on Monday and couldn't believe she'd slept so long. She was sore, it seemed, everywhere.

He's gone, she thought with a start. Of course. Why would he stay? But would he tell them where she was? She looked for the gun that had been on the nightstand; it was gone.

She started to get up when she heard a noise. Somebody coming down the hall. Him or someone else? Again, she had no gun.

Suddenly, a figure appeared at the door. "You're awake. How do you like your eggs?"

She smiled. *Now that's a better way to wake up,* she thought. "Scrambled light is good. I can't believe I slept that long."

"How soon?"

"Give me ten minutes," she said.

"How do you feel?"

"Like a truck ran over me."

He smiled and left. She figured the longer they were together, the more likely she had him for what she had in mind.

After breakfast, they talked about Gatts and decided to go to Markleeville later that night and see if they couldn't find the guy, then figure out how to get his cooperation. Marco told her not to worry about that.

"Give the place a call," he said, "and make sure it's still open. I'm gonna crash for awhile." He pushed the Beretta across the table, plus the clips.

After he was gone, she called her police-reporter friend and asked him to run a serious background on Marco Cruz. "I need this pretty fast. And check on the Mountainview Restaurant. Make sure it's open and that Gary Gatts runs the place. And if you can get me an address, I'd appreciate it."

"And you won't tell me anything about—"

"No. You're a sweetheart." She hung up and then went out to

look around, make sure things were okay. She decided to sit out on the side deck so she had a good view of the water and of the feeder road that led to the gate.

Sydney felt better and better about her connection to Marco Cruz. They had something powerful in common—guilt. It's something that comes with the territory for cops, soldiers, or anyone working tight with somebody who ends up dead. There's always the sense you could have prevented it, or should have been the one to go down instead. It's a big part of what drove her, and she figured he had that in his backpack as well. Life's load is much heavier after something like that happens.

***

Marco stared at the band of light coming in from the side of the curtain on the wall and, tired as he was, didn't know if he'd slept or not.

He didn't like that they had delayed. He'd wanted to get to Gatts quick, before his uncle—whose suggestion it was—could use Gatts as a trap. He didn't know, under the circumstances, how far he could trust his uncle. But in the end, he had no choice. Sydney had needed that sleep. He didn't want her in a weak state and now he was the one exhausted, who needed a few hours himself.

Tahoe was a terrible place to be hunting somebody while you were being hunted. The basin is surrounded by mountains with only so many roads coming in and only one that circumvented the lake. The towns around the lake—like Tahoe City, Incline, even the casinos in South Lake—were all basically one-horse. If you traveled by car, you were always vulnerable, with no running room. It helped that they had use of the Range Rover, but he still worried about getting spotted.

The one big thing they would have had going for them, before his decision to talk to his uncle, was that the logical thing for them to have done was leave the area. He questioned his decision to meet Tony. And Sydney's decision to hang around.

But there was a big additional problem. He could handle the terrain, the threat, the lack of resources and all that. But the woman was a whole different deal. Girls, even beautiful, smart ones, never were a serious threat to him. He had a good way with the ladies and never had a shortage of opportunity. They were something he worried about when they were around. He typically had a girlfriend for however long, then, when it was convenient for one or both, he'd move on. So much other stuff was always going on that he just never got into anything that might lock him down or send him in a direction he didn't want to go.

This was different. This lady wanted to use him in her mission, her crusade, or whatever the hell it was. Under other circumstances, when some hot little something started trying to drag him down her dark path, he'd enjoy the quick fruits of his labor, then quickly shake free and get the hell on down his own road, avoiding without regret some nightmare he had no hand in making in the first place.

But right from the start, from her attitude, her whole deal, and the way she was somehow so different, he felt a little overwhelmed. Something about her was like a magnet to his inner deal. And now he saw really serious trouble ahead and the escape hatch getting smaller and smaller. He wanted the hell out of this before it grabbed him. And he didn't want to get any too close to her precisely because the not-so-bright part of him wanted just that.

With that unpleasant threat looming, he did, in spite of himself, eventually slip off into a ragged sleep that, as was common, was filled with plenty of equally unpleasant activities related to combat, conflict, and incarceration.

19

Leon, suffering jet lag from flying in from New York, lay on the small, circular bed in the Celebrity Cabin Monday afternoon. The cabin sat below the pool and on the edge of the lake. As he waited for the client to come, he chatted with one of the loves of his life, Marilyn Monroe. He asked her who did the deed—who'd murdered her—and was thinking about what her answer might be when he heard the client coming through the tunnel.

First thing the client says—coming out of the closet, out of the secret tunnel that Sinatra had built so he could go to and from the kitchen of the Cal-Neva and Marilyn's room in secret—was, "How are you?"

Leon was amused. Guy breaks all protocol just coming here. Acting like a big shot. Right away, Leon knew what he was dealing with. He nodded.

The guy strutted to the window, looked out, then came back acting like he was some kind of mafia boss. Like he was Brando. Thing is, he didn't have the look, the voice, or the mannerisms.

"I'm glad you could get here on short notice," the client said. "We have a big problem out there and we need it resolved fast."

Leon sat back against the pillows on the circular bed beneath a picture of Marilyn Monroe and stared at his client. Unbelievable. The man was breaking all the rules.

What he knew about this guy from his Vegas connection was that this Thorp's great-great-great-grandfather had cleared the Sierras of Indians, hung gold mine thieves, and brought in Chinese for the rail line to Silver City. So Leon was interested in the guy's history. At least he was until he met the asshole. The guy didn't live up to expectations.

Great generations aren't followed by even greater generations, Leon thought. And this guy was proof of that. So, somehow, this guy manages to get the tunnel opened up and comes up through it like the old days, like he's a chip off the JFK, Sinatra, and Giancana block. *Yeah, right.*

Leon never met clients, but this guy had insisted. What, maybe they would be friends? Leon didn't do small talk, so he just looked at the guy. Listened to his rant. All the people he wanted dead. The guy was tall, thin, tense, everything on his frame top of the line.

Listening to him jabber, Leon reclined on the bed propped up by pillows, his amusement turning a little sour. The cabins had porches and views of the lake. They were small. Not all that great, but this one had history, and Leon liked history. But then the guy started this whining song and dance about the big screwup he wanted cleaned up and how it had to be done and done fast and how he'd make sure Leon was very well compensated above and beyond his normal fees…and on and on the guy ranted.

Leon waited.

Finally, he got to specifics. Mentioned a guy named Cillo. The uncle of some lowlife who had the girl they wanted dead.

"He's the key. You get him to talk to you, he probably knows where his nephew is holed up. You find the nephew, you find the girl. He's got her somewhere. I got a feeling they're not all that far away. Then get rid of Cillo."

Leon said nothing, just listened. Multiple kills weren't normal, but money for these guys was apparently no object.

The guy rambled on about the woman, and then about the guy she'd brought, some kind of ex-con. Then about his crazy cousin. Finally, the client sat down, one leg up over the other. In the silence, on the lake, Leon could hear the drone of a boat's engine…still closer, the cry of some loud bird.

All the information the guy was giving him, Leon already had. The lawyer had provided the details, and now he had to listen to numbnuts repeat everything.

Then he started again. On and on this guy went about this woman, the blogs, how she was hurting his family's reputation, single-handedly trying to stop Tahoe from becoming what it was meant to be. Then the maniac said he's got this old lion. Bought it from a place in Texas where they take in retired circus animals. Said he wanted to get the bitch alive if that's possible and put her in the cage with his lion that he said is named George. Then he wanted to know, by any chance, did Leon play golf?

Leon had been asked many things but never before had he been asked about golf. He shook his head. Never had he run into a stranger cat than this guy. He was nervous. That was it, Leon concluded. He's nervous and excited at the same time. Like a kid on a first date.

But instead of that being the end of it, the guy went off on handicaps and how he met somebody on the Nullabar Links in Melbourne who may have been in Leon's profession. Guy hit the ball like a pro.

"It's the damnedest golf course on the planet. Takes, like, four days. You cross two time zones. All along this highway through the deserts and kangaroo country, you have to drive your car from tee to tee. It's eight hundred forty-eight miles long. And nobody is sober after the first two holes, and that's when the guy told me about some of his wet work."

He waited as if this was where Leon should jump in and join the conversation. Leon wasn't in the mood, so he just continued to stare at the guy.

"I want constant updates," the client said, a little bit exasperated. Like Leon had disappointed him in some way. "You have my lawyer's throwaways. You let him know what's going on every step of the way. You need men, hookers, whatever, you name it. On the smartphone in the package he left for you are the pictures and addresses. Everything you need. Keys to the car. If you need men for casing or whatever, he'll make sure you're provided with what you want."

Finally, thankfully, the client finished, got it all off his chest. He thought the guy'd be there till midnight yapping.

Leon hadn't said a word until now. "You can leave now. Have them seal the tunnel. Anybody comes through there, I'll kill them."

"Yeah, yeah. I understand," the client said, vigorously nodding his head. And then he left.

Leon bent his head back and looked up at Marilyn. "You believe what you just witnessed? Because I don't."

He considered for a moment refusing the job. The client was exactly the type he'd rather kill than work for. Still, all in all, Tahoe might be fun. He'd never been to Tahoe before, and he appreciated the beauty of the lake and how big it was. You couldn't even see the south shore from the deck of the cabin, it was so far away.

He said to Marilyn, "The bastards murdered you. I'm sorry I wasn't around then. I'd have taken care of all them. But at least you aren't around to deal with this crew." He laughed and imagined her chuckling. He loved the woman.

Leon had never actually had a woman since he was nine and his mother's boyfriend made him and the girl next door try and fuck so the bastard could jack off watching. That guy turned out a few years later to be his first kill, his first suicide creation. He forced the guy at gunpoint to call the suicide hotline, confess his sins, and apologize.

Then he died in a fiery self-emulation. Died with lots and lots of pain and regret. The suicide, much like those monks in Vietnam, got lots of attention. Leon thoroughly enjoyed it and never regretted it for a moment. Killing, he'd discovered, wasn't just easy, it had a certain joy. He became a philosopher of the hunt and the kill.

20

Sydney and Marco left after nine Monday night for Markleeville. He had on a jungle-type hat, she a baseball cap. Very minimal attempts at disguises in case somebody got a look in the car under a streetlight.

He told her she looked cute in her safari outfit. "Women can disguise up easy enough—change of hair, hats—but for men, it's different."

"Not many people have seen you in seven years. You probably don't have to disguise up much." He'd gotten a bag of safari-look items from Bernie Shaw's closet—big jungle hat and wide sunglasses. "You look like a gold prospector from the old days."

They laughed. She was doing much better after the sleep. It also helped that the entire Tahoe Valley was packed with tourists, and the drive down Highway 89 and up into the mountains avoided all the towns around the lake. Bikers, motor homes, and cars jammed the 89 and 50 intersections. It took them nearly an hour to get out of Tahoe and up into the mountains.

"Maybe we'll be sleeping in the car," he told her.

"Tell me about you and Gary Gatts," she said.

"I remember he was always into some con or another. One of those guys who look at the world as something you're always trying to hustle."

"Sounds like him."

In the scheme of things, Markleeville, in the mountains southeast of Tahoe, was nothing much, a half-horse town in the mountains south of Tahoe. Quaint. Old.

"I used to like this hotel," he said, pointing out the window.

By the looks of it, the hotel, the Creekside Lodge, wasn't a hotel anymore. One-block town, that was about the sum of it. The sign said the population was 165. It was on the Indian Creek Reservation, not far from a small airport, Alpine County Court, Monitor Creek, and the East Carson River. The road led over the pass, down to 395. Would be a great ride on a motorcycle.

"You have some good times up here?" she asked.

He smiled. "You won't tell, neither will I."

She figured March had seen plenty of good times all around the lake. This particular mountain town was an unpolished gem that lay at the merge of the Monitor and Wolf Creeks on 89. Popular with bikers and people coming over the pass, they had a courthouse, sheriff's office, and a general store.

"The Cutthroat Bar," Marco said, looking toward a shabby building. "I can't believe myself sometimes. I never connected it to the fish. I always thought it was some pirate thing."

"You didn't—really?"

"Really."

Sydney said, "When the shooter came in, that's what I was holding in my hand. A Cutthroat fingerling."

"Then this is appropriate." He pointed again and said, "There's a sign that says rooms. I'll check it out."

He went in through the back entrance to see if any rooms were actually available. He learned there were, located in the building next to the bar in a motel-like building. He paid cash for a room back off the street.

He let her in, then went on a coffee run to the bar.

Back in the room, when he sipped his coffee, he winced and swore. "Damn!"

"It's that hot?"

"Not really, but I have sensitive tissues in my mouth."

"What from?"

He sat on one of the beds, a small table separating the two twins. She was lying with her arms slung across her stomach.

He said, "My mouth never fully recovered from *la tehuacan.*"

"Which is some kind of hot Mexican sauce?"

"Well, yes and no. You won't find it in a restaurant. During my time in that Mexican prison, when they wanted better conversation, they introduced you to *la tehuacan.* Carbonated mineral water laced with the juice of chili peppers."

"Sounds nasty."

"Then, when your mouth was burned out, they stuck it up your nose while your mouth was gagged. That happens, you tend to become very cooperative."

"Sounds really nasty. What did they want from you?"

"Whatever it was, they didn't get it. I wouldn't have made it, but I had some outside powers interested in me. I ended up in *apando*, a punishment cell, but under the protection of the most powerful man in the prison, the *Tio Mafia*, the prison godfather. Something was in the works. About a week after that, I'm walked out by this *federale*, thinking they might just drive me up in the hills and kill me."

"Our boys?"

"I was met by the guy who put me there. They had work for me in a very deep task force."

"An offer you couldn't refuse?"

"Yeah. When I walked out, I'm standing there blinded by the sun, one of those hard glare days. I'd been in the hole for a long time. No light. I'm not believing anything he says. I'm thinking, *That's it for me.* The air stinks like a welding shop, and this guy's smiling at me and the *federale* who escorted me out says, 'You go home, my friend.' I remember his gold tooth flashed at me like a strobe. He said, 'No more trouble for us, no more trouble for you. *Tomelo facil, amigo.*"

"You have a habit of getting in and out of bad situations."

"So far. So, this gringo gets me out of there. Had Federal or Homeland agent written all over him. He was one of a kind. A real trip. I finally get my vision back. He's standing there like the prison warden in *Cool Hand Luke.*

"So this guy thinks he's funny. He starts talking to me in this phony Southern accent as we walk to a waiting car. 'Let's get you the hell outta town, boy. A town without pity.' At that moment, this *autobus de la prision* passes, kicking up a dust storm, and I'm choking on the dust. He says, 'You need to learn to stay off the bus, Cruz, and we're gonna give you the opportunity to do just that.'"

"What did he want?"

"A job. Turned out to be a few others after that."

He told her about the guy in prison who'd protected him. He was a great mural painter. "They let him paint murals all over the prison. A real genius. This one, the biggest of them and the most brilliant—I wished I'd had the means to take a picture of it."

"Describe it."

"Well, in the center, you had peasants searching among grotesque bodies sprawled on splotched orange terracotta tiles looking for those they could save. On one side, this Mexican Indian woman wept over an open casket, and around her men were laughing and dancing and firing rifles into the air, many dressed like the paramilitary *Guardias Blancas*. Overhead in the fire-red sky, small hawks with boomerang-shaped silver wings—drawn more like knife blades—tacked in the breeze, swinging this way and that, some down in the fields, some riding the thermals he had a genius way of painting. It was like the whole thing was alive. You could see so many things when you studied it."

"Sounds like he was really good."

"He was. I remember was a funeral procession in the fields outside of buildings that represented *San Cristobal*. The women were dressed in black, homespun cloaks, their mouths covered against the smoke and cold, weeping for the dead on the road. In the background, fierce *Chaumla* warriors rose from the smoke among the caskets that lay everywhere. Beyond them, the burning rain forest, the *Selva Lacandones*, and in the fields, thousands of mummies, tiny mummies from the museum in *Guanajuato*, tiny, baby-sized *pistoleros* climbing from the fish raceways led by naked, wounded, bleeding soldiers. A young girl's eyes wide and dark as dying suns…"

She was transfixed by the description, and by his passion for the mural.

At some point, he fell asleep. She didn't. Her mind was in a real spin. She kept thinking the door would burst open and killers would come in. She had the Beretta next to her. Close.

21

O n a "hunt" day, Leon didn't eat. He believed that predators were much more alert when hungry. So he saved eating until after the job was done. If it took long, he'd eat bites of a protein bar, drink coffee and lots of water. It kept the edge.

He went up the mountain in the provided Ford SVT Raptor, the best off-roader in Leon's opinion. He had a little trouble finding the roads that led back to Cillo's place, but Leon eventually left the Raptor a hundred yards back in the trees off the logging road, way up on the mountain. He fixed the silencer to his Glock.

He noticed the outstanding way the reddish moon looked. It reminded Leon of a bullet hole in the sky. And he liked the way the night smelled here in pine country, high in the mountains, that lake black as oil after the hot day.

Great place, Leon thought. It was so pure, nicely tucked away up in the mountains. Vast water below, pure darkness—a primitive magnificence. He breathed in the aroma of heavy pine tinged with smoke from some distant fire. It filled the air as he walked along the dirt road, his gun with silencer at his right side. From time to time, Leon stopped because he had such an outstanding view of the whole basin. He appreciated it more than he thought he would.

Near the house, he spotted two cars: a small one, a Prius; the other, a Jeep Cherokee. The house looked dark save a small light from the back. He moved through the trees toward the porch, then a big, ugly dog rose slowly and came down off the porch to greet him. The dog, looking half-wolf, didn't bark.

"Hey, boy," Leon said in a low, confident command voice to show authority without hostility. "C'mon, here..." He stepped closer, open hand out, palm down. If the dog barked, he'd have to shoot it.

Without much of a sound, the dog displayed teeth and came snarling toward him. Leon shot him in the head. Close up, he confirmed that it looked half-dog, half-wolf, a violation of nature.

"You miserable fucker. You come at me!" Leon said in a low voice. He kicked the big, dead animal in the head. Kicked him a couple more times. "I should skin you, you piece of shit. Attack me, damn you. I'm an animal lover."

Now he'd have to get rid of the creature. A suicide wouldn't look so good if the dog was shot in the head.

He waited to see if the silenced shot had been picked up by any other ears. Still, he saw no movement in the mostly dark house. Porch empty.

Then he heard voices, but they were coming from up in the woods. A girl giggling. Laughing. Somebody having some dirty fun.

He grabbed the dead animal's hind legs and dragged the flea-bitten, half-dog fraud out of sight fifty yards down into the woods so he could be food for natural creatures. Then Leon went up on the porch and in through the unlocked sliding glass door and said, quietly, "Don't shoot. I'm just here to ask you something. Your friend from Incline sent me."

No answer. There was the stink of cigarettes in the house. Maybe pipes and cigars. Leon left the house and followed the stone path lit by a few Malibu lights up through the trees, leading to a stone hut.

The old man he took to be Cillo was playing stud with a young girl in the rock pool in front of some kind of building. The lovers played in the water like kids. Leon, hidden in the trees, wondered how much she cost. There, in the pool, the old man sitting on a rock with the whole of Tahoe below, the girl was giving him a blow job. And she had to work at it. She jerked and blew on him, him trying like hell to get to the end of it all and then finally appearing to.

Leon got a little excited and a little sick. He waited, hoping the little skank would leave so he didn't have to do something with her body. He wasn't in the mood for complications. That was the whole problem with not having time to plan, track, assess, predetermine. These guys were in a panic to shut down the threat, and that led to haste. And haste always, always, brought on unforeseen, unplanned complications.

Fortunately, half an hour after getting the old man off and having finished a drink, she climbed out, then got a towel from a little shed next to the hut. She mumbled something about the night and went down the hill toward the house, wrapped in the towel. A few minutes later, dressed in shorts and a halter top, she crossed the porch and disappeared down the steps. Moments later, she pulled out in the Prius and left.

About damn time, Leon thought. He figured the old man would slip, hit his head on the rock, and drown. Nice, fitting end. They'd find him in a week or so. Instead, the old man smoked a cigar, naked in his rock pool, enjoying that his ancient cock still had some life in it.

"Nice place you got here," Leon said. "I take it you're Tony Cillo, master of this domain."

The old dude turned, not showing as much shock as you'd think. Anger was more like the expression. Looked a little high on something.

"You on Viagra?" Leon asked, smiling.

"Who the fuck are you? What are you doing spying on me like some kind of sick voyeur?"

"I see where the damn half-breed dog got his attitude," Leon said. "So far, everybody I've met in Tahoe has some kind of messed-up attitude. People up here in paradise should have more chill. You're either a dog or you're a wolf. That in-between shit doesn't make it."

"Get the hell off my land!"

"Soon as I get what I came for. You got a nice pad here. Isolated. View of the whole basin. Sit up here getting stoned, having some skank getting you off. Hard work for her."

Leon loved to see how people lived. How big they made their lives. It was so meaningless. Life was short and you were dead forever; all the shit you built up meant nothing.

"I'll tell you what," the old man said, showing no fear. "You best get outta here."

Leon smiled. "Tough old bastard, aren't you? I gotta ask you a question, and you better have a good answer. I'm not here by accident. There's this dude thinks he's God's gift to the planet sitting in his pad at Incline Village. He brought me all the hell the way out here to get some answers. I'm a kind of a liaison between him and you. So let's cooperate so I can get out of your way."

This information changed Cillo's expression. Now he knew the name of the game. His voice went down to a more civil tone. "All he had to do was call. What does he want to know?"

"Where your nephew is. The one who has the woman who's causing all this trouble."

"I don't know."

"Now, now," Leon said. "Let's be smart. I didn't come all the way out here, put up with assholes and mean dogs, for 'I don't know.'"

"It's the truth. I don't know where he went," Cillo said. "I tried to bring him in, but so far, he's out there, and you'll have to go find him. I can't help you. If I could, I would. If he contacts me, I'll let your boss know."

Leon frowned. The nice-guy attitude didn't last long. The bastard couldn't resist getting back to his tough prick self. "Let's get something straight. I haven't eaten in a long time. Makes me mean. I don't want to get mean. Like I said, I didn't fly three thousand miles to hear any bullshit. I asked you a question, and I want an actionable answer."

"He cut me off. I got no idea where he is. Now get the hell out of here," Cillo said. "This conversation is over."

Leon left his Glock on the rock and stepped into the pool.

The old man tried to get up, but Leon was fast on him, grabbing the guy under the chin to lock his head and partially choke him out before he intended to bounce his head on a rock, then drown him. But the old codger, in spite of age and fat, had some fight in him. He pushed off with one foot against the side of the pool and Leon slipped back, hitting the protruding rocks. Now, enraged, he grabbed the old man and put an MMA chokehold on him.

Leon leveraged the bastard, worked him around, and got the hold he wanted. He kneed him in the crouch to get him off balance, then slammed him back against the side of the pool, smashing his skull on the rock. As the man slipped under, momentarily out cold, Leon held him down. Scene still looked good for a slip and an accidental drowning.

Accidents look as good as suicides. No real follow-up.

But then the bastard came alive like some horror-movie dude, grabbed Leon's ankle, and tried to drag him down with a seriously strong grip, forcing Leon to back off. The way Cillo came up coughing, spitting, and fighting, Leon had to smash him in the face repeatedly, then jump on him with his knee against the bastard's throat, pinning him under. Even then, the old man showed remarkable fight, and it took a hell of a long time to get him to settle and get done with it.

Finally, the kicking and struggling stopped. The last gurgle and bubbles came next. Leon knew soon the bowels would let loose, and he didn't want to be in the water. He got out, breathing hard, soaked—amazed at how strong and determined the old fool was. Probably the damn Viagra.

Leon cursed himself for being lax. The last guy, so willing to die, so beaten, had affected him in dealing with this guy, and he wasn't happy with himself about that. If it was to look like he slipped and fell in, he must of slipped a couple times.

Dripping wet and staring at the dead guy, Leon said, "You miserable old son of a bitch, you had some life in you, I'll say that. All I did for you—even let you get your last blow job. And you got to give me a bad time. You and your fucking wolf-dog."

Before heading back to the house, Leon went through the dead man's robe and found his cell phone. So far, nothing had gone smoothly. First he met the asshole client. Then he ran into this crazy old bastard and his dog. Now he was wet, hungry, and pissed.

He had a lot of work yet to do. Not a good start to the night. Leon left Cillo's and hiked back to his Raptor. He had his travel bag in the vehicle. Leon never left anything in a hotel room.

He changed, draping the wet clothes in the back seat. Then he headed for Jesup's condo on the other side of South Lake. He wanted to get a hold of Jesup's computer, notes, and files.

All the fun had gone out of the night.

22

Marco was asleep when Sydney got the call from her police-reporter friend. She went into the bathroom.

"Hi. Thanks for getting back to me. What did you find out?"

"Not a lot, but enough. You were right about this guy. His records have been sanitized. Wiped clean. I talked to a very solid source who knew all about Marco Cruz and his problems."

"Federal?"

"Yes. He wouldn't tell me anything real specific, for obvious reasons. Cruz ended up in a Mexican prison for unknown offenses. I'm not sure he was even charged, but if he was, it's been cleaned. This was after he took out the guys who killed the border agent. It may or may not have been connected to the gun-walking deal."

"How did he get away with being in Mexico?"

"He has relatives in Mexico. Some with questionable associations. Anyway, he ended up in prison for a time. All under a tight wrap. Can't confirm anything about what happened. Then he's out, vanishes for over a year. Now, apparently, he's clean and in Tahoe. According to my source, he survived in prison because he was friendly with the big dog in there. Maybe the guy was a relative or a friend of a relative. He got released suddenly, without any explanation. Who got him out, and what he did to earn his freedom, or what he did for his benefactors, I don't know. Whatever he did, somebody with lots of power liked him for it. And the only people who can clean records like that have a lot of federal power. Could even be the CIA. He was a perfect candidate for whatever they wanted—his military and border background, shady family ties. Like he was designed for clandestine activity."

"Thanks. I appreciate your help."

"Syd, how you're connected with this guy, I don't know…and maybe don't want to know. But he's not exactly someone you want to take home to Mom. Look, I know some rumors, and I don't much like to deal in them—"

"What?"

"Well, this is rumor. After prison activities—and this is speculation because of timing and location—but it might be connected to the fall of one of Mexico's most powerful families. That's very much undercover as well. Information surfaced about connections beyond the cartels, reaching all the way to the Middle East. Somebody got that information and there's this rumor—and that's how it was put to me—that Marco Cruz was involved in the operation. People died. People ended up disappearing. It was supposedly a major operation. His role in it, I don't know. But be careful—"

"I will. Thanks."

"Syd, I don't know what you're doing, but—"

"Don't ask. I won't tell."

Sydney hung up. When she walked back into the dark bedroom, Marco was still dead asleep. She stared at him, that rugged but handsome face, the scar on his neck, the mouth and nose, the curly hair, the dark skin.

He's my guy, she thought. *My dark knight.*

She smiled. If he was half as bad as it appeared, *Well,* she thought, *maybe he's exactly what a girl needs when the most powerful people in the Sierras are trying to kill her.* It wasn't like she was marrying the guy. And it wasn't like he didn't do this kind of thing. But, she admitted, he needed to come to it himself. If all he wanted was the shooter, so be it.

At some point in her ruminations, she realized he was awake and staring at her.

"You looked stressed out about something," he said, shifting in the bed, propping his pillow to sit up a bit.

"I had my police-reporter friend, my only real friend up here at the moment, check you out. His advice was to get the hell away from you."

"Sounds like he's a wise man. You don't strike me as someone who doesn't take good advice."

"I don't." Sydney Jesup looked away from him, her gaze on the wall, the window curtain, the old furniture in the room. "I never, ever thought of myself as crossing certain lines. Always by the book, by the law. And then I did."

"Let me tell you something," he said. "You take the very best, law-abidingest person on the planet and you stick them in the midst of massive and brutal corruption that has even the law in its grasp, and that leaves a simple, if unfortunate, choice. You have to submit and become corrupt, as many cops do—if not most in Mexico and quite a few in this country—or you have to rebel and cross that line. You took the right moral path in my mind. It comes with costs and high risks, but it leaves you your soul."

"And your Shelby Mustang," she said with a smile.

"That's right, and I'm going to get the bastard who put bullet holes in it."

No, it's not ending there, she wanted to tell him. *You might not know it yet, but you're in this, and you can't get out that easy. You're going to help me get those bastards.*

I'm not a cop or DA's investigator anymore, she told herself. *And he's not a soldier or border patrol agent.* But what did the things they were going to do—because she was confident that the deeper he got, the more locked in with her he was—make them? Criminals?

No. We're not criminals, but we aren't going to use the authorities, and we're probably going to commit crimes. There needs to be a third category.

Staring at him, she made a decision: at some point in the not too distant future, she was going to climb into his bed if he showed interest.

23

Shaun Corbin was freaking out, yelling at himself in his head, coming apart.

You are such a moron! Jesus, man, you're a dead man, Shaun Corbin. Sonofabitch. Is this how it ends?

His first panicked thoughts when he woke up in the dark in his pickup were, *I got to get the hell out of here. Pack, get money from Kora, hit the road.*

He'd been sleeping in his truck on a side street near the ski run. He drove the short distance to his house. Earlier, he'd been afraid to go home, but now he needed to pack up and get ready to run.

He parked and stood outside for awhile, looking around for something amiss. Something that would tell him somebody was there. But he realized he was alone on the lonely road. He wasn't even entirely sure it was the same night. He went inside and put stuff together in a backpack and suitcase. Just the essential stuff—his laptop, some files, the travel junk, some clothes.

Should I take it with me now? No, I can't leave it in the truck and go up to see her. If she can't get the money until the bank opens, then what?

A million damn questions and problems. He separated out everything with Kora North involved—the videotapes, photographs. It was what he would trade for the cash. He put it all out on the coffee table.

Kora was his greatest find. She was now the top call girl in Tahoe and worked exclusively for his cousin's party set. But it was late—he assumed she'd have to go to the bank in the morning, and probably bring the money to him. By then, he'd make up his mind what to do. And she could find out some things for him, like when his damn cousin was coming back. Maybe she'd even know something about what was going on with the pro Gatts said was coming.

That scared him. Last thing he wanted was to be in Tahoe when some stone-cold killer showed up.

I'll be gone by then, he told himself.

He sat for a minute, his brain all messed up from the binge he'd been on. But to get himself straight, he needed a drink. And he needed to go see Kora.

On his way to her place, like a broken record, his mind played the hatchery shooting again and again and again. He'd been so close, fired so many shots. Then the chase and her escape in the Shelby. It was the worst moment of his life when she'd gotten out of there. It didn't seem possible. It was like the universe conspired against him. Hated him.

Instead of being on the hunt, he'd been riding the bottle. He'd messed up big time and it was over. He had to get out.

He was drunk and miserable. His greatest opportunity kicked him in the gut and mocked him. He hated himself for wanting so desperately to be accepted by the goddamn Thorps. All he did for them…the party girls, the drugs. God, he hated the whole arrogant elitist bunch of assholes. But he knew he'd screwed up big time. He was a dead man if he didn't get the hell out and get far away.

Once he had some running money, he was thinking of Florida. He'd get what he could from Kora and from a guy who owed him. Then he'd pay a visit on his way out of town to Gatts, maybe, and relieve him of some cash and drugs and be on his way.

For sure, Kora North had become the star. Nothing like the demand for her. She had become the mother lode for Thorp and Rouse's ambition to get everyone on sex tapes for future use. She was a sex magnet. Tahoe's new Monroe.

He turned onto her street. Kora lived in a place at the trendy Tahoe Keys condos. Top of the line, all the way. Sixty to a hundred grand was what he figured he needed to get things going, but he doubted he could get much more than thirty out of her.

He parked. The Keys had fingers of land reaching into the wetlands they'd drained and made into boat docks, condos, and houses. He went up to her place, a corner unit with a nice view of the lake, and started with the doorbell.

After no response, he started pounding. "C'mon, bitch, wake up!"

24

Who the hell...? Oh, Jesus...

Kora North, on her bed writing in her journal, wearing her running pants and a T-shirt, heard somebody pounding on her door in the middle of the night and knew who it had to be. She went out into the living room and heard Shaun Corbin, the nemesis of everyone's life, out there yelling for her to wake up. Looking through the peephole, she confirmed it, then opened the door.

"Shaun, what the hell are you doing here? It's, like, one-thirty in the damn morning. You look like shit."

He pushed his way in. "That problem I got is too big to argue with you. You didn't talk to me. Hung up on me, you bitch."

"What problem? You're drunk. Get the hell out of here. You want me to call security or the police?"

"You got anybody here?"

"No. And I don't want you here, either. Goddamn, you're drunk and you stink."

He went over to her bar, his gun sticking out in the small of his back. *He shoot somebody?* she wondered. She watched as he poured himself a half-glass of vodka.

"You got anything to eat?" He opened the little bar fridge and pulled out some string cheese.

"You're pathetic. What do you want, Shaun? If it's about your big screwup, don't come to me. And don't break anything. Who'd you shoot?"

"What do you know?" he said, giving her a look of concern.

"That's the point of the question, isn't it, genius?"

He looked almost relieved. "I got a serious big problem and I need some help."

"You are your biggest problem. You did something, and I don't care about it, so why are you here? Go. Get the fuck out of here. You mess me up and you know what'll happen to you. They'll hunt you down like a rabid dog, and it'll go bad."

"Kora," Corbin said, turning, giving her his nastiest look, "you better shut up and listen to me."

"And why is that?"

"Because I'm not pissing around. I got to get out of here and I need some cash."

"What, exactly, did you do?"

"Don't worry about it. I'm leaving and I'm not coming back."

"You serious?"

"I am. So we need to settle up."

"If that's true? You're leaving, I'm celebrating. As for the cash, forget that. I don't owe you shit."

"Hey"—he moved closer—"you bitch, all that money you have is my money. I put you on your back in the right crowd. I hooked you up. You'd still be pole dancing in some stinking club if it wasn't for me, sweetheart."

"Shaun, back the fuck off. I'm warning you."

"You forget. I have something you don't want spread around. And I know you have a lot of cash somewhere. Thirty from you will do to get me where I'm going. Travel expenses. I'm collecting from everybody owes me, and you owe me big time."

"Screw you. I made you the asshole big shot you think you are," she said.

"That right? Kora," he said, "that video of what happened at the lake—you and the senator, half a dozen other big shots—you don't want that out on the goddamn Net. You'll get dead fast. So you want those tapes, you better dump the attitude."

She knew Corbin, and he was a vindictive little bastard. He'd do it, and that would be the end of things for sure.

"I can't give you what I don't have."

"Fine. See you on the Internet." He turned to leave.

"Shaun, look. What I have is in a bank box. I can't get anything until morning."

He stared at her. "Morning ain't all that far off. Get it and bring it over to my place pronto. And don't get stupid. Don't talk to anybody about anything."

He downed the vodka, eyes closed for a second, then opened them and took a deep breath.

"What you did must have been really stupid," she said.

"Just get my money."

"This isn't good, Shaun."

"Don't worry about it." He slapped the glass hard on the bar. "I need to use your bathroom."

"Jesus, can't you just go home or to a bar?"

"I need it right now." He headed down the hall.

She had a gun in a drawer in her bedroom. She had an urge to get it, shoot this prick, call the police, and say it was in self-defense. Mess the place up. Cut her lips. Give herself some bruises. But she had to get those tapes first. She was certain he'd do just what he said he would. The real question was, why didn't the real slut—his mother, who'd dropped this abomination on the world—have enough sense to abort him? In her mind, Shaun Corbin was all the argument the pro-abortionists would ever need.

He came back and walked to the door. The man couldn't do anything he didn't find a way to make a little bit gross.

"Eight tomorrow morning with the money, Kora, baby?"

"Don't be an idiot. Banks aren't open that early. I can't be there any earlier than nine."

He stared at her. He was close enough that, besides his breath and the ugly mole in the center of his stinking forehead, she noticed how bloodshot his eyes were, and that he was afraid of something in a big way. Whatever he'd done, it had to be bad.

"You messed up good this time, didn't you, hotshot?" she said, taunting him. "What did you do?"

"Don't worry about it. You know when Oggie is coming back?"

"No."

He left, throwing the door open and leaving it. Kora thought again about shooting the bastard. She could go over and just put a bullet in his peanut brain, then get the tapes and whatever he had and set his fucking house on fire.

Being part of his little escort business was one of the biggest mistakes of her life. Maybe the biggest—and she'd made plenty of them. To calm herself down, settle her mind, she poured herself a very large goblet of Merlot. Then she fetched her .32 Smith from the bedroom and returned to the living room. She aimed it like she intended to do. She pointed. She imagined shooting Corbin in the head, shooting out that fucking mole. Beauty kills the beast.

Then she'd do what she had been planning a long time—get the hell out of Tahoe.

I hate my stupid damn life, Kora thought bitterly. She knew three things about herself: she had a high IQ, she was knock-down hot, and she was living a totally phony, rotten life. She didn't believe in killing animals or eating meat, but killing assholes was definitely on her *to do* list.

Bang bang, motherfucker!

25

Leon, in post-kill euphoria, left the mountain and headed past the casinos.

"You talkin' to me. Are you talking to me?" He smiled that same crazy De Niro smile in *Taxi* as he drove from Cillo's to the GPS address for Jesup.

He parked down the street from Jesup's. She lived a quarter-mile from the government complex that housed the courthouse, police, sheriff's and DA's offices. His client already had one of his goons sitting on the street in case she made any attempt to come home. Leon found him asleep in his car. He didn't bother to wake him.

Leon used a simple lock-shock to get in. No alarm system on. Once inside, he went about his task fast and methodically. Before leaving Sydney Jesup's bedroom, everything in piles, neat piles, Leon thought about what her clothes, the outdoor gear, and the pictures she'd taken of nature and stuff told him.

The girl he had to hunt and kill was lean and something of a minimalist and a mountain girl. No excess. Nothing very sexy except for some short shorts. He held a pair up, felt the material against his face. But the tight-ass cop didn't fit his model. Mountain girl. Cop family, from the pictures. She run to family in Sacramento, maybe?

"Probably a nasty dike bitch," he said his thought out loud.

The facts about her behavior didn't make much sense. She hadn't reported the shooting at the hatchery. At Cillo's, according to the report his client had gotten, she was sitting up in the car and nobody seemed to know how bad she was hit other than what the nephew, Marco Cruz, had said. Why did the guy not get rid of her, get away from the whole thing? Made no sense. What was that about?

People are hard to figure, Leon thought. Why would this guy risk everything for some low-level DA's investigator on a short list to get the bus for the scenic ride to eternity?

Normally, Leon didn't give a damn, the "why" about somebody

to be taken out. But everything in this case hinged on the whys. Why was she anywhere around Tahoe, unless she was hit pretty bad? That made sense. But why was Cruz sticking with her?

He used her tennis bag to collect her iPad, notebook computer, handwritten journals, and flash drives. He'd look at it all later and find some answers before turning it over to Thorp.

There were a few pictures of the outdoors, of her and her lesbian girlfriends up in the snow.

Some books. Law stuff. Stuff on the environment. Her furniture was simple and Ikea-cheap. Pictures on the desk of family, he assumed. Fucking cops all over the place. He smiled. That's where she'd run—Sacramento. Home to the protection of family? Maybe.

But they'd gone first to the bad boy's uncle. Strange place to run. And her cop relatives might not be all that thrilled she was hanging with a criminal. And then this Marco refused to cough her up, refused to come home. They were up to something. Did they know each other before?

Tracking was all about their past, their habits, comfort zones. Any good hunter knows running off in the woods is a waste of time. You need to understand the quarry. Maybe they'd headed back to Mexico.

Maybe this Corbin, the wannabe, could tell him what the hell was going on. That is, if he was even still around.

Runners are two kinds—those who planned ahead of time, expecting to be on the run, and those it happened to without warning. She was the latter, and they usually left trails, contacting friends or relatives. But, this was a woman from Cop World. Ex-sheriff's deputy, DA's investigator. So she didn't fit into any normal profile.

Corbin, on the other hand, looked like a real fool. He botched the hit and was probably out there looking to fix it. Get it right. If he had half a brain, he'd have gone. Be on his way to South America.

Leon left Sydney Jesup's place and followed the GPS to the address he'd been given for Corbin.

26

The boy lived back in the hills about two miles or so from the center of South Lake. Hard to find at first, with all the curling roads. No fucking streetlights. Houses hiding back in the trees. But he found it eventually.

Leon parked out of sight of the house, on a feeder road just off Needle Peak Road, and walked. He took the tennis bag with him to add to it if the PI had anything of value.

He slipped up into the woods behind the unlit house and came down toward it slowly, his cougar on the hunt walk, as he liked to think of it. He stared at the little nondescript house. No vehicle out front.

Where are you, boy? You gone? You best be long gone.

It was a dark street with no traffic. The houses in here were a little ragged. Not very active. Not the ski-bum crowd. Poor whites working the casinos, most likely.

Leon, the tennis bag slung over his left shoulder, weapon in his right hand, went into the backyard, past a car up on blocks, and found a side door with not much in the way of a lock. He put the tennis bag down in the kitchen and searched the house. Shaun Corbin proved not to be home, but he hadn't run off. His bags were out and packed, and it looked like he had plans on taking a long vacation. Even had a map on the table. Florida.

You're still here, boy. How dumb are you?

Leon brought the tennis bag into the living room.

"You got to come back for your stuff," Leon said to himself.

And I'll be here. We're gonna have a little chit chat about how this mess happened.

He didn't expect to learn much about the whereabouts of Jesup and her new buddy, but he could learn a little more about the client and the situation.

Why hadn't Corbin gone? Hanging around to say goodbye to

friends? Or was he out on the hunt, hoping to fix things.

Too late for that, boy.

Leon wore a Black Diamond headlamp with two tiny LED bulbs. Gave him a small amount of light, but didn't create a beam the world could see.

Unlike Jesup, this boy was a pig. His place was a fucking disease incubator, a biohazard zone. Jesup had been minimalist, if a bit messy. This guy was a junk collector. Everything was shoddy. Man never dusted or cleaned. You could smell the mold.

Leon opened windows just a quarter inch—not far enough they would notice, especially at night—to let in some fresh air and allow him to hear anyone approaching.

"Well, let's see what a PI has in his collection," Leon said. There was a bunch of stuff out on the coffee table, but first he opened a backpack he'd noticed and pulled out computer disks, dozens of paper files, notebooks. There were dozens of CDs with dates and names. He opened some of the manila envelopes. Man had pictures of young girls doing bad things to older guys. Blackmail kind of stuff.

Busy little PI bugger, aren't you?

Some of them looked like the same motel rooms. Or cabin rooms. Serious porno stuff going on. Leon chuckled. A couple of young pussy looked like prison bait. Even some gay stuff. Kinky scene, this Tahoe underbelly.

Then he turned to the stuff out on the coffee table. More photos, tape recorder, videos.

"What have we here?"

The photos were all of the same girl with various men. Not your run-of-the-mill hooker. This lady love was in a class by herself. This was serious stuff. Marilyn with an even better body. No surplus on this package. Stop a fucking train. "The best for last, my boy."

Some girls just had that combination of sweet kid looks and a shape that wouldn't quit. On the back of one photo, her name: Kora North. The more he stared, the more enraptured he became. There was something about the girl. Perfection, to be sure. But in a unique way.

Figuring it could be a long wait and, being jetlagged, Leon moved to the recliner, but he didn't like the looks of it. He went into the kitchen and got a towel, wet it, and cleaned off the leather recliner. Before sitting down he tightened the curtain, then began to look over what he had on Jesup.

The more he read from her files and from the PI's, the more he began to wonder what the hell was going on here in little old Tahoe. What the client was up to his eyeballs in. Who was the PI gathering all this stuff on, and for what, exactly?

He went back to the hot chick, the train-stopper. Some of these dudes in the pics had to be among the rich and powerful set. Lake Tahoe, with its bad-boy history…looked like some of those bad habits were back in vogue. What was the little snoop up to? Must be some blackmail goin' on. This guy was up to his eyeballs in the muck.

C'mon home, Corbin. Can't wait to meet you.

He found a file on Jesup. Pictures taken with a telescopic lens. Had a couple partial nude shots in her place. Man had been tracking her. Had all kinds of records on her. Even tapes of phone calls. A big investigation. Newspaper clippings of a girl named Karen Orland who'd drowned in Fallen Leaf Lake.

Corbin had a big profile on the woman. Her past in Sacramento. Her friends and relatives. Habits. Mountain rescue skier in the winter. He knew where she worked out, ate. Had a picture of her coming out of a breakfast place called the Red Hut Waffle Shop.

Leon couldn't wait to get to the computers. He finally turned off the tiny light. Settled back in the recliner, his weapon on his lap. He was a light sleeper, but right now, he was a little more exhausted than usual. Still, he kept going back to the photo of Kora North. Never had he seen a more beautiful, more perfect woman. He wondered if, in person, she was half as fine.

He drifted off with his usual sleep protocol. He loved to imagine himself hunting down world leaders, killing them, feeding the news cycles, and playing with the government agencies hunting him. Taunting them. It was a kind of masturbation of the mind for Leon.

But on this night, after enjoying his kill in New York and his battle with the old man, he went to Kora North, having various forms of sex with her in his mind until he finally drifted off.

27

Just before sunrise on Tuesday morning, Marco and Sydney slipped out of a still-sleeping Markleeville.

Sydney felt guilty about dragging Marco further into this. She sensed he was already in deep yet was still serious about dumping her and going to his uncle, hat in hand. He was angry about what had happened, but she knew she was growing on him. Now a lot depended on what Gary Gatts could tell them—if it turned out the shooter was some random guy and not coming from Thorp, then she couldn't expect Marco to join her "crusade."

The Mountain View Restaurant squatted off the side of the snaking mountain road in the pines about six miles from Markleeville. A sagging dining hall, faded red paint, and a sign over the screened-in porch announced that you could "catch 'em yourself" along with a colorful drawing of a fish.

"Is that the place?"

"Yes."

The sun began its rise and would come with a vengeance. Another hot day ahead.

Suddenly, a small horde of leathered, tattooed bikers came roaring around the bend from the opposite direction and pulled into the parking lot of the restaurant. It was awkward for a moment, as Marco slowed as if also going into the restaurant but then continued on, the bikers no doubt assuming their presence was enough to scare off any regular citizenry.

They drove around the curve; Marco found a place just off the highway in the woods, on a feeder road, and parked out of sight of the main road and the restaurant. "We arrived a few minutes earlier, it would have gotten uncomfortable," he said.

"Timing in love and war is everything," Sydney said.

Marco secured his piece under his shirt, and then they hiked down through the trees, where they had a view of the restaurant and parking lot but were well hidden. They waited about thirty minutes. Two girls were outside by one of the bikes. They were joined by the rest of the crew: four males, two more females. They stood talking for a moment, then mounted up, kickstands retracted, engines turned on and cranked up.

"Dogs on hogs probably making a delivery, or a pickup," Sydney said. "The Hell's Angels used to run the trade until the Mexicans took over. They work for them. Next they'll all be working for the Chinese. A new world."

Marco smiled. "You're cynical."

"Usually depends on the time of day."

With the biker bitches clinging onto their road warriors like fierce female bats, they roared off down the winding mountain road toward Markleeville, their shiny black helmets gleaming in the early morning light.

Sydney and Marco walked across the parking lot and went on inside, greeted by a fragrant waft of chilies and old grease. A sign on the wall next to the empty hostess stand explained that you could catch your own fish down in the creek, bring them up to be cleaned, then cook them yourself, or have the cook do it.

Fishing poles and bait on the porch, the sign read in big red letters across the bottom, with an arrow pointing to the porch.

The man they were looking for wasn't in the dining room or in the kitchen. A plump, attractive Spanish woman emerged and cast anxious glances at them.

"I guess we don't look like customers," Marco said. He nodded to the woman and said, *"Cómo es usted que hace hoy a señora."*

She looked worried. Marco assured her they weren't ICE. *"No somos gobierno."*

"I speak English," she shot back, eyes fiery like he'd insulted her. "Probably better than you do."

Marco smiled appreciatively at her feistiness. "We're looking for Mr. Gatts. He around?"

A flicker of anxiety shadowed her eyes. "No."

"Where is he?"

"I don't know. He comes, he goes. Doesn't tell me when or where."

Sydney glanced at the small kitchen table with two coffee mugs and two dirty dishes, then out at the tables. No evidence the bikers had bothered to eat or drink. Looked to her like they'd picked up or delivered and left.

"You just get a delivery?"

"No. Deliveries come on Fridays."

"I'm not talking about food."

"I don't know what you mean," the woman said, eyes now showing some real apprehension.

"Who's down at the creek?" Sydney asked. She went over to the stove. "I assume you have the right credentials of citizenship. Or at least a green card."

Marco said, and without any humor now, "*No te echarás. Dónde está Gatts?*"

"Yes, that's him down at the creek. He should be up in a few minutes."

Marco nodded. "We'll go on down. He's an old friend. Be a nice surprise."

"He has friends?" she asked, with a wry raise of her eyebrows.

Marco and Sydney exchanged looks.

"We were in prison together," Marco said.

Sydney thought the woman's suppressed smile would have been laughter had they been sitting at a bar, and if the woman wasn't frightened for her own safety.

Sydney said, "Sweetheart, you might want to take off, close the place for the rest of the morning. Silence is golden. *And* a way to stay in this country."

The woman grabbed her purse and a canvas bag from under the counter and beat it out of there, the screen door banging resolutely behind her. Moments later, they heard a car engine cough, then start. They saw from the south end of the building an aging, wounded, blue Ford Focus sputter out across the parking lot and stumble down the road beyond the trees.

Sydney hung the CLOSED sign on the door, locked it, and they both took out weapons, holding them down behind their legs. It was time to shake some information out of Gatts and find out if an old friendship had any weight, and what that might mean.

28

*S*ydney's got game, Marco thought. He liked the way she handled herself. Big city law way out of her true element in a small town like South Lake Tahoe.

As they crossed to the steps, Marco glanced at the fishing poles and rubber boots that cluttered the back porch. A broken refrigerator leaned against the wall, next to it, a sign in large letters: BAIT. A cheap hunting knife was stuck in the wall.

He paused as Sydney got out her phone, he guessed to make a recording of the interaction with Gatts. Then they went down a series of stone steps that led to the stream below. She had to go easy on her wounded leg but seemed to not be in pain.

The creek was narrow but active. Had to be a pool somewhere that Gatts kept stocked. They made their way carefully, the murmuring of the creek over rocks loud enough to mask their approach.

They found him at a turn in the creek maybe fifty yards from the steps. Gatts squatted at the edge of the creek, feet in the water. He wore tan shorts from which dropped skinny legs, no shirt under his black leather vest. Skin and bones, the overall look of somebody who lives more on chemicals than food. A bulge in the pocket could be a handgun.

Gatts was next to a sluice box popular with gold rockers, oblivious to their approach. But it wasn't the sluice box he was messing with. As they got closer, Marco could see a thick metal tube. He was pushing something inside before screwing on a cap, then pushed the metal tube into a pipe imbedded in the bank. A rock soon covered the hiding place.

A perfect hidey-hole, Marco thought, *especially when the water rose to normal levels and covered the whole deal.*

"Neat," Marco said quietly. "Guy's got himself a little safe right here in the creek. No dogs would sniff that out. No DEA would think to look under rocks in the stream."

They moved closer.

"That's pretty damn nifty, Gary Gatts," Marco said. "How you doin', boy?"

Gatts jumped up, startled, nearly falling over, his eyes wide, as if he expected to die right then and there. He tried to collect himself.

"Jesus, you scared the hell out of me sneaking up like that. The fishing poles are up on the porch. Ask the lady in the kitchen." His mouth uttered the words, but his eyes showed concerns of a different sort. He knew they weren't looking for fishing poles, knew they'd seen what he was doing, and this was not a good situation. He didn't appear to recognize Marco.

"We wanted some fish," Marco said, noticing the dragon tattoo on Gatts' right arm, the tiny gold studs in his ears that caught a spike of sunlight dappling down through the trees. "We'd have you catch, clean, and cook them for us."

The expression on the man's face said run, said get the hell out of there, eyes big as an owl's.

"Settle," Marco said. "Things better that way. You don't remember me?"

"Holy hell...Marco Cruz. Damn, I heard you got killed in Mexico. Hey, dude, good to see you." He said it but didn't look like he meant it, eyes all jumpy and dilated.

Then Sydney removed her sunglasses—did it in a cool way—and the little guy recognized her. She did this little rise with her eyebrows coupled with a gotcha smile.

Gatts mumbled through his shock, "Sydney Jesup," like she was the second to last person on this earth to have come back from the dead.

"How are you, Gary?" Sydney said. "Nice little place you got here."

Marco said, "I hear you've come a long way since your pot-dealin' days. Nice setup. People make deliveries; you put them here in your secret little safe. Pretty neat, Gary—your own full-service restaurant."

Gatts rubbed his temple with his left hand, his right drifting back of his thigh.

"What do you want?" Gatts asked, and then, rodent quick, he spun around and started to run, his hand going to his pants pocket under his shirt.

Marco fired a warning shot in the water ahead of him. Gatts stumbled and struggled with whatever he was trying to get and Marco fired a second shot in the water. Gatts abandoned his struggle with his weapon, rolling half in and half out of the water as he screamed and grabbed his wounded foot.

"Get under control," Marco said.

Gatts rocked back and forth as both hands clutched his right foot, his eyes wide and staring at Marco, who was on him fast, grabbing the little guy's face and pushing it under. Marco removed the weapon from Gatts' front right pocket, where it had gotten hung up. He lifted the gasping drug dealer's head up out of the water.

Sydney reached for Gatts' gun. "Finally, one of my own. Thanks, Gary."

Marco dragged him up on the side of the rocky bank, the little guy squirming and pleading.

"Settle, Gatts!" Marco said.

Gatts, on his back now, his leg pulled up to his chest, his hands on the wounded foot, moaned like a baby.

"Nobody told you to run," Marco said. "You try and pull a gun on me and you're still alive, makes me wonder what I'm coming to. Maybe it's because I need some information bad enough to forgive you. Once."

Sydney took a nearby seat on a rock just above and out of sight of Gatts' eyes, saying, "Listen to your old buddy, Gary. He's not the nice guy you once knew. He's the nastiest bastard I've ever run into, and I've been around the block. He'll hurt you slow and mean before he kills you if you don't listen to him and answer his questions." She prepared her cell phone to capture whatever transpired.

29

Gatts struggled with a nod of submission. Water bounced off his head, dripping onto his face. He muttered plaintively, crying out in pain and fear, "What do you want? I got some cash. Take it. C'mon, man, take my stash. Anything. Whatever you want, just don't kill me. Don't kill me, man. We go back, you and me. We had fun. Memories, you know. Good memories."

Marco dragged him back to the bank, next to his drug cache. "You're hardly worth a bullet. I might just drown you, though. Let's see what you got. And get calm. I hate talking to excited people. Brings out the worst in me. Before you know it, the vultures will be circling."

"Take it, man. It's yours. I just make the connections is all. It's pretty big money there. Take it. Just let me get out of here. I'm begging you, man, don't kill me."

"You don't shut up, I'll have no choice."

Gatts shut up. Marco pulled the rock aside, pulled the tube out, unscrewed the cap on the end, then reached in and pulled out some plastic bags. He laid them on the nearest flat rock.

"What we have here," Marco said, dumping the remaining contents of the cylinder out on the flat rock, "is a CVS pharmacy of hardcore drugs."

"How do you think," Sydney said as she wiped down the small revolver, "a guy like Gatts would do in prison?"

"He'd become popular fast food. Be buying and selling him the way he buys and sells these joy bags."

"Where are these headed?" Sydney asked. "You provide for the big parties?"

Gatts didn't respond. He was in obvious pain and afraid he was going to be killed. Marco gave him a little tap with the gun. Gatts yelped, one hand leaving his foot to grab his head.

"Yes. Yes."

The bullet had cut through the outside of his left sneaker from top to bottom, just behind the toes. He was sitting half in the shallow water, tears rolling down his cheeks, blood trailing downstream, curling with the flow of the water.

"These for the big bash next weekend?" Sydney asked. "Thorp's Great Gatsby Gala?"

Gatts nodded. "I'm just the delivery guy. I don't even own this place." He nodded to the restaurant. "I'm just managing it for some people."

"Some people?"

"I really don't know who they are. Just some real estate company. I think the lawyer, Rouse, has some connection to it."

"That's Thorp's buddy, partner, and next door neighbor," Sydney said. "He's the real power behind the throne."

"Jesus, my foot hurts bad. Damn!"

"You once worked for Shaun Corbin when they came in by seaplane to Fallen Leaf Lake, didn't you?" Sydney asked.

Gatts looked like he didn't want to answer that, but a little move by Marco altered his attitude.

"Yes."

Sydney moved a little closer and, now behind Gatts, said, "You want to stay alive, don't you?"

"Yes."

"Okay. I have a few simple questions for you." She massaged the back of his neck with the gun. "You answer them correctly and you'll have a good chance of getting out of here alive. You don't, I'm going to leave you two alone. I'm a little squeamish."

Gatts had a look on his face, the skin drawn back, nostrils wide, fear crawling out his pores.

Marco leaned down and smiled as evilly as he could. "She's not kidding. I'd answer her questions. And the thing to remember is, we already know a lot. We talked to people. She catches you in a lie, she'll walk away. She walks, you're completely and royally screwed."

"Who ordered Karen Orland and her unlucky boyfriend killed?" Sydney asked.

Without hesitation, a very scared Gatts said, "You know it was Thorp."

"Who did the killing?"

"I don't...I'm just tellin' you what I heard, what went around. I don't know who the doer was. That's the God's honest truth."

"Tell me what you know about me getting shot at the hatchery Sunday afternoon," Sydney said. "Be careful how you answer. You make a mistake, lie, there's no coming back from that. Don't contradict things we already know. We just want corroboration."

The expression on Gatts' face made it seem he'd decided it was best to get on their side and find a way out. "You probably want to talk to Shaun Corbin about that."

"And why is that?" Sydney asked.

"That moron came up here—"

"Corbin?"

"Yeah. A week ago...gets drunk and starts shootin' off his mouth how he's gonna be a big deal. Settle issues. You being the issue he's gonna to settle. He's got a small brain, big mouth. I didn't buy it. I didn't think he would actually go after you."

"Thorp wasn't behind it?" Marco asked.

Gatts hesitated. "Well, yes and no. This is gonna get me killed for sure."

Sydney said, "Better later than now." She turned to Marco. "You think now he's going to start lying? Maybe a bullet in the other foot will get him to tell us what we want to know."

Sydney cocked the revolver.

"Wait, wait! Okay. Don't shoot," Gatts cried.

Marco said, "She sees that little telltale hesitation that precedes a lie, she'll put another bullet in you."

"Corbin was mouthing off about some heavy hitter coming in to take care of her," he said, nodding back toward Sydney. "It was set up for after the big Gatsby party next weekend. I didn't know if he was talking out his ass or what. He's a major bullshitter, but sometimes he knows things. He's got a string of hookers who work the party circuit. He finds out all kinds of dirt on people. So he's talking how he's gonna save his cousin some money. Starts blabbering how he can do the job and make himself a hero. Like I said, he's a moron."

Marco glanced up at Sydney. "You know Shaun Corbin?"

"Yes. And he fits the description perfectly. Short, fat, not the brightest star in the galaxy. I didn't think of him, but he's perfect. I think we got our guy."

"See?" Marco said. "That may have just got you some more time on this earth. You might want to make good use of it and get the hell out of Dodge."

Sydney said, "By the way, who set up the security system for Rouse? Was that Dutch Grimes, by any chance?"

"Dutch Grimes sets up the systems for all the bigwigs. High-tech stuff."

"He still live in South Lake?" Sydney asked.

"He's got a place up Keller Road where you make the turn to go to the ski resort. He's not that far from where Corbin lives."

Marco looked at Sydney. "We got what we need?"

"I think we do. Gary, I don't want you leaving town right away," Sydney said. "I want you to get that foot fixed up. Go to a hospital in Reno, tell them you shot yourself accidentally. Then, for the big Gatsby party, you go ahead and make your deliveries as usual. That way, nobody's gonna get all worked up and start hunting you down. After you finish, you can take a nice, long vacation. Let me show you something."

Sydney came down where Gatts could see her. She showed him some of what was on her smartphone video. "You do like you're told. Otherwise, this will be everywhere you don't want it to be. You cooperate, in time, I'll get rid of it. We have nothing personal against you."

Gary Gatts, utterly beaten, nodded. They left him sitting there in the water next to his drug cache, holding his wounded foot.

As they climbed the stone steps, Sydney said, "We do good work. Bad cop, worse cop."

"How's the leg?"

"Not bad. Sore. How are you?"

"I'm adjusting to my new reality," Marco said. "In some ways, it's a lot like my old reality."

"Sorry about that."

"Yeah, well, it's what you get picking up strange girls on the road. They all come with some kind of baggage. What are you thinking of doing with Corbin?"

"I want some information and, like Gatts, I want him on video. That video, I'll use to pay him back. I'm not up for killing him myself. But I know who wouldn't hesitate. Once we have that, you're free and clear."

"You?"

Sydney threw a look at him. "If Corbin has all this inside information, I want it. If it's good enough, I'll find some way to use it. I'm going to get to Thorp one way or another—or he's going to get to me."

"Maybe it'll be enough, you'll just have to give it to the right people."

"Maybe," she said. "We had some very good information once before and it just sort of vanished. This time, I'll be more careful."

"I might not be there to pick you up after the next hit attempt."

"I thought you were starting to like me?" Sydney said in a seductively mocking way.

"Oh, I like you just fine. Maybe even a touch more than just fine. But I promised myself no more crusades. Shaun Corbin shot a Shelby, and for that he has to pay. It's my last stop on the road to freedom."

He sensed that she didn't believe him, and he didn't know how convinced he was either, but it sounded good. As they headed back to where the car was parked, he said, "You asked him about some guy, Dutch, who installed a security system. What are you thinking?"

"We'll talk about that after we talk to Corbin. Once I understand some things, then talking about Dutch might make some sense."

30

Nine-thirty in the morning, the sound of stones crunching, a vehicle coming into the driveway startled Leon awake. He moved slow, carefully lowering the recliner to avoid noise.

He couldn't believe he'd slept that hard. He was upset with himself. It had to be the jet lag and the mountain air, and maybe the extra exertion of the fight with the crazy old man on the mountain. Assuming it was Corbin coming home, he said in a barely audible voice, "About damn time you showed."

He checked the chamber in his gun and seated the clip. The silencer was in firm as he moved to the side of the window and observed the target coming up to the door talking loud on his cell. Man had any sense, he would have been long gone. Listening, Leon heard him say as he started to unlock the door, "Just get the fuck over here with my money, Kora, right now, or I'm gonna make your life more miserable than you can imagine. I'll destroy you with a couple clicks of the mouse."

A short, fat guy came in swearing under his breath, dropping his keys and phone on the table by the door, muttering ceaselessly. He looked like shit. Like he'd been on a major binge, stains on his shirt and pants.

"About time you dragged your fat ass home," Leon said, sitting back down in the recliner, smiling at the man, the compact HK with silencer resting on his knee.

So this poor excuse is the cause of the mess.

Corbin froze, his eyes locking on Leon's weapon with appropriate shock and fear. Then he glanced at the things Leon had pulled out of his suitcase and his backpack that were now spread all over the tables, ottoman, chairs.

"Relax, boy," Leon said. "I'm on your side."

Corbin couldn't find his tongue, seemed to be considering a run, but where? How fast could fat boy go before a bullet caught him?

Two feet?

"Don't even think about it," Leon suggested. "I'm not your problem. I'm the solution to your problem."

He paused to let it sink in, then said, "I'm not familiar with this area, so I'm gonna need your help. You being a hotshot PI and all." Leon waved his gun, Corbin still fixated on it, not looking like he was feeling any relief from what Leon was telling him.

"After that, I'm going home and you can carry on," Leon said. "I figure you'll be groveling and apologizing for a year to two."

Give the fool a sense of survival. Unlike the old man, this yokel didn't seem to have much attitude besides fear and stink. Guy was coming off an epic bender.

"I'd have you fix breakfast, but I don't trust anything in this place. You're a real pig, my friend," Leon said, then added, "Go ahead and breathe. While you're at it, remove your piece, slow, fingertips. You know the drill. Put it on the table there. You got a backup, do the same. You move too sudden, I'll kill you sudden."

Leon smiled his much practiced De Niro *Taxi* smile, eyes wide, evil grin.

Corbin did what he was told, hands trembling, confirming Leon's thought that he was coming off a serious binge.

"Sit here," Leon pointed to the wicker chair with the filthy cushion.

Corbin lowered himself awkwardly into the chair across from Leon, eyes glancing at the coffee table full of tapes, pictures, and notebooks.

"I'm curious," Leon said. "How is it that the DA's investigator is still walking around? How'd that happen?"

Corbin finally got his vocals working. He said, albeit meekly, "I shot her…point blank."

Leon nodded. Played with the HK. "Somewhere between point and blank, you didn't get the job done. What I hear, you weren't the one who was supposed to do the job in the first place. You botch a hit, it just makes it all the more difficult for a pro to come in and clean up your mess, don't you think?"

Corbin seemed uncertain how to answer. What he finally said was, "It was a target-of-opportunity kind of deal. So—"

"Target-of-opportunity kind of deal? Interesting way to put it. What made it such a deal?"

The guy hesitated, thinking, unsteady. He had tiny hands with stubby fingers. He said, "She was alone in the hatchery. Perfect situation."

His goddamn hands are freaky.

Leon studied this fool for a moment. "Perfect, was it? Government property. You kill somebody there, it brings in the feds. What kind of deal is that?"

Corbin said nothing.

Leon, his De Niro smile splitting his face, said, "You got your stuff packed like you're headed on a long vacation."

Corbin stared at him, and he noticed the guy had a nasty mole in the center of his forehead. Leon said, "How come you never got that mole taken off?"

"What?"

"The mole. That ugly mole in the center of your forehead. Why didn't you get it removed? You don't look in the mirror, see how ugly that damn thing is?"

I'm gonna take that fucking mole!

"I…I guess I just got used to it. Didn't notice it."

"Relax, molehead. Nothing's going to happen. We're just going to talk, straighten this out. You're family. That's makes you safe. Nobody wants to kill family. Thorp doesn't kill family."

Corbin didn't appear to buy that. Whatever was going on in that addled brain of his suddenly landed on an idea. His face lit up. He said, "I'll tell you what. You want to make some real money? I'm talking millions."

"A deal?" Leon asked.

"Yeah. I mean something really big. Listen, man, I got all the skinny on what goes on over at Incline. The big gambling tournaments. Whatever you're getting paid is peanuts compared to what's available to somebody wants to get rich and get rich fast." While he talked, he made all these little twitches, like a teen girl on her first date.

"Big?"

"You wouldn't believe," Corbin said.

Beads of sweat popped out on the guy's nose, forehead and upper lip. Fear ran riot through his veins.

"I'm talking maybe fifteen, twenty mil. I can work something with you. I know where that cash will be, and I know how to get to it."

"That's big money, alright," Leon said. "Where is all that money? Under the house? Buried in the desert? A gold mine you know about?"

"No. Listen, the man you're working for…Thorp…his lawyer is like the secret Swiss bank of Tahoe. This big Gatsby weekend coming up, there'll be so goddamn much money rolling in here, you won't believe it. Look, we can work something out."

"You got the skinny, right?" Leon asked.

"Yes."

"Isn't that like the whole *naked* truth. No clothes covering the truth. By the way, that thing on your forehead is distracting as hell. Like you got three eyes. I mean, Jesus, man, the only people could stand that, wouldn't be distracted, is some dot-headed Hindu."

Corbin said nothing.

"Write down the password to get into your laptop," Leon said. "I think we can work out a deal."

"Why is that necessary?" Corbin asked in a pleading, little girl's voice.

Leon smiled cold. "I want access to your laptop. Don't ask *why* ever again."

Leon tossed a small notebook on top of a pile of sex photos on the coffee table. Then a pen. Corbin, hand trembling, wrote the password down.

Then Leon took the notebook and pen back, and he tapped the top nude picture. "What's with this girl?"

"Kora North. She's on my string. Party girl. Top of the line. She owes me some money. Wants some of her…pictures and stuff back."

"That who you were yelling at on the phone?"

"Yes. She's on her way over. And she can confirm what I'm telling you about the big payday."

Leon picked up the picture. "Nice. Very nice."

"Top of the line. Prime. Kora North is hot as they come," Corbin said, sounding a little hopeful now. "She's Thorp's favorite party girl. Gonna play Daisy at the big party next weekend. The Great Gatsby Gala. Half the rich assholes on the West Coast will be there. Look, I'm tellin' you there's gonna be a ton of money to be had, things are done right."

Leon put the picture down, switched hands with his gun, and picked up Corbin's Glock. "Perfectly fine weapon. You aren't too good with this. You don't practice, or were you drunk?"

Corbin started fumbling around for a good answer but Leon cut him off, saying, "Tell me about the big party."

Corbin started to tell him about the party, how everybody dressed in Roaring Twenties outfits, about the outdoor band and the big poker game down in the game room, but Leon was sick of him now.

"Sounds too good to be true," Leon said. He brought Corbin's Glock up, leaned forward, and shot the man in the head, aiming for that mole.

No decent reflexes in the guy. He just stared in disbelief that he was about to be killed. He never moved.

Got it! Blew the damn third eye back into the man's brain. It vanished quick as an eel pulling back into its hole when a shark swims by. Not the usual place a suicide would shoot himself, so, if the girl came, it would be that she killed him before she committed suicide. It would be a murder/suicide, and it would work nicely.

Corbin's head had hardly moved at all when the bullet hit. Man didn't have enough brain matter even to slow it down. He just kind of slowly tilted back, his head resting on the corner of the chair like he was taking a nap, yet his eyes stayed wide open. The chair had a bullet-hole exit.

Leon said, "You thought you were cut out for the trade, did you? You're not even in the same world. You insult me."

Then he texted the client's lawyer as he was instructed to do after each event. After sending the message, Leon then settled back to await the arrival of this hottest of all hot chicks, Kora North.

31

That Tuesday morning, when the message reached them, Rouse and Thorp were in the foothills, ninety miles down the mountain on the west slope of the Sierras. They were about to head back to Tahoe after having attended funeral services for a friend of the Thorp family.

The service was at the old, white church that stood stiff as a constipated Puritan on a hill north of the ancient gold mining town of Jackson. The graveyard, with headstones in jagged rows like rotting teeth, held many bodies from battles a long time ago.

It was dry and hot under the relentless sun, the hills burnished with the color of overcooked tortillas. After the funeral, they'd paid a quick visit to the ancestral Thorp estate, where his mother still lived, just off historic Gold Route 49—down from Thorp Lumber and Mining, a massive complex of corrugated-roofed buildings, mountains of logs receiving a mist spray to keep them moist in the summer heat.

"It's our boy," Rouse said, looking at the screen as he drove his Mercedes SL500 into the foothills. "Damnit, I don't like this. Jesus, it's like the wild west."

"He's cleaning up the mess," Thorp said. "About time I got rid of the family idiot."

"I don't like it," Rouse said again.

That made Thorp smile. They were passing the origin of his power and name, Thorp Lumber and Mining. In the big yards, the mist drew rainbows in the sky. Giant hoses, like anacondas, lay across the piles delivering the spray. The air trembled with the constant buzz of saws and thundered from the endless procession of logging trucks coming and going past the fifty-foot water tower that had a giant black T painted on it.

That's me, Thorp thought. *I own it. It's mine, all mine.* He liked that he was the big dog. And in his mind, he hadn't even gotten started yet.

As they headed up through the back roads, Thorp said to Rouse, "It'll all be history. A new day. The future begins. The future Tahoe deserves."

"What *I* don't like," Thorp said, "is that crazy bitch is still out there with this nephew of Cillo's. I don't like it. He finds out his uncle is dead, he's going to be angry. Our boy has to get to them quick, so he has to do whatever it takes."

"You can't just have a rash of suicides. Who the hell is going to believe that?" Rouse whined. He was in his grumpy, nervous mood.

A hawk sailed high in the desolate sky in front of them.

"Don't worry about it. That's my business. I don't care how many suicides there are. Nothing will track back to the killer or us because nobody is interested. This guy's the best in the business, so you said. When he's finished, it all works out, I'll see if I can keep him on retainer. Or, make him head of our security operations."

Rouse scoffed. "You don't hire guys like that on a permanent basis. This could turn into a real disaster, bodies turn up all over the place."

"You need to get some balls," Thorp said. He thought of the days they were kids, he and Rouse playing among the ruins of places with colorful names like *Musicdale, Slabtown,* and *Blood Gulch.* Most were nothing more than historic landmarks, remnants of a few stone buildings where miners and "digger" Indians once resided before Thorp's ancestors kicked them out and turned the land over to people who knew how to use it.

"Progress," Thorp said, "doesn't come cheap, or without a little blood. It's the way of the world. Always has been, always will be."

Having a killer on the payroll gave Ogden Thorp a sense of power and strength that was different than anything he'd known before. He had an instrument of death at his disposal. He could take care of anybody who got in his way. That was a big ego trip. He loved it. Put a big smile on his face. Now he understood the big boys in the big game. Didn't matter if you were sending out a lone killer or a whole army, it was the same. And it was beautiful.

This is a great day, Thorp thought. *This is the beginning of the greatest week of my life.*

"We need to get back to the Cal-Neva," he told Rouse. "I have guests arriving soon for the tour. Step on it."

But in the back of his mind, there was one serious nag. Rouse was right about one thing—Cillo's nephew. Once he found out his uncle was dead, he'd be on the warpath, and Thorp didn't know exactly what that might mean.

So he chose not to think about him. That was his hired gun's problem.

32

After leaving the restaurant and going back through Markleeville, Sydney and Marco passed the bikers' motorcycles parked in front of the Cutthroat Bar. *Appropriate,* she decided.

Twenty minutes later, when Marco turned off 89 onto the Pioneer Trail, Sydney said, "I'd like to shoot the bastard a couple times, let him know how it feels."

Marco smiled. He followed her directions, heading through a sparsely populated, heavily wooded area into a narrow ravine. Tight place. Hard in the winter back here.

"That's it," Sydney said, pointing to a nondescript wood-frame, brick-bottom house tucked into the hillside.

A familiar pickup was in the driveway. Marco said, "Looks like we're in luck. Our boy just might be home."

He followed the narrow road around the bend and looked for a place he could park in the trees, well out of sight of the house. She took a pair of binoculars from the glove box, and they hiked around the neck of the hill through the pines and a patch of aspens, the ground still soft from the spring runoff.

Sydney said, "Of all the places to build a house, he picks the spot the sun pretty much misses all day long."

She couldn't believe that with all that sun out there, these people chose the shady gloom, their small, plain, clapboard house hidden in trees along the gully like a poisonous mushroom. Below, behind the back of a house, stood a dilapidated garage with two beat-up garbage cans leaning against the side and a half-inflated, above-ground pool filled with stagnant water and leaves and crap. A mess of a place. Nothing looked cared for.

Marco appeared to be studying the house looking for signs of someone moving around.

"Nothing happening I can see," he said.

"Maybe our boy's sleeping. Been a tough night."

The garage protected their approach as they slipped through a copse of lodgepole pines, moving now at a quick-step, keeping the garage between them and the house.

A cat shot from under a rusty piece of tin roofing behind the garage and vanished around the side. Marco nearly shot it.

Christ, he's jumpier than I am!

Behind Corbin's, there was a banged-up camper shell next to the dilapidated garage.

"Look at that, it's a crime," Marco whispered, pointing at a gutted-out car.

"Sixty-eight GT 390 Fastback," Marco said. "Steve McQueen's green machine. Same as the one in *Bullitt.* McQueen has to be turning over in his grave." Marco shook his head at the lack of respect this guy had, letting that car rust and rot. He moved forward.

She noticed how he avoided everything on the ground that might trigger noise. Moved light for such a big man. She followed in his footsteps.

Farther on, Marco paused, stared at the kitchen window. No action. They waited there for a minute before moving forward, but Marco found the back door locked. He took out his pocketknife and removed the nearly rotted wooden frames of the closest windowpane, removed the glass, reached in, and opened the door slowly to minimize any hinge squeak. He was good at this.

The hall and steps to the kitchen had crap everywhere. Weight bench with dumbbells. On the floor, empty dumbbell bars and all kinds of stacked boxes. A Coleman outdoor barbecue. Coats on a rack. Boots below. Shovels and a rake. Barely a path to walk.

He stepped in, paused, and listened.

***

Leon was impressed with the perfection of the bullet hole, how it had taken out the entire mole. *That's real art,* he thought. *It should hang in a major gallery.*

He picked up Kora North's nude. The murder/suicide would work, of course, but he'd never killed a beautiful woman before. Not that it would really matter. Still, if she looked anything like the photos of her, well, it would be a challenge of sorts. He'd do it, of course. It was the profession. Still...

But first he'd interrogate the woman. Make her feel she had a chance if she gave him some information he could use to find Jesup. Plus some understanding of the whole show here in paradise.

In the midst of these thoughts, something caught his attention. He'd gotten acclimated to the sounds of the PI's world. Now there was something out of place.

Maybe just a bird on the roof.

Maybe wind.

Squirrel on the roof?

Or his imagination. He figured jet lag was still bothering him and maybe affecting his awareness. He listened. Then he got up and took his weapon and stood quiet, waiting for some indication he'd actually heard something not quite right.

He decided to make a house check. Back door first. He moved back into the kitchen, standing with one hip against the refrigerator, stared out the kitchen window toward the garage, and listened. A man in his line of work trusted nothing. Not even his senses.

Instincts are what keeps a man alive when he can't trust anything he hears or sees.

33

Sydney followed Marco into a tight, junk-filled hall.

Moving in carefully through the boxes, weight rack, and garbage bags, Marco reached the second step and was almost at the floor into the kitchen when a man appeared. He came so fast and quiet around the corner, the two men bumped into each other with startled mutual grunts. One shot went off and Sydney ducked as the men locked up and twisted violently into the corner.

Sydney tried to stay free of them, but in the small hallway, that was impossible. They forced her back. She tripped, hit something round and hard, and, trying to stop her fall, her hand struck iron and her gun went down.

No, damnit!

Marco spun, his gun hand passing by her face as he tried to get it around, but the guy hit him hard and they locked up, knocking her into a weight bench. The two men crashed against some boxes, and then the three of them got locked in a violent wrestling match, stumbling over boxes, the weight bench, junk. They slammed from wall to wall, falling into junk, headbutting, elbows flying like sledgehammers. They were like a couple of pit bulls in a small cage, jaws locked on each other's throats.

The men blocking what little light there was in the battle against the door, Sydney scrambled on the dark floor looking for the gun. Instead, she came up with something that felt like an empty dumbbell bar. She grabbed it in both hands, got up against the wall, and looked for a chance to use it.

Their opponent leveraged Marco into Sydney and one of their guns fired again, the shot so close to her ear she could feel the heat of the bullet. The ferocious battle between the men once again knocked Sydney back and into boxes and a bench, but she didn't lose her grip on the metal bar.

Marco and his opponent were locked up and smashing into one

wall, then the junk against the other wall with such fury and speed, it was hard for Sydney to get into the fight. When Marco snapped his arm down, freeing his hand, he then tried to bring his own weapon up but took a vicious elbow in the throat and a knee as they twisted back and fell against skis and a snowboard. Marco tried to regain his footing, spin the guy back into the wall, but took another hard elbow.

Sydney finally had a target and swung the dumbbell bar, but it hit a glancing blow off the man's shoulder. The two men fell against the steps. As the assailant twisted around toward her, Sydney found another chance. She swung the bar like a baseball bat.

The dumbbell bar hit with a sickening crack of bone. The guy let out some kind of wild-sounding moan and backed to the door, his hands flying to his face, his gun hitting the floor. She tried to get him again but he thrust out both arms and pushed her violently back into Marco, and the two of them went down against the steps.

The man fled out the back door, sunlight bursting into the narrow, junk-filled hallway.

"I lost my gun," Marco said, frantically scrambling away from her and trying to find it.

She located the gun their attacker had dropped, then went out the door. Marco, having found his weapon, came right behind her. At first they didn't see any sign of the guy.

"He could be close. Have a backup piece," Marco said, inching toward the side of the house.

But then Sydney saw the man run behind the garage, his hands cradling his face. She fired three shots. It was a long way for a snub nose to be accurate, but she saw him stumble, and it looked like he fell in the shrubs just inside the tree line.

"Looks like you got him," Marco said. "He's not short and fat."

"That's definitely not Corbin," Sydney said.

She figured he wasn't going to survive the breaking of his skull and the bullets. It hit her that she'd never killed anyone before. Everyone involved in law, or the military, was ready to do the obvious if necessary, but the fact of it would be something she'd think about later. It wasn't that he didn't deserve what he got. That was never the issue. It was just that it was something that, when it happened, was significant. *Or should be,* she thought. But maybe for some, not so much. Or maybe it was all context. She didn't know.

That would all come later.

"Let's clear the house," Marco said. "See if fat boy is there. The guy in the woods with the broken head might be able to talk on a cell phone, get help, so we need to get out of here. Bastard could still fight."

Marco, his mouth bloody as well, spit some to the side and then wiped his mouth and nose with his shirt tail. "You had to have ripped some of those stitches."

"We'll deal with that later."

She had the Colt and handed him the Heckler and Koch compact with silencer. They headed into the house slow and cautious, just in case Corbin lay in wait.

34

A hundred yards up the hill from the house, Leon leaned against a tree, feeling sick, the pain shooting spikes through his skull.

Jesus, Jesus Christ, I'm dead. The bitch broke my fucking skull. It's her! Jesus!

The pain was like nothing he'd ever known before in his life. Had to have a broken face.

The three shots hadn't hit him, though one bullet had taken a piece out of his left ear. Fucking bitch was crazy. He stared down toward the house, tears welling in his eyes, blurring his vision, blood dripping from his nose and mouth.

I messed up. I took a job on short notice and messed up.

Enraged, he pulled out his cell phone and found he couldn't talk. He put it away and reached for his ankle holster. But the effort spiked the pain and any thought he had of going back into the fight vanished.

He found himself trapped between his desire to get down there and kill these people, put an end to this, and the excruciating, immobilizing pain that became so intense he wanted to scream.

He'd gotten a glimpse of her and seen enough pictures to know that was Jesup and Cillo's nephew. *Jesus, tough sonsabitches.*

He couldn't believe it. They weren't running and hiding—they were on the hunt!

Everything now flipped over on its back. Tahoe had suddenly become a very dangerous place.

He sat on a fallen branch on the hillside in the pines trying to get his mind settled, get himself calm, his skull on fire. Pain spiked and shot in waves through his head. What had she hit him with? That bitch had tried to take his fucking head off!

Everything they said about her was true. She was crazy. The woman had gunshot wounds and was still on the hunt and in the fight. What kind of crazy-ass woman was he dealing with? No wonder everybody wanted her dead.

You got to get them now, he told himself.

But he couldn't move, couldn't think of anything beyond his misery.

Off in the distance where the road appeared over a rise before dipping back down into the ravine half a mile or so away, he saw a car coming. He wondered if it was the hooker, Kora North. Everything in Leon's world was going to hell.

When the car slid down around the curve, reappeared, and slowed, he knew it was her.

***

Sydney and Marco found Corbin slumped, listless, in a chair, eyes open, blood on his forehead, a startled look on his face.

"Rigor from a bullet isn't exactly cosmetic surgery," Sydney said. "Doesn't improve the look. But he's not been dead long. Maybe an hour or two."

Marco, his senses on high alert, trigger finger flexing like a coiled snake, readied himself for any hostile target.

They quickly cleared the other rooms. The occupant had bad habits. Filthy toilet, mold, dirty clothes. Cracked paint. Smudges soiling the carpets. Smells. The small house clear, they came back into the living room.

The hole in the man's head had a filigree of red around it. "*Flor roja la Muerte,*" Marco said.

"Meaning?"

"Death's red flower. Something that happens very frequently in Mexico. Whole bouquets. We need to get moving. You want to use the bathroom, go ahead."

Sydney let out a dark chuckle. "Funny. I'd piss in the woods before I'd sit my ass on anything in this shithole." Then she said, "Son of a bitch," as she pulled out files and a notebook computer from the open tennis bag. "My bag, my stuff. Our boy has been busy."

Marco came over and looked. "Well, he didn't get far with your stuff. Or Corbin's. Which means he'll be back if he's capable. Or he'll send somebody. You have blood on your nose. Looks funny."

She went into the kitchen to find paper towels to wipe blood from her nose and mouth while he picked up some photos.

"Tapes and a folder with pictures of various sexcapades," he said.

Sydney looked at the photos when she'd come back into the living room. "I know this girl."

Marco heard a car and went to the window. "You want a little surprise? It's her. Just pulled up in her BMW."

Sydney came over and looked out the window. "No way. It is. One and the same. Kora North, one of the highest priced girls in Tahoe, who now works exclusive with the Thorp Incline crowd. What the hell's going on? And she looks pissed off and in a big hurry."

The tall, striking female left her shiny black Beamer and came up the walk past the pickup truck. Long legs, gold hair, and substantial breasts in a halter top, the calendar-girl body swung toward the steps with aggressiveness. She clutched her shoulder bag like she was afraid it would swing off her shoulder and run away.

Marco went to the door to invite the high-priced bombshell in.

Sydney said quietly, "This should be interesting."

Everything had changed now. He knew that, and so did Sydney. There was no way out of this. Whatever Sydney had in mind, it now included him. He felt a lot like he was back in Mexico.

35

Through a slit opening in the side window curtain, Sydney watched Kora North walk up to the door, where Marco was ready to welcome her.

Kora looked stressed and angry. She started to knock, but Marco opened the door, grabbed her arm, and yanked her inside so fast she didn't have time to resist. When she struggled to get something from her bag, Sydney ripped the bag out of her hands.

He kicked the door shut.

"Easy girl," Marco said as Kora fought him with cat-claw ferocity, wild eyes, and screaming curses.

After taking a couple of hard blows to the face and shoulder, he subdued her by grabbing under her armpits, pinching off the nerves, and angling his hips so she couldn't get a knee to his groin.

"Easy! Nobody's going to hurt you."

"You *are* hurting me, asshole!" she yelled.

Kora North had a Hollywood body and a viper's disposition. Marco grabbed her wrists and pinned them in front of her. Sydney caught a whiff of perfume that smelled like fresh-baked apples and cinnamon. A little surprising.

"Don't panic, and don't try and head-butt me or I'll really get pissed and mess you up," Marco said in a calm but stern voice.

Kora's eyes widened. She stiffened when she saw Sydney, then Shaun Corbin's body. She tried again to break away, but Marco swung her around and slammed her back against the wall.

"Calm down. We're not the killers, and we're not going to hurt you."

The wildcat Barbie hunched her shoulders and arched back, rigid and defensive, ready to go off on him again.

Sydney said, "He's telling you the truth, Kora. Relax. The guy who killed Shaun, I put some bullets in him. He's lying somewhere up in the woods."

Kora, realizing the situation was out of her control, smartly ceased her futile struggle.

"You," she said, now recognizing Sydney.

"Right," Sydney said. "Me."

She put the shoulder bag Kora had been carrying on an end table and opened it. "Well, looks like we have money. Lots of it. And we have a gun."

"Girl came prepared," Marco said.

Sydney held up the gun. "Nice." It had hardwood grip plates with a ruby embedded on either side. "What is it you came prepared for, Kora?"

"I don't want anything to do with this," Kora said. "Give me my bag, my money, and my gun and let me get out of here. I didn't see anything. I couldn't be happier that bastard is dead. I have some things here I want back, then I'm out of here."

"If only things were that easy," Sydney said. "Like he already said, we didn't kill Corbin. When we got here, the man who did kill him was apparently waiting for somebody, and that somebody looks to be you. He had your nude shots out on the table. We got in a fight with him. He got the worst of it. Took off."

"Why would he be waiting for me?"

"Maybe to have some fun," Sydney said. "Maybe to kill you. We don't have time to argue. What's the money for?"

Kora said, "I was being threatened by Corbin. He had stuff on me. Bad stuff that would put me in trouble with Oggie Thorp and the law. I was buying it back. He did something bad, wanted to run, and needed running money. If you just give me what I came for, I won't say anything to anyone."

Sydney packed the big tennis bag with everything on the coffee table, then put Kora's gun back in her shoulder bag. "Just be thankful we're here and not the guy who killed Corbin. And the stuff that Corbin had on you, we own that now. So maybe we need to have a little talk. Just not here."

Kora glanced at the body. No shock in her face seeing the guy dead. More like she was looking at some road kill.

"I'm not going anywhere with you," Kora shot back.

Marco said, "You want that back—your money, car keys, and the tapes you came for—you'll talk to us. You'll cooperate with Sydney. Otherwise, you'll be walking"—he held up her keys—"and your car will be parked in front of a dead man's house. You'd be lucky if the cops got to you before somebody else did. So let's go have a nice little chat."

Kora stared at Marco.

Sydney said, "Let's get out of here."

Outside, heading for Kora's BMW, "Sydney said, "Why was Corbin killed? What did he do, he was so scared he wanted to run?"

"I don't know."

Sydney stopped at the back passenger door as Marco got in behind the wheel. She grabbed Kora, turned her, and then showed her the bandages under her shirt. "Shaun Corbin tried to kill me. You know nothing about that?"

"No. All I know is he did something he was running from."

Sydney studied her for a moment, then said, "Get in the front."

Sydney got in back with the tennis bag and Kora's shoulder bag. Marco keyed the engine and they left.

Sydney, leaning forward on the seat, said, "Kora, the guy who killed Corbin robbed my place and was apparently waiting for you for whatever reason, which means you'd be dead if we hadn't shown up. Then he'd have come after me. So, the way I see it, we have something in common."

"Where are you taking me?" Kora demanded, looking at Marco.

Marco said, "Just a ways up the road, where we can talk and see what's going on down here in the valley."

***

Standing in the trees two hundred yards up the hill from the house, Leon, still in brain-freeze, pain, and shock, watched as the threesome left in Kora North's BMW, Cruz driving, Kora North beside him in the passenger bucket, Jesup in the back. They had the tennis bag. He couldn't believe it. He'd lost his Glock and the bag with all the files, laptops, and videos. And his face was broken.

Everything in the neat, ordered world of Leon, in the way he usually planned, prepped, did careful surveillance, following a precise methodology in order to get a clean kill—all of it out the window. Trashed from the minute he'd set foot in Tahoe. And now this. He stared in shock as the BMW headed around the bend in the hill and disappeared.

What the hell's going on? He ignored his misery for a moment. *Is she with them or did they just take her?*

He walked across the nape of the hill and down to his car, each step sending spikes of pain through his skull. He waded through dry pine needles and pine cones, then stopped, leaned against a tree, and felt sick.

I can't die here. I won't die here, goddamnit!

To ease and calm his mind, he entertained violent visions of revenge, getting the Jesup woman and giving her live to Thorp on the condition he got to watch the fucking lion rip her to pieces. Only violent fantasies tended to relax him. It had always been that way for Henry Craven Lee, aka Leon.

The pain exploded across the tangled wire of synapses in his brain like an electrical storm. He suppressed a scream. He couldn't move his jaw. With tears fogging his vision, Leon cried inside, cradled his face, and tried to will the pain away.

He hadn't taken a beating like this since he was a kid and one of his mother's many boyfriends beat him on a pretty regular basis. The worst was the one who made him do things. The bastard who made him try and fuck the neighbor girl, the bastard jacking off as he watched two nine-year-olds. Then later, he beat the crap out of Leon to convince him never to say anything about it. He threatened the girl with death to her whole family.

At least Leon had gotten even afterward, when he'd thrown him out a sixth-story window. He still relished his first suicide kill, still the one he remembered with the most pleasure.

Breathing hard through his nose, Leon finally made his way to his car, every step pure agony.

They came for the PI to do what? Kill him?

Thorp was right about Jesup. She was a nut case. And what was this with Kora North? She come to pick them up? Had she dropped them off? Was she working with them?

He considered calling in some of Thorp's goons, but that wouldn't solve the problem if it was big and included other people. He had to understand it first. This was his problem now. His alone.

He had to get back to the cabin. Get the lawyer to bring some pain pills. Right now, he couldn't move his jaw without sending white-hot lightning bolts that fired splintering pain up through his face and head.

36

"What do you want from me?" Kora asked when they parked up in the trees above the ravine near their car, just far enough away so Kora couldn't see what they were driving.

"Like he said, we're going to talk to you about something," Sydney said to this beautiful stick of dynamite.

"Talk about what?"

Sydney said, "The big party next weekend. You're part of that, I assume. Miss Daisy?"

"Yes," Kora said. "Look, I just want my stuff, and I want to get out of here. I don't care if you killed Corbin or some mystery guy you're talking about. Just give me what I came for and let me go. This is kidnapping. You can't do this shit."

Sydney let a moment's silence hang over the conversation. Then she said, "We have you by your short hairs, Kora. Don't tell me what we can or can't do. People are trying to kill me. I'm in no fucking mood to put up with any shit from you. I hand this stuff over to the right authorities, you'll do serious time. Except you won't get the chance to do time. You'll be dead. You know too much. You'll be as dead as Shaun…and Karen Orland. And she's very fucking dead, girl. You remember Karen, don't you?"

Kora gave Sydney a gelid stare.

"Help us out," Marco said. "And by helping us out, you'd be helping yourself. We're what stands between you and a very bad ending."

"Help you out how?"

Sydney said, "The Great Gatsby Gala."

"What about it?"

"I hear Rouse closes down his place and spends the weekend at Thorp's. Plays poker around the clock. That true?"

"So?" Kora's belligerence was somewhat tempered by curiosity.

"Rumor has it, Tricky Dick has a lot of blackmail tapes on a lot of people. Plus a huge bankroll in that office of his…"

Kora emitted a cynical little snort. "You're crazy if you're thinking of breaking into Rouse's. Forget it. He's got a top-of-the line security system. His place is like Fort Knox. He pulls out his cell phone, he can see every room anytime he wants. He's paranoid because of that office he calls his sanctum sanctorum."

"During the party, where does he stay? He have a room at Thorp's, or does he come back to his place?"

"His place is closed down for the whole weekend. He never leaves Thorp's. He never actually leaves the poker tournament. He plays poker with all those stars and big shots. Thorp has a replica of the poker room in Tombstone where guys like Doc Holiday played. Same kind of tables. Little rooms there for the hookers so they can take a break, get laid, nap. They play big games all weekend. Believe me, cash like that—and it's all a cash deal—they have security and they're armed. Most of them are ex or current cops or sheriff's deputies. It's like a million-dollar buy-in. Crazy amount of money."

"Where's the money kept?"

"Right in that room. You won't get anywhere near it, believe me."

"We're actually not interested in it. What about this office of Rouse's? There any money in there?"

"Sure. If somebody got into Tricky Dick's safe, what's rumored, they'd find a fortune. Being one of the world's biggest asshole thieves, he doesn't trust the banking system. But you must be joking. Nobody gets in there without tripping off all those sensors and alarms."

"Maybe the guy who put the security system in would know the weak points," Marco suggested.

Kora looked from one to the other. "Jesus, you're serious."

"As serious as Corbin is dead," Sydney said.

"With that great security setup, does the lawyer have armed guards around his place?" Marco asked.

"No. Doesn't need them. It's all electronic. Even if you could get into Rouse's place, you couldn't get in his office. It's a fucking bomb shelter. Steel door is, like, ten inches thick or something. And then the safe—"

"Kora," Sydney said, "Let us worry about our problems. You need to worry about yours."

"What, exactly, are my problems?"

"You're going to be our inside girl," Sydney said.

"You're kidding me, right?"

"No, I'm not," Sydney said. "Once you leave here, you stay close to home for the next couple days."

"This is—you can't make me do this."

"We can," Marco said. "It's the alternative to destroying you."

Sydney said, "You don't get involved with anyone unless it's Thorp and he wants you for something. You were never here. You don't know anything about what happened to Corbin. You know nothing about us. We'll be in contact with you. Later tonight or tomorrow, we'll let you know what we want. If there's a lot of money involved, you'll get your share, plus the dirt Corbin had on you. If what I want is there, it'll protect all of us. It's time to turn the tables on those boys."

Kora said, "You're going to get me killed."

Marco said, "Consider yourself a dead girl already unless we find a way to save you. It's much easier that way."

"Even if you get in the office," Kora said, "what if you can't get in the safe he's got in there. Maybe there's some kind of time lock or something?"

"We'll deal with that when and if it becomes a problem. We might have to find a way to get the man to come over and help us out," Sydney said.

"Without bringing a whole security force with him?"

"Would depend on what he thinks is going on. You let us worry about that," Marco said.

Sydney added, "Life isn't fair. Right now, we own you, and you don't really have a choice. But you're lucky. We'll be very generous and fair with you in the end if you do your part. And we'll let you know what that is in the next couple of days."

"If there's millions in that safe, I want half," Kora said.

"We get in, and that safe is, like you say, a well-stocked bank, you get a million-dollar buy-out," Sydney said.

Kora said, "A million dollars isn't what it once was."

"We'll work it out. Maybe two mil," Sydney said. "By the way, were you going to kill Corbin yourself? Or do you always carry a piece?" She pulled Kora's gun out of her bag.

Kora took a moment, then smiled faintly and shrugged. "The

thing is," she said, "maybe I was going to shoot that miserable bastard right in the mole in the center of his forehead. I can't believe that's what the guy who killed him did. How weird is that? It's like he stole my play. Why Corbin never had that cut off is beyond me."

"He was waiting for the right surgeon," Marco said. "We'll be in contact."

Kora said, "I want my gun back. It was a present, and it's kinda like a piece of jewelry."

Sydney emptied the gun before putting it back in Kora's bag with the money and handed it to her.

Marco said, "Don't shoot anybody. Have a quiet week. We'll be in contact. Do something stupid, you won't live to regret it. That's your new reality."

"It's my normal reality," she said with bitter sarcasm.

Sydney and Marco got out of the BMW, taking the tennis bag with them.

"Go the long way home," Sydney said. "You were never here. You know nothing."

"Maybe they already know I was coming here. Maybe Corbin told somebody."

"Don't overthink it," Marco said. "Go home. Stay home. Play the role they want you to play. You're Miss Daisy; nobody's going to kill Miss Daisy."

A very unhappy Kora North eased her BMW out onto the back road and disappeared past the trees.

Sydney said, "Real sweetheart. I hate that this whole operation could end up depending on a high-end hooker."

"Believe me," Marco said, "I've been in operations that depended on a lot worse than Kora North. Let's get the hell out of here. I'd like to talk to this Dutch. You know how to find him?"

"I can find him. My police-reporter friend will track him down. Let's go somewhere we can get a few hours rest. Come back to Tahoe after dark."

They walked back to the Range Rover. Marco said, as he pulled out, "Looks like you got yourself a partner and an inside girl."

"Hopefully."

"You know what the end game looks like? We hit that place, no matter what we get, nothing is admissible."

"I have an end game in mind," Sydney said. "And it has nothing to do with the law or the courts."

"I'm starting to like you," Marco said, "and that scares the hell out of me."

"It should," Sydney said.

37

All the way home, Kora North debated with herself about what to do. Run? Tell somebody? Jesup and her boyfriend were nuts. No way in hell they could pull this off.

She figured the damage she could see on their faces—the bruises, cut lips—wasn't caused by fat-ass. He couldn't whip himself. So their saying it was some killer who'd taken out Corbin and then nearly them made sense, and that they'd killed the guy.

I'm screwed, she thought.

Seeing Corbin dead didn't affect her as she thought it would somebody else. She wasn't horrified in any way. She was actually satisfied that the universe had finally gotten sensible and killed the nasty little weasel. Her only regret was that she didn't get to pull the trigger herself.

But now what was going to happen?

They're gonna use me and then what?

Feeling like she was in a crazy nightmare, Kora drove to her condo depressed, seeing no way out.

I hope the bastard died knowing it, feeling the whole fear and pain, she thought. *Payback.*

She watched people walking toward the Ketch Restaurant by the boat docks. She wondered if she had it in her to do it. She thought she could. She'd fantasized about killing a whole bunch of assholes who'd messed up her life. Someday, she'd pick one of those miserable sonsabitches and do it. Maybe hunt down the punk bastards who'd raped her when she was fourteen. In her mind, it wouldn't have been murder. It would have been eradication of a disease.

This guy with Jesup, whoever he was, looked like the real thing. Where'd he come from? Cute in a badass sort of way. Jesup hire him?

If Dutch Grimes was actually working with them, they just might be able to pull off something crazy like this. Maybe that guy had all the information on the security system and the safe. Hell, he put it all in.

She sat in her car for a time staring at the waterfront condos. She was trapped for sure. No way out. Jesup and her buddy had her.

What if they were good to their word? Would they really cut her in? Part of her hoped they succeeded and somebody finally took down Thorp and Rouse. Those miserable bastards needed to be brought down, all the people they ruined.

Not likely. But how cool would that be?

Had her turn finally come around and she'd hit the damn lottery? Or would she just be a tool to be disposed of? This was getting crazy. There'd be killers running all over Tahoe after each other.

Gonna be a Chinese New Year around here, *she thought, this gets out of hand. What's that saying…you want revenge, dig two graves? How about a whole fucking cemetery?*

Why in hell am I always in this kind of shit? Kora wondered as she got out of her car.

Her greatest curse was that she'd been born sexy, kept getting sexier, and seemed to have no defense against a world that wanted that. Since she was little, all she really knew was how men reacted to her, reached for her, used her. Next weekend, the highlight of the damn party would be when she, as Daisy, ripped off her clothes and jumped into the goddamn fountain Thorp had built. Other girls would join her. A real fun fest.

That's my life, she thought, *entertainment for jack-offs.*

She knew the feeling of powerlessness and hated it worse than anything else. She'd really wanted that moment when Corbin looked down the barrel of the gun in her hands, and even that had been taken away from her. But she wasn't done yet. She was breathing, wasn't she?

She thought of Jesup and decided she was like a role model for a girl who doesn't take shit from the big boys.

I wish I was a killer like the guy who did Shaun.

She thought about Thorp and Rouse and the big weekend coming up. Jesup was no fool. If you did know the security system and had somebody could deal with it, then getting to the mother lode was possible.

Damn, she thought, *this isn't impossible.* If there was one time a year when it could be done, the party was the perfect cover. She started getting worked up about it. She'd been trapped for a long time on a train going nowhere. Maybe in some bizarre way her time had finally come. She sure as hell was due.

How strange would it be if the one who got her out of here with a ton of money was the most feared and hated woman in Lake Tahoe?

38

Thorp's lawyer grabbed him by the arm. "Oggie, I need to talk to you right now."

Rouse was wild-eyed like he was on the verge of a nervous collapse.

They were in the hallway at Cal-Neva lodge, where Thorp was giving a tour of the past and the future. He pulled his arm away. "Calm down. In a minute."

Thorp continued his tour with a group of investors. He pointed to the wall of history, a line of pictures leading to the main ballroom. "Sinatra, Marilyn, Robert Goulet, Lena Horne, Jack Benny. Back in the day, actually, the heyday, yes, indeed…but a new day is upon us, and we have to make changes or we'll lose out."

Rouse had that panic twang in his voice as he whispered in Thorp's ear, "This is an emergency. Come out on the deck."

"Gentlemen," Thorp said, "make yourselves at home. The bar tabs are on me. I'll be right back."

"What now?" Thorp uttered with a low hiss as he followed Rouse down the hall and out past the bar. He'd been back from the funeral less than three hours and in the midst of an important tour for a small group of big investors and wasn't in the mood for interruptions. But he could see it was serious. Maybe the body of Cillo or Shaun had been found and there was a police investigation or news reports.

Rouse led him outside on the patio above the swimming pool, his face all tight, a weird, frantic look in his eyes.

Thorp stopped. "What?"

"Your boy is back," Rouse said in a low voice. "He's down there in his cabin, and he's in bad shape. Got his face broken."

"What in hell—?"

"Happened at Shaun's place," Rouse said.

"I thought Corbin was out of the picture?"

"He is. You're not going to believe this. He was there going through some of Corbin's stuff when Jesup and Cruz showed up."

Thorp couldn't believe that. He was stunned. "What the hell are you talking about? Speak up, for Christ's sake."

Rouse said, "What I could get from him, he got into a fight and he got the worst of it. Got hit hard in the head with a steel bar or maybe a dumbbell."

Thorp couldn't believe what he was hearing. Something like this was impossible. Insane. Sydney Jesup and the criminal nephew of Cillo's still in Tahoe, and they beat up the pro? It was beyond comprehension. It couldn't be true.

Thorp asked, "He sure it was them? How does he know it was them? I don't understand."

"Ask him yourself who beat the hell out of him. He was lucky to escape. He wants to see you. And he wants painkillers," Rouse said. "I sent for some and a gun. No way I'm going down there again." He pushed a package at Thorp.

"What's this?" Thorp, in a daze of disbelief, took the package.

"He wanted OxyContin. What he needs is an X-ray or MRI and medical treatment, but he's not interested in that right now. He's crazy. He's mumbling about broken bones in his face. They got everything."

"Everything what?"

"Corbin's computer and files and whatever he had. He's nuts right now. Threatening to kill half the people in Tahoe. He wants a replacement for his gun. It's in the bag. If I were you, I'd consider shooting him. Bring in somebody to clean up."

"He lost his gun?" Thorp couldn't believe this. It was unacceptable. The idea that Jesup wasn't all that shot up—that she had this Cruz with her and they were on the move *and* had gone after Corbin—was just not what he needed right now. The whole deal could blow up in his face.

Rouse said, "Yeah. This greatest of all"—he lowered his voice—"hit men got his ass kicked in a fight and lost his gun. This guy you want on retainer, or to run all your security operations, is waiting for you."

"I don't believe this."

"Believe it. This Cruz she's hooked up with could be real trouble. He needs to be dealt with soon. You want, I'll get them to open the

Sinatra tunnel."

"No. He said he'd kill anybody who came through there. He didn't like it when I did it the first time."

"You have the gun," Rouse said. "He's incapacitated."

"Then maybe you should deliver this."

"No. He wants to see you."

Thorp looked down at the Celebrity Cabin. Going down there wasn't something he wanted to do. He glanced up at the veranda and saw concerned faces looking at them. He turned to Rouse. "Go entertain them. Tell them I have to deal with a relative. This is a fucking nightmare."

39

On the way down the hill, Thorp glanced toward Incline across Crystal Bay. At this moment on the main lawn of his estate, though he couldn't see anything from where he was, the band platform for the weekend Gatsby Gala was under construction. Already one of the big tents was laid out and ready to be raised.

Thorp swore bitterly, his blood pressure maxed out. He struggled to breathe, his chest tight as a fist, his mouth clenched. He wasn't happy at all about going down there to meet this greatest hit man of all time, this top of the line, this crème de la crème who got his ass kicked.

He knocked on the cabin's side door and heard a mumble. He went in.

"—took long enough," the killer, sitting on the bed, muttered in a thick whisper, his jaw not moving when he talked, like a ventriloquist.

Thorp, trying not to shake, to show fear or weakness, handed him the bag.

The face of this greatest of all hit men was a bloated mass of distorted flesh around the mouth, eyes, and nose. Just looking at him made Thorp extremely uneasy. Something really nasty had happened to this guy. Thorp shook his head, all kinds of terrible scenarios whirling around.

The killer clenched and unclenched his left fist, his right hand at his face. Then he rolled his neck. A man in terrible pain.

Out on Ogden's lake, as Thorp liked to think of Lake Tahoe, sailboats and speedboats darted about at play, awaiting the next big thing to hit Tahoe.

The suicide specialist stared at Thorp, right eye bloodshot, swollen. He was holding an ice pack against his face. Up close, he looked like a freakish, inflamed gargoyle.

"Goddamn!" Thorp said.

"Pills," the killer muttered, fishing around in the bag. He came out with the OxyContin.

"Richard said they hit you with a dumbbell. Jesus, that's like getting hit with a damn sledgehammer."

Leon took the bottle, dumped a couple OxyContin tablets out, and slipped them one at a time between his teeth, apparently not able to open his mouth. He picked up a drink he had sitting on a table to wash them down, but most of the water fell down his chin.

"The woman with him—definitely Sydney Jesup?"

Leon nodded.

"You need to get your face looked at. I can get you someone who won't ask questions or remember the visit. Take a look and see if you have broken bones." Thorp thought as he spoke of getting more guys up here fast to deal with this mess.

Leon shook his head. Waited a minute before whispering, "Later."

Blood bubbles formed at the corners of his mouth like the froth of someone with rabies. He said, "I got work to do tonight. One of your girls…"

"One of my girls?"

"Kor…ah…Kora North."

Thorp had to lean in, get uncomfortably close just to make out what he was saying, the noise of a powerboat all but drowning him out. "What about her?"

"Showed up," the killer said with a tight grimace, swearing under his breath. "At Corbin's…they took her. I need address. Find out why."

"I don't understand."

"…kidnapped. Or working with them." His eyes flashed in rage.

Thorp backed off. He saw the killer in the guy just then. That look in the eyes like a cobra.

"Kora North," Thorp said. "Are you sure?"

"Address," he whispered. "Give me her goddamn address."

Thorp, so buoyant a few minutes ago, now began to feel cracks developing everywhere around him. He saw a massive conspiracy rising. At the root of it, this insane woman who'd linked up with this criminal nephew of Cillo's. That he hadn't killed her a long time ago…the biggest mistake of his life. Rouse's fault. The nervous fool had counseled against it. Weak. Pathetically weak.

"Look," Thorp said. "We can get you help. But you don't look in any condition to be doing much of anything. We can bring up a couple of Vegas boys to deal—"

"You bring nobody," he whispered in a guttural snarl. "You just do what I ask. You hear me?"

Thorp stared at the killer's eyes. Like looking into gun barrels. He nodded.

"Her address?"

Thorp said, "She lives in the Tahoe Keys in South Lake. You want the speedboat?" Thorp said, "I have a guy who can get you over there fast."

The killer shook his head. "Last thing I need is to be slamming across water in a fucking boat."

"I don't want her dead," Thorp said. "Get this settled. This girl is my Daisy, playing the Mia Farrow role at my party. Don't mess her up."

The killer's expression grew reptilian cold.

"Look," Thorp pleaded, scared of his guy, "she's worth too much. One of my best assets."

The killer stared at him.

Thorp had to make the guy understand. Kora was important. She got men to do things they wouldn't ordinarily do. The best films, the best arm twisting came from her. Men fell in love, went nuts, did what they did, and paid the price. Thorp controlled himself. He was famous—and had been all his life—for his tantrum-like outbursts when frustrated. But not with this guy.

Thorp said, "She's too valuable to me. Find out what you need to find out, old sport, but I need her. She's a favorite of some very powerful people. She's expected at my party."

The guy waved him out.

This top professional in the business had gotten the shit kicked out of him by Marco Cruz. Thorp thought about that as he left, and it didn't improve his mood. He wished Corbin was alive. He'd take the son of a bitch down into the tunnel and feed him to George.

Thorp stood for a moment looking at his lake. The black ring of mountains. His world. His family's world. They had cleared the Indians out of here. Built the railroads. This was Thorp's world on the verge of greatness, but now on the verge of destruction if things continued downhill. And he was about to expand that legacy, that birthright, to include the greatest vacation resort on this earth.

And on the verge of the biggest, most important weekend of my life—the Great Gatsby Gala—now this.

***

Leon took another pill. He waited. Finally, after long minutes, he felt some change. Some relief.

He checked the replacement gun, a Glock 23-40 with concealed clip holster and two 17 round mags. Nice weapon.

The hunt had taken a turn, and now it was war. He could get his face fixed later.

40

Sydney and Marco drove back into South Lake a little after ten that night, using back streets to keep off the main boulevard. They'd spent the afternoon and evening in the Range Rover thirty miles from Tahoe up in the mountains, seats back, trying to get some sleep. Marco didn't know how Sydney was holding up. She kept saying she was fine, but he could tell that wasn't exactly true. He'd taken some big shots from the guy he'd fought and was feeling the effects now, putting him in a grim mood.

Something seemed to be bothering Sydney.

"Maybe the guy who killed Shaun lived long enough to call whoever his contact is," she said. "Maybe he told them about us, about Kora."

"Not likely. I head his skull crack and I saw him drop. That boy survived long enough to make a call, would be something, especially since he left this behind." Marco pulled out the cell phone. "Forgot in all the rushing around that I'd picked it up. So quit all this worrying."

She nodded. Sydney had made contact with her reporter friend, and he'd called back and told her where to find Dutch Grimes. A watering hole called Pop's, two blocks off the main drag. Sydney said she knew the place from having passed it many times but had never been inside.

"Been a long, strange day," Sydney said as they drove into a back parking lot of Pop's Place. "From Gatts to Corbin and now Dutch Grimes. I don't know if we're moving up the social ladder."

Marco drained the coffee they'd stopped for, nodding to that. He put the cup in the holder and prepared to go get their target. She'd given him a description of Dutch. He got out and left her to watch for anybody coming into the parking lot they might not want to encounter.

He entered the bar through the rear door. He wore sunglasses and the wide-rim hat, an Airflow Tilley that he'd borrowed from Shaw.

The place was moody—no music, dark, one of those old joints that hadn't gotten upgraded. A place where you expect to see sticky flypaper dangling from the ceiling. No Monday-evening crowd here, no dancing girls. No *Bada Bing*. A low-end joint for the pool players and serious drinkers.

In the center of the establishment stood two pool tables getting some action. Players, bottles, cigarettes, and a couple of over-the-hill girls still trying to get around the block a few more times, but with lesser dudes to choose from. The place had that end-of-time look and feel. The last hurrah.

Sydney had described Dutch as a geeky-looking guy, tall and skinny. Marco picked him out at one of the pool tables, then went to the far end of the bar. At a booth, three other guys silently worked on their drinks.

Marco, being a stranger in a local watering hole, was put on hold by the "busy-in-conversation" bartender, a guy who looked like he'd fallen off a prison bus, weighed down by excessive tattoos. Marco took the time to write a note in the small notebook he always carried, then ripped it out.

Finally having decided to wait on the big-hat stranger, the bartender ambled over, cleaning a glass as he did. "What can I do for you, partner?"

Marco handed him a note, told him it was important. "Give it to the tall dude playing pool. The one in the blue shirt. He needs to see this."

Before the bartender could react one way or another, Marco placed a twenty on the note, turned, and walked out. The note he'd left was simple: *Message from Incline. Next week's Gatsby Gala. Come out back. Now.*

***

Sydney sat in the Range Rover fiddling with the .38 and watching everything and everyone who came near the parking lot. The bar was a couple blocks from the casinos.

This has to work out with Dutch or we have no chance, Sydney thought. Marco would be out, and she would be on her way somewhere.

She wondered how long it would be before somebody found Corbin's body. And what was Kora thinking, maybe doing? So many things could go wrong.

Finally, she saw Marco come out and walk back to the SUV. He leaned in the open window on the driver's side. "He should be coming out."

"You talk to him?" Marco looked on edge, as stressed out as she was.

"No. Left him a note he couldn't turn down. He brings trouble, comes out with some friends, it won't be good."

"He's coming out," she said, her eyes shifting to the bar's back door.

Dutch emerged, tucking in his blue, short-sleeved shirt and hitching up his pants over his skinny hips like maybe it was Thorp himself he was going to meet. Dutch stopped, looked around. Didn't look like a guy who thought his enemies were closing in on him. More like a man who thought he had life by the balls, and it was about to get better.

"Over here." Marco said.

Dutch looked his way. "What's up?" he asked, glancing left and right.

"I got something for you from the man. Something he wants you to do."

Marco held up the small pocket notebook and held it out.

"What's that?"

"Read it and celebrate your next gig. It's a Mexican subpoena," Marco said with a smile.

"A what?"

Dutch, curiosity getting the best of caution, reached for the notebook. As his hand closed on the notebook, Marco, apparently in no mood for pleasantries, came up under it with a short, quick left hook powered by a strong push off his left foot. Got his whole body into the punch, the fist deep and hard into Dutch Grimes' unprotected liver. It took the air out of the man's lungs and dropped him like he'd been shot with a heavy-caliber bullet.

The man looked really hurt. He got slowly to a sitting position. Marco ran a quick weapon's check and found none. He retrieved the notebook, then helped Dutch to his feet.

"You're alive," Marco said, standing over the guy, looking around to make sure they were still alone. "Stay that way."

Marco opened the car door, pushed him into the back seat, and climbed in with him, a gun stuck in Dutch's ribs. He then tapped the boy lightly on the head, enough to keep his attention. "Relax. We're not here to kill you."

Sydney pulled out. "I know your address," she said. "Show me the easiest way."

"Take Ski Run to Needle Park and go left." He was having a hard time adjusting to the pain. He hesitated a moment, then said, "Needle to Keller and go right to Regina. Couple blocks on the right."

"Now that we've been properly introduced," Marco said, "let's have a conversation. Here's how it goes. You play it my way, you'll benefit. And there's no other way."

Recovering slowly, the security expert looked past Marco. His eyes lit up with shock when he finally realized who was driving.

"What," Sydney said glancing in the rearview mirror, "you thought I was dead?"

He didn't reply.

"How are you, Dutch?" Sydney smiled. Then she said, "I'd answer all this man's questions if I were you. He's a really nasty mother when he's not angry. Right now, he's angry, and that just makes him crazy mean."

Dutch's eyes shifted from one to the other. He looked sick. "What is this? What do you want?"

Marco nudged him with the gun barrel. "*No me jodas.* Which, translated, means don't fuck with me. Don't ask questions. Just provide answers to the ones you're asked. Got that?"

Dutch stared at him and nodded.

Marco said, "You didn't answer me. I hate killing people who don't need killing, but I get over it. Are we communicating?"

"Yes."

"Good."

Whatever testosterone the guy had went underground with the liver shot, Sydney thought.

"Give up a name," Sydney said. "You don't, he'll take your balls. You know how these half-Italian, half-Mexican killers are. They like to cut. You should know the difference between a civilian and a *condottiere.*"

Marco gave her a smile. Bad cop, worse cop.

"Who's at home?" Marco asked.

"Just my mother. She'll be asleep. Uses heavy sleeping pills. She won't wake up."

He sounded very cooperative.

Dutch's small, neat house stood in the pine trees on Regina Street below the Heavenly Valley ski area.

She glanced at him in the mirror. "You have a problem gambling? That why they have such a good hold on you?"

He seemed unsurprised.

"Yes."

They parked and went inside, greeted by two cats.

Marco, a gun in the man's back, said quietly, "You're going to show us everything you have on the electronic security system Thorp's lawyer uses at his place. All that high-tech stuff. You were the principle installer, if my information is right. What company?"

He didn't like looking at Marco. He looked down and off to the side. "I worked with a company from San Francisco. Secure Systems International. SSI. I did the installation for a lot of high-end homes."

"I want the layout of the lawyer's house. You can provide me with that?"

"Yes."

Once Dutch got into this thing, he was very thorough. He explained in detail how it all worked and how it could be taken down. He was a man proud of what he could do with security systems.

"You're being helpful," Sydney said. She showed him the recording she had of his cooperation.

He didn't like that. "You're going to get me killed."

"Not if this never happened."

"They'll know."

"They might not be in a position to do anything to anybody," she said. "Just hope we're successful. If we are, your debt problems will vanish. I'll put this with a good friend of mind. He'll know to destroy it when I tell him to. In the meantime, best stay sober. You get talking, you might not like the consequences."

Marco studied the laptop file with the security info. He had Dutch show him how to deal with the iControl System Interrupter and the code sequencer. Strangely, Dutch began to show some enthusiasm, more than just his pride in a job well done. He was gaining some interest in the caper. He displayed no great love for Rouse or Thorp.

"Sorry about hitting you hard like that," Marco said. "I thought you'd be more resistant."

"I think I'll survive it," Dutch said.

Sydney said, "This works out the way we anticipate, we'll have what we want and a hell of a lot of cash. You have gambling debts? House debts?"

"I do."

"Maybe a few hundred thousand will help you out?"

"Do more'n help me out. My mother needs some medical stuff done. It'll help her out as well."

"We get what we're after, well make sure you get reimbursed for your help. You won't have to worry about anybody finding out or being able to do anything. You just have to handle the money with some discretion."

"I'll do that."

He gave them night binoculars, meters, and a commo set so they could walkie-talkie each other without using the cell phones all the time. For the torch work he added welding glasses and a powerful torch kit.

He dug out printed Google shots, then made a few notes with some suggestions how he would approach it. He gave them the control system, putting it all in a large work bag he used when out on a job. Twice he wondered out loud if Marco was some kind of ex-soldier or agent or something, given all he seemed to know. He didn't get an answer but he seemed intrigued by the idea.

After assurances and warnings, they thanked Dutch for his cooperation and left.

41

When they pulled away from Dutch's place well after midnight, Marco now behind the wheel, Sydney said, "I never saw a man go down so fast from a single body shot like that. You do some fighting?"

"You don't fight, you don't live long in a Mexican prison. I'm sorry I did it now—he was really helpful. Nothing humbles a man and commands his attention like a liver shot," Marco said. "Dutch wasn't in any kind of shape to take a punch. It hurts bad, closes the lungs, cripples the will. That was the shot Bernard Hopkins used to take out Golden Boy, De La Hoya, out in the ninth at the MGM in Vegas. Another great body-shot-maker was Ricky Hatton. A jaw shot can knock a man out, but a liver shot cuts a man down."

They headed up the eastern side of the lake on 50. Marco had said he wanted to drive past the Thorp and Rouse estates, see what they would be dealing with.

"How are you doing?" Marco asked.

"I could use a bath, a massage, and a glass of wine."

"I think we can handle that."

Sydney felt worse than she was letting on. The fight at Shaun Corbin's had aggravated the wounds.

Even with Marco with her, she couldn't shake the feeling of being vulnerable. The windows of the SUV were lightly tinted and at night they were invisible, which helped. But she figured Thorp would bring in all kinds of security and who knew what else. And she didn't like his relationship with the police and sheriffs, especially on the Nevada side—where they were now. Marco wanted to see if access was feasible by land. If not, they'd have to go in by boat, which was definitely Sydney's preference. She wouldn't have security to deal with on the lake. And the noise of the party, and the lights, would provide cover out on the dark lake.

They drove past Zephyr Cove, up past Glenbrook, and through

the tunnel, leaving 50 and heading up 28 past the Ponderosa Ranch turnoff, into Incline Village and Crystal Bay.

Sydney said, "If we come in by boat, it'll be right out there."

"They really think they can get hold of George Willett's Thunderbird Lodge and all that property?"

"They think they can do just about anything. You have the right friends here, in Vegas, and Washington, there's no limit to what you can get away with. You just make deals. Build everything Green to placate the Greens, and who knows? But they aren't going to get the chance if I have anything to do with it. The plan is, they'll start with the old casinos around the Cal-Neva. Work from there. I'll show you the piece of land he wants as his starter property when we get over there."

He turned down Shoreline Boulevard in Incline Village.

"Half the homes along here were in foreclosure," Sydney said. "Thorp and Rouse ended up with many of them. They'll be worth a lot more money once the resort is in place."

He slowed down on Lakeshore Boulevard. Now they were passing the big Incline estates. Grand houses behind trees, gardens, gates. No lights on the street, the residents not wanting the ambiance disturbed by streetlights.

"We have a checkpoint," she said, "better pull over and douse the lights."

A limo passed. "Guests arriving already," she said.

"They block off a whole street?"

"No, they're just checking. That gate, that house—what you can see of it, anyway—is Thorp's. The next one is Rouse's. They actually have a tunnel that connects the two. Rumor has it, he keeps a lion down there just like the guy who built the Thunderbird Lodge did back in the thirties. George Whittell brought in Hughes and the movie stars of the day. That's Thorp's game plan. He wants to be George Whittell. The man couldn't carry Whittell's piss bottle. He was the real playboy of the Western world."

He stared at the houses partially hidden back in the trees, prime lakefront. They switched places, and she got them back on the road. They went a few more blocks down Lakeshore Drive, turned up to the next street, Southwood, and started going back.

"The help they use, Mexicans mostly, live in these apartment complexes," Sydney said. "They cut the lawns, do the gardening, run the households, kitchens."

"What's with the satellite dishes?" Marco asked. Every apartment seemed to have one. They looked like a vertical field of mushrooms.

Many Mexicans were out and about, lots of kids in the street playing.

"No streetlights?" Marco said.

"No. They city doesn't allow them. It takes away from the ambiance."

They headed back to the Shaw house. Going through the Cal-Neva highlands, she slowed. "Right up there. Used to be a big casino, then it was torn down and was going to be rebuilt, but it never was."

A security or cop car, she couldn't tell which, turned toward them and Sydney eased on down the road. They turned back up to the main highway and headed back.

"You're right," Marco said. "The only way will have to be by boat."

"Right now, I need that Jacuzzi and some wine." She couldn't help thinking maybe a massage wouldn't be a bad idea, too, though she hadn't said it again. A massage would be really nice, and she had an idea he would do a good job on her abused body.

What the hell? she thought. *We came this far—maybe we should seal this relationship while we're reasonably alive and well.*

42

Nothing clears the mind like a long shower, Kora North thought, lifting her face up into the rush of water as if it might wash away this crazy day.

A little earlier, she'd briefly contemplated suicide, but not too seriously, though she did have hypnotic sleeping pills and figured she could take a bottle of them with enough vodka to kill a couple truck drivers. But suicide wasn't her thing. So, changing her mind, she chose a shower and a big glass of wine to help her think about the mess she was in.

Because, why did everything in her life end up like this?

I'm cursed, she decided.

In the shower, she again contemplated running. Playing it out. Back and forth. Where? How long before they hunted her down? Girl like her couldn't hide easily. She'd have to get a protector and, once again, she'd be under some guy's control until he got tired of her.

She reached her arm out and found the glass of wine on the vanity. She drank half the glass, then put it back down, returning to the shower for a moment, luxuriating in the flow of water over her perfect body. The feel of a thousand tiny fingers on her flawless flesh.

So many grubby, grasping fingers on her, in her—no water could wash those memories away!

She dried off and entered her bedroom, fresh and feeling better, wearing nothing, the nearly empty glass of wine in her hand. And there stood a shocking, frightened creature in the middle of her bedroom. He had a bloated face like some movie monster.

"Jesus!"

"Not quite," he muttered.

Naked, glass in hand, she stared at this horror, the man's face all discolored and swollen. Then she saw a gun hanging in his hand by

his side and she knew she was dead. She knew it had to be the guy
Marco had beat up, the professional who'd killed Shaun and got into
that fight. Shaun must have told him she was coming over. Maybe
he'd seen her there from up in the woods.

Fuck, it is him, she thought. *Is this how it ends?*

She couldn't deal with that, so she threw the wineglass at him,
ran back into the bathroom, and locked the door. Then she went to
the window, wondering if she could get out. She'd probably kill
herself on the sidewalk or break something and he'd just kill her
there.

Her body naked, bloody. People staring. We knew it would end badly
for her, *they'd say.*

She didn't even have time to formulate a real plan. The man
kicked open the door and stood there looking at her, rheumy eyes
raking her body. She swung at this mad clown's wrecked face. He
grabbed her hand with one hand, put the gun to her face with the
other.

"Go ahead!" she screamed at him. "You bastard, you want to kill
me, do it! I don't want any sick shit while I'm alive, okay? Just know
this, I'm glad you did that miserable prick Shaun Corbin. I
appreciated that."

That seemed to have a strange influence on him, because he
released her hand and stepped back, as if surprised about something.

Her .32 was still in her bag, along with the money, and was on a
chair in the living room. She tried to remember if she'd even
reloaded it. Damn that Marco guy. He'd taken the bullets out. They'd
left her defenseless. They hadn't protected her. So much for being
their inside girl.

Horror-face tried to talk, seemed like he couldn't. He waved a
gun at her, motioning her to go to the living room. She grabbed the
silk robe from the back of the bathroom door and put it on as he
watched. He followed her into the living room, then settled gingerly
on the couch against the far wall, facing the small bar. She sat on the
chair at the end of the couch, their eyes fixed tight on one another.

"They really fucked you up, didn't they?" she said.

He stared at her for a moment longer, then glanced at the large
picture above the small bar. Cost her three grand. A western scene—
bunch of cowboys in a bar fight over a big-breasted girl wearing only
a black cowboy hat and black boots.

He got up, went to the bar, and made himself a drink, but that didn't work out very well. Ended up all over his chin. She told him there were straws under the counter.

He got one and was able to get it in his mouth. He sucked the alcohol in with a slurping sound. When he finally spoke, his lips hardly moved at all, his jaw didn't move at all. She had to lean forward to understand his garbled voice.

"You…" He paused. Gathered himself. "Jesup. How are you and her…connected?" His voice was raspy and low like an old, dying man's voice.

"We're not connected," Kora said with defensive anger, shifting her legs, pulling the thin robe tighter, trying to maintain an icy, calm demeanor. "They grabbed me and wanted to know things. I don't know things. They left me here alone. Fuck them."

She was furious at them for putting her in this situation. If they wanted to use her so bad, they should have done more to protect her.

He looked at her and she thought that's wasn't a good enough answer. She'd given up nothing to trade with. She added, thinking fast, "That's not exactly true." She had to have something he needed, something he needed right away before he got crazy on her.

She said, "Actually, they want me to help them out…this plan they have. I know exactly what they're going to do and when they plan on doing it. They have a hold on me for my cooperation. It's not like I want to help them out. They have recordings, video that might put me in prison."

He stared at her. A black and yellow swath of ruin ran from his lower jaw right to the corner of his bloodshot eyes. He looked like the face from hell.

"What are they planning?" he murmured, voice barely a whisper and his eyes jumping weird, like the lights in his brain were flickering. Fucking guy was something out of a monster video game.

"Yeah, like I'd tell you so then you kill me and go your merry way. That's gonna happen. I need something in return."

She studied him the way you'd study a coiled rattler. The distance of the potential strike.

He was deciding something. Was she valuable enough to keep alive or not? What was it he wanted most? He didn't kill her right away. So it wasn't her. It was *them*! *He's after them, not me,* she thought.

I'm just a means to that end. She had to play that card.

He couldn't kill Thorp's Daisy. No way.

Desperate to keep him on the track of her survival, she repeated herself in case he didn't get it the first time. Then she said, "They want me to work with them. They threatened to kill me if I didn't. Then they told me what they have planned. Don't think you can beat it out of me. Or scare me. You can't. If I'm gonna die…one thing I'm not going to do is give another asshole any satisfaction. You need to understand that."

He almost smiled, tried to anyway, then mumbled, "Tell me…"

Screw that, she thought. *Once he gets whatever information I can give him, this psychopath bastard is going to put a bullet right in my forehead like he did Shaun.* Maybe that was Thorp's order. He could find fifty Daisys to replace her if he wanted.

She changed direction. "You have a name?" Kora asked. Anything to connect.

He whispered something she couldn't make out. Sounded like *Lee…On.*

I'm going to be killed by a guy with a fucking Chinese name? Behind that wrecked face, was he Chinese? No. Maybe it was just he couldn't get it out.

She'd had moments in her life like this. The first time she was raped and thought the guy would kill her. Somehow she'd got free of him, fighting and biting and clawing—and he'd given up and ran off. And there was the time somebody stuck a gun in her mouth and threatened to blow her head off. She was fourteen. She'd known these and many other moments, and surviving them made her street tough and street smart.

But this was the first time she'd come face to face with a real professional killer. The kind like you see in movies. Only those are just actors.

She needed to keep talking, get him thinking her way, so she said, "I'm assuming Thorp and Rouse are the ones who hired you to get Jesup. That's your mission, isn't it?"

He stared.

"I might be able to help you with that. You want to know how they're going to take them down. And when. Then you need to play it my way. I'm in a position"—this occurred to her like a flash of genius—"where I can hand them to you on a silver platter. Make your life a lot easier. But it'll cost you leaving me alive. That's a fair trade."

"You can do that…silver platter?" he whispered.

She thought he wanted to smile at the idea, but couldn't handle the pain it would bring.

"I can. I think you know by now they aren't some joke like Shaun was. This guy you're up against, he's the real deal."

She was playing him now. Challenging him. She pushed it.

"This guy is a badass. Maybe worse than you, by the looks of things. He's a Mexican stone-cold killer. You want to take him on without knowing anything, in the dark about what they got planned, good luck to you. I can help you, but do I look like a girl does things for free?"

He waited, the gun now resting on his thigh, eyes fixed on her. Fixed on her eyes, her mouth, drifting up and down.

"I didn't get your name. Sounded Chinese."

She leaned in when he said it this time.

"Leon."

"Leon. Got it." Then she said, "What they plan will surprise you. To say nothing of Thorp and Rouse. Jesup's determined to get Thorp if it's the last thing she does in this life. I know what they're gonna do. You can kill me, but what good will that do you? Like I said, you can't scare it out of me. I've been down that road too many times."

She figured she had his full attention now. Working him. "Those two have some tapes, things that can hurt me real bad, and I want them back. They're using them to make me help them."

"Blackmailing you…help them."

"That's exactly right. That's the name of the game around this stinking lake."

"Beautiful eyes," he said.

This psycho gonna shoot me in the eye?

She was thinking fast and coming up empty now, not sure how to play this. If she had to use a weapon, if her play didn't work, the only weapon she could see was the corkscrew wine opener. If she could get to that and jam it in his throat, or his eye…

But he suddenly zoned out, his eyes glazed over. Then he snapped back. He reached for the bottle, poured himself another JD, and pulled out some pills. He put two of them in his mouth, pushing them in with a finger, then used the straw and sucked down some whiskey.

"You got a cigarette?" he asked.

"Yeah, but I don't like people smoking inside. I always go out on the patio."

He waved the gun at her. "Get me a cigarette."

"I have a pack in my bag."

"What's that?" he pointed to the table behind her. "Oh," she said, hating that she'd left a pack of cigarettes on the bar.

She lit a cigarette and handed it to him. Then one for herself.

"Like I said," as smoke drifted from her nostrils, "Whatever happens to me, just know I'm glad you killed that prick Shaun Corbin. I want to thank you for that."

She wasn't kidding about that one bit. This killer looked really bad, like he was drifting off. "I'd give you the best blow job of your life for doing it, but you don't look like you could take anything too exciting right now."

He tried to smile. Tried to talk, but he wasn't looking like he was all there. Then the killer suddenly laid his head back against the corner of the couch.

What the hell's this?

The killer was out cold. The gun on his lap, cigarette about to burn his stomach. She grabbed the cigarette and put it in one of the big shell ashtrays on the coffee table. Then she eased the gun from his hand.

Kora North had thought a thousand times what it would be like to put a bullet in some bastard's head. And now she had the opportunity. It gave her a giddy feeling, but also one of uncertainty.

How to dispose of the body and how not to get blood all over her beautiful couch? She couldn't decide what to do. And that seemed in her mind to sum up her miserable life. *Why?* It made no sense not to do it. Yet something held her back.

Then she nearly laughed out loud. The guy had fallen back and she realized he had this erection blooming in his pants. Her sense of dark humor gripped her. The utter absurdity of her existence and her effect on men stunned her at times. A guy comes to kill her but falls unconscious with a hard on. She'd tell the girls in the bar she did a goner with a boner, or something like that.

Whack-city is where I live, she thought.

Then it was decision time. She had to think this out. Consider all the ramifications of whatever she chose. And why it was even a question in her mind.

To kill or not to kill.

Do it! she told herself. *Do it!*

43

The Jacuzzi and massage never happened, and neither did any kind of sealing their bond doing something pleasurable. Instead, Sydney got a call from her police-reporter friend right after they returned to the Shaws' telling her that Cillo's body had been found.

Marco didn't want to talk about it right away. He sat in the kitchen with a tiny headlamp and went over Dutch's files, notebook, computer, and his security workup sheets—all of it on the kitchen table.

When he finally joined her on the deck, he decided to talk about it. They sat in the dark, nothing on the lake but the moon.

Sydney said, "According to the Douglas County Sheriff's Department...an accident. He fell getting into his rock pool. Hit his head. Knocked himself out and drowned. Apparently, he'd been lying in the pool for at least a day or two."

Marco said, "Your police-reporter friend believes the accident theory?"

"I don't think he's got any contradictory information."

"Who found him?"

"One of his friends couldn't get ahold of him. Went up and found him."

They were silent for a moment.

Marco said, "Damn, that's really hard to get my mind around. Some people you grow up with, they seem indestructible. He was like that. One of my favorite stories as I a kid was how he survived the bombing of Harvey's casino back in 1980. He was one of the guys who continued to play even as they were evacuating before the bomb went off. Sometimes you get lucky, sometimes you play one hand too many. He was a to-the-bitter-end kind of guy. A family trait."

"Didn't he win the Tervis Cup once?" Sydney asked. "I heard stories about that. And some controversy?"

Marco said, "He courted controversy, for sure. He was nothing if not provocative in everything he did. But the Tervis Cup was one of the highlights of his life. He talked endlessly about it. I was about twelve when he won it. He'd tell you every mile of the hundred-mile climb over the mountains, always prefacing it with the fight he had with some guy in Squaw Valley at the start of the race. Then the miserable climb in the heat and dust up twenty-three thousand feet and how cold it got at night, and then the drop down to Auburn over miserable switchback trails. I heard that story a hundred times. Got better with every telling. If he'd lived to ninety, I'm sure he would have added Indians he had to fight over the Sierras to the mix of things. It was the highlight of his existence, winning that race."

"What was the controversy?"

"Somewhere between Devil's Thumb and Murderer's Bar, just as they were heading down toward the final victory lap at the Placer County Fairgrounds, they got into it again. The controversy was over whether some foul play was involved. The guy he beat out never finished the race, but he never talked about how he got a broken arm and cracked ribs. Never lodged a complaint."

"Maybe he got a little drunk and slipped," she said.

"Maybe. He definitely gave me some good moments in my life. But he had a real dark side, for sure. I can't help wondering if maybe because he didn't bring me in, he had to be punished." After a long pause, he added, "I'll think about him and that part of my life later. Right now, we have work to do."

Marco took out his cell and called Kora North. No answer. Called her again. "C'mon, Kora, answer the goddamn phone."

"She's probably drunk and asleep. Or she decided to run," Sydney said.

"We have too much on her. And she wants that money. I'll go with sleeping. But when their *Sicario* doesn't return, there'll be more guys out there looking for him. And us. We travel by boat at night from now on."

They stayed up until morning. Marco tried Kora twice more and got nothing. Sydney sent her a text. If they were going over there, it meant waiting until dark. They needed some confirmation from her.

***

Kora stared at her phone, then at the comatose killer. He'd been out a hell of a long time. It was already daylight. She knew she couldn't continue to ignore the texts she was getting from Jesup and the calls from her boyfriend. She tried to decide what the hell to do. Maybe she should just tell this Marco guy that the killer was lying there on her couch unconscious. Let him handle it.

The humming of her phone, mingled with the killer's snoring, had her getting crazy. Leon was in a sleep so deep that when she nudged him, he didn't show any signs of waking up. Maybe he was dying. She realized if he died, that was a problem. If he lived, maybe a worse one. If she killed him, Thorp would get her one way or another for it.

She now had Leon's gun and her own. She had all the power. Just didn't know what to do with it.

Make a goddamn decision, she admonished herself.

She fought off a sense of panic. If she shot him, she had to do it in a way that wouldn't mess up her expensive couch. She loved the couch. She had expensive tastes.

She wondered if he was brain-dead or something. Then it occurred to her that if she didn't answer the texts or phone calls, Marco and Jesup might just show up.

I can't kill a man while he's sleeping, she thought. *That's not fair. He's got to see me, look into my eyes and know he's about to die.*

Then she wondered why she thought that. What the hell did it matter? *I'm nuts,* she thought. *Can't make up my goddamn mind about anything.*

She stared at her fish tank. The fish swimming lazily. All damn day, every day. Trapped. No exit.

That's when she looked at the buzzing phone and knew she had to answer this time or the guy might just come over to find out what was wrong. She picked up the phone.

It was the boyfriend, Marco. He said, "If you're not okay, say you have the wrong number and hang up."

"I'm okay. I was sleeping."

"Okay. Look, I need the drawings so we can begin...construction."

"I'm working on them."

"Do the best you can," he told her. "Inside and outside, down to the water. The inside is the most important. Where the office will be located. On the outside, where the fishpond, gazebo, boat dock, and that kind of thing should be."

"When do you want them?" She spoke to this stud, wondering where he was. Maybe right outside close. She stared at the killer. He was now snoring fitfully.

"Tonight. Make them detailed as you can. Contractors will be coming in a couple days."

She wondered if he really needed them, or if he was just testing her. All this code language like the fucking FBI was listening in or something. And again she wondered if she should just tell this Marco guy and have him come over and kill the guy. *Go ahead, tell him,* she pleaded with herself. But she didn't.

Be real easy to kill the killer and then let Marco get rid of the body, wouldn't it?

She couldn't think clearly about what it would mean. She was in a state, caught between the killer, the guy on the phone, and Thorp. It always amazed her how she got into this kind of shit.

Meanwhile, Marco was telling her he'd let her know when he was there. Asked her again if everything was good.

Good? *No,* she thought, *not exactly.*

"Yes. Everything's good. At least as good at it can be under the circumstances," she said, walking to the window, back to the couch, then to the bar as she talked.

"Sorry 'bout that. It's how things go. Contractors are undependable. Let me deal with them."

Yeah, right, she thought sarcastically, looking at this killer of men, and maybe of women. She was so tempted to tell Marco she had the killer right there in front of her. But what would that accomplish? How many more were out there?

Don't tell him. No way, Kora thought. *Not yet.*

"Okay, I'll be in touch."

She closed the phone. Men and their bullshit.

She again looked at the fish tank. She saw herself in there as a tiny fish swimming against glass walls in a permanent trap.

To hell with that.

She picked up the guns and tried to decide which one would be best to finish this with.

Shoot the bastard in the head and be done with it.

Then call the police and say some madman broke in and tried to rape her. He sure as hell fit the description of a madman.

She pointed one gun, then the other, at his face. All her life she'd wondered, since the first time she was raped, what it would be like to kill some sonofabitch. Now she was about to find out.

Bang-bang, motherfucker.

Still, she hesitated.

She hadn't made up her mind, and that really bothered her. *I've fucking got to decide,* she thought. *If he doesn't die, if he wakes up, then what?*

He kills me.

That's what.

What is wrong with you, damnit? Either kill this bastard or…or what?

44

Marco said, "Kora's good to go. She's looking at the end of the rainbow."

Marco went back into the files and tapes Corbin had on her. It was heavy stuff.

Sydney pulled her chair next to him and said, "These guys she and the other girls are partying with, they're some of the most important people around the lake."

A couple tapes later, they found a senator, two congressmen, and other politicos. "This outfit was busy," Marco said. "No wonder they got control of things. How far is it to Rouse's place?"

Sydney said, "From here, in that speedboat, about half an hour. You know what's so scary? I'm now my opposite, my dark alter ego. I was this straight-laced law chick, but now I'm a full-fledged criminal. It was so easy and doesn't really seem to bother me. That's scary. You went through some of those radical changes, didn't you?"

"Here's the thing. The way I look at it, there are two kinds of law breakers—those who have no moral justification and those who do. It's all a matter of context. If the law can't bring justice, well, maybe somebody has to do whatever it requires."

"The end justifies the means?"

Marco said, "Sometimes the means force the issue, determine the end."

They went over all the negative scenarios. They worried Kora had gone to Thorp and there would be people waiting for them. But given they had so much on her, so much of what she wanted, in the end, they agreed that was unlikely…but they still needed to plan for the worst.

***

Sydney dug out Bernie Shaw's many maps, and they looked at the keys. The condos and house were on fingers of land that had been created out of the wetlands. It looked on the map like a cluster of germs.

"I nearly bought a condo here when prices dropped," Sydney said.

"It looks like a nice place. What stopped you?"

She told him how unaware she'd been of some of the history of the place. That it was carved out of Truckee wetlands, much of the building material supplied by none other than Thorp's grandfather and father. It triggered one of the great battles over the destruction of the environment in the fifties and sixties.

"You and the Thorps go way back."

"I guess so. They stuck thousands of condos and houses right on top of one of nature's necessary places. This is where she lives, on Capri Drive."

"It seems like a big place," he said, looking more closely at the map.

"They dredged the wetlands so they had all these fingers of land, so everybody gets a little waterway out front. Seven miles of interlocking waterways."

"It *is* big."

"Would have been even bigger had they not been stopped. They altered the natural channels that filtered the water before it reached the lake. The paving and building on the Keys eliminated that filtering process, and that had a lot to do with the lake turning gray-green. From high in the air, the place looks like a big pond with amoeba-like creatures frozen in place. If Thorp and his investors get their way on the North Shore, who knows if they won't come back and finish this? It was Thorp's father and grandfather who supplied much of the building material for some of the first homes. And across the lake, if they find a way to open up any part of the Whittell legacy, Tahoe will just be a really bad copy of Vegas."

"Funny how my uncle changed," Marco said. "He was a big fan of keeping the lake in its natural state. You would have connected with him back then."

"It's difficult to protect a place as beautiful as this," Sydney said. "Those who own property don't want anybody else coming in. They want an exclusive. Others want to turn it into Vegas North. But I see it as a big park where everyone has a right to come and enjoy it, but no one has the right to destroy. How you do that is the issue. But one thing I do know is that Thorp has no interest in the lake. Just himself. He's the opposite of George Whittell, the man he supposedly worships. And he's willing to do anything to get what he wants. And has."

They put everything that was spread out on the table away, then decided to get some rest before heading over to see Kora at twilight.

Between the fight at Corbin's and his uncle dead, Marco was now totally committed to the mission. It was very simple—they would find a way to get Thorp, or he would get them. And like it was in much of Mexico, the police didn't much matter.

45

The killer moved, shifted, let out a heavy breath, almost like a sigh, and Kora backed up.

Shit! He's not dead or dying.

He was alive and going to wake up. She pointed the gun, pointed it at the killer's temple, ready to do it, willing to do it.

Something was happening in her mind. An idea—one she knew was completely nuts yet excitingly powerful—began forming. And that slowed her down, made her stop, think.

She felt the heft and the power of the gun. It had a weird trigger. She'd shot guns before. At the range, and when she went camping once with this nutty cop from Reno who wanted to marry her so bad he was willing to give up his wife and four kids. Mercifully for her, and them, he died in a bad accident while chasing a drunk.

But then, she didn't know what she wanted. She shifted a little so the bullet wouldn't go through the couch.

If you're gonna do it, she told herself, do it now. *End this crazy fucking day with a killer's dead body on your seven-thousand-dollar couch.*

On the other side of the lake were two assholes who wanted to control the universe. And then there was Jesup and her ex-con boyfriend, who was probably a killer as well. It was a lot to think about. Overwhelming.

On the one hand, there shouldn't have been anything to think about. This killer was at her mercy. She could kill him and call Jesup and they could get rid of the body.

But she didn't do that. She was getting some other idea. She felt it forming, emerging, growing.

It occurred to her they had something in common. She sold sexual services to rich men. He sold murder services to those very same rich men. Sexual services. Murder services.

That's what they were. Highly paid service workers for rich and powerful assholes. They got no respect. They were dark secrets nobody would ever admit to.

I'm not going to kill him, she thought, enlightened, as if it was a powerful epiphany. *So what am I going to do?* And that's when a new idea began to emerge in her agitated brain. A crazy, beautiful, new idea. Maybe the craziest and potentially greatest idea she'd ever had in her life.

***

Leon had flirted with consciousness a couple times. Now, he was awake for a moment and unsure of where he was, what was going on. He lay on a couch, staring at the ceiling, not at all sure even who he was for a moment. He struggled to put the pieces of his mind back together, remember where he was, what had happened. He opened his eyes.

A female vision materialized through the swirling brain fog. His vision struggled for focus. Breasts, mounds of white sweetness, thighs swelling in front of him, rich and full. And a gun.

Memories started coalescing slowly, bits and pieces, streams of memory looking to solve the puzzle of consciousness. Reality reforming into understanding.

His gun! The instrument of his power and authority, the pen with which he wrote the epithets of his conquests. For the second time, he lost it.

His memory bubbled up out of the mental swamp, inchoate, confused, fighting to free itself of the tangles, the predators of his mind. He found himself staring at his Glock, the weapon's nasty eye staring back at him, ready to take his life.

Kora North, this hot chick behind the gun, said, "You're finally awake. Christ, I thought you were in a coma getting ready to die on me. Then what? Getting rid of your body would be a big problem and what was I gonna do? I couldn't call the police, given my problems," she said. "Then I thought, just shoot him and call Jesup and her boyfriend and let them take care of the body."

Jesup and her boyfriend! That's right, he thought. *They took her. Was she with them? But…but?*

Kora, hopped up, all wild-eyed, then said, "So, how's the face?"

He didn't understand.

Then she said, "I was going kill you, but then I decided you're more valuable to me alive than dead, in case you're wondering. And right in the middle of thinking about it, I got a call from Marco Cruz. He wanted me to draw some maps for him. Here I am thinking whether or not to kill you, I got this other badass on the phone. Been one of those days. Then I got an idea."

She was dressed now in shorts and a midriff-revealing T-shirt as she sat at the bar sipping from a large ceramic cup, the Glock lying next to her hand. Her knee moved back and forth, revealing the smooth silk of her inner thigh. *The highway to heaven or hell, depending,* he thought.

Leon forced himself to sit up, which influenced her to bring up a second gun. A small caliber. Looked like a .32.

"You look like a vampire that's been run over by an eighteen-wheeler," she said. "You're wondering why you're alive. Why I'm going to give you your gun back. Well, it's because you and I are going to make a deal that's gonna make us rich."

Jesus, another deal! Everybody up here is crazy. Got to be the air.

"The biggest deal of our lives. It's time we form an alliance, you and me. An alliance that can make us rich and protect us at the same time."

Then she starting talking—that sexy smirk on her face—about what he was getting paid and how that was nothing compared to the possible payday she had in mind. Then she started telling him he didn't know what it was like being on top of things.

"You're always working from dead-man paycheck to dead-man paycheck. Doing other people's dirty laundry. Like some Mexican hitman with no life beyond what he's told to do. A working dog for the man."

She was insulting him. Trashing him. He couldn't believe this woman.

Then she said, "Maybe you don't want to be one of the big boys…Maybe"—she flipped her hair back from her forehead with her gun hand—"you like being the hired help, cleaning up their shit and getting paid like a janitor compared to what's out there. That what you like, cleaning up some asshole's crap? 'Cause I got a feeling you're a better man than that."

This would have been the point where, he wondered, had he his weapon, he'd have just flat out killed the lady to shut her up.

"How long was I out?" he mumbled.

"A long damn time. Which is a good thing. It gave me a chance to think things through."

Then, to his utter disbelief, she got up, walked over, dropped the Glock next to him, put the .32 in her back pocket, and walked over to look out the window. He realized it was dark outside. *How the hell long have I been asleep?* he wondered. Then he realized he needed a pill. And there was his gun, right there.

He picked it up and aimed at her.

She turned and looked at him. No fear blossomed in her smoky eyes. The chick had liquid nitro in her veins. The second badass female he'd run into. These fucking women up here...

Kora said, "No, I'm not scared. You wanna know why? You want me to help you and I haven't given you the information you really need. And because I turn you on. And because I have a proposition for you. And because you strike me as a smart man who's sick and tired of being nothing more than a gun gardener mowing other people's lawns. That's why you won't pull the trigger."

She walked over and he saw that her gun, which she now pointed at him, was a Colt NP Cobra, aluminum frame, two-inch barrel. She handled it like she knew how to handle it.

"Killing me," she said, "would only prove one thing—that you're stupid. Too stupid to live."

He couldn't believe this.

Then she said. "Let's put the guns down and get you fixed up. I'll get some ice to take down the swelling. You need an anti-inflammatory. And maybe a little food. A protein shake. And stay off the booze. We can talk. I got everything you want, including Jesup and her boy toy."

That's when he realized the gun was empty.

She said, "Here's the thing. We need to learn to trust each other...hard as that is for two people who don't trust anybody."

She got the clip from the bar and put in on the table next to the couch. All he had to do was grab it. But he figured she'd pull that little popgun and shoot him before he could get locked and loaded.

She chuckled, came over, and planted a light, delicate, warm kiss right on his bruised mouth, like he was a child, or maybe a dying patient.

She said, "I got a feeling we're gonna make one hell of a team."

Her smile widened, like a new dawn flooding into the dark world of Leon, the Professional. It was like his fantasy world, the one he needed so desperately in his isolated existence, had suddenly become his real world. Emotions, feelings, foreign and strange, moved through him like an alien invasion. She seemed highly amused by his situation.

"You want to hear me out?" she asked.

He nodded that he did.

This woman had a plan. And she started telling him what her plan was, how all this money was involved, how Jesup and Cruz were going to rob the lawyers. How they had the plans and were working with some security installer guy named Dutch. And how she was the inside girl. Then she went off on his clients like they were the two worst people on planet earth.

"I know it violates your sense of self," she said.

Kora North spelled it all out like this was her thing. He'd watched movies that featured female killers and badasses and that was fine, but he never really believed they could actually exist. Just something for the imagination. Comic-book chicks. But he was looking at something very different here. If ever the real thing existed, he was looking at it.

"Jesup and Cruz are coming over to pick up the interior drawings of Rouse's place I drew for them."

She showed him the drawings she'd done on printer paper.

"You can kill them, but you'll be killing the greatest payday of your life."

She's got it all figured out.

She took a sip of whatever she was drinking and then told him the rest of her plan. At first he resisted the implications of it, but the more she talked—the more she added what the future was going to look like for *them*—he found himself actually paying attention. And it all came from the mouth of the most beautiful woman he'd ever laid eyes on.

Then, in the midst of this, her phone rang. It was them. "Now he wants me to meet him at the dock near the restaurant," she said after ending the call. "So you need to decide. You can kill him now, or you can kill him twenty million dollars richer down the road. It's not just money. It's all that dirt they have on people. Imagine the power behind that. Think for a second. Instead of a hired gun, a grass cutter, what it would be like to be the big dog for once in your life.

That's what I want. I'm sick of working for other people."

Henry Craven Lee, presently Leon the Professional, had become mesmerized. Dazzled. A little disoriented.

He felt an overwhelming desire to surrender to this crazy woman and what she was up to. He'd never felt anything like this before. He was in love. It was a very strange, very exciting feeling.

46

Waiting for dark, Marco suggested maybe, with the big party coming up and the hired gun out of the picture, Thorp might have a temporary change of heart.

"Sending out a bunch of goons right now, with the guests coming in, might not be something he wants to do. I'm sure he'll have major security at Incline, but he might wait until the party is over."

"That makes some sense," Sydney agreed. "But where Thorp is concerned, sense doesn't always rule. I'm not relaxing."

They waited until the lake began to settle down, after some speedboat races, before heading down the coast. Sydney drove the speedboat fairly close to the western shore past Tahoma and Rubicon Bay before crossing Emerald Bay and turning southeast toward the Keys.

They passed the lake's two behemoth paddle-sternwheelers, the *Tahoe Queen* and a little later the M.S. *Dixie II,* plodding along on the way back to dock with their dinner guests.

"If she's not going to work out, what's plan B?" Marco asked as they slowed.

Sydney said, "I hear Rio is booming."

She said it with a sense of dark humor, but Marco figured it wasn't far off the mark if Kora flaked out on them.

Sydney eased the speedboat down the Keys' east channel into the Keys Village and main boat slips. She found an empty slip near the channel entrance where, if need be, they could make a fast run out into open water.

"I hope you're right about Kora," Sydney said as they checked their Bluetooth communications, compliments of Dutch Grimes.

"She's gonna play," he said. "We have too much on her and she's looking at the money."

There were a lot of people out and about. Most of the crowd

gathered near the Ketch Restaurant. Marco glassed the area, the parked cars, people coming and going from the Ketch. There were a lot of boats to hide in, and the parking facility stretched all along the harbor and the cove. But it was the best time to make an appearance. The last of the boats out on the lake were coming in, so there was nothing unusual about them docking.

Marco gave Sydney the night glasses. "Keep me posted if anybody looks like they don't belong."

He took his cell and made the call. Kora answered immediately. He told her to come over to the Ketch area and toward the entrance channel. He closed the phone and started to climb out.

Sydney said, "Tell you the truth, I thought she'd be gone."

"Kora's looking for that big payday. But I was a little worried."

***

Kora North left Leon and her condo. She walked across the street to the Ketch and headed down along the line of boats moored along the inlets. She didn't know if she'd convinced Leon or not. Maybe he was just playing her.

She was nervous and struggled to make the walk your basic evening stroll at the end of another great Lake Tahoe day. Let the men check her out, their women get irritated. People over on the tennis courts, talking at the docks, waiting to be seated at the restaurant.

This could end in a bloody shootout, or this Marco could see that she was playing games, and then what? So many things going on. All those big shots coming into Incline Village. All the money.

And here she was between two badass killers, one in her condo, the other waiting for her, and the most powerful man in the Sierras wanting her to be his Daisy for the weekend Great Gatsby Gala.

It doesn't get any better than that, Kora thought sardonically.

***

Marco, now up on the dock, spotted Kora rolling toward him through the lights on the dock, those long legs making her real hard to miss even in a crowd. Hips snug in black shorts, blouse tied across the open midriff, a big-money body, but his focus shifted to the people she passed, people moving around the docks and the boats. He studied the crowd in front of the restaurant looking for a particular type but not seeing anyone who looked suspicious.

Marco tested the Bluetooth on his ear, "Clear?"

"Clear," Sydney's voice came back. "I see her."

"Yeah, I got her," Marco said.

"Nobody to worry about I can see."

Marco climbed over a rail and positioned himself between one of the dock buildings and a storage shed.

He called Kara on her cell when she was a good fifty yards away. "How are you, Kora?"

She looked around. "Okay, I guess. Where are you?"

"Any problems?"

"If you mean other than this whole situation, no. I'm good." She'd stopped walking to answer.

"Keep moving," Marco said. "See those large boats ahead?"

"Yes."

"Go there. Wait for me."

The lake had a near full moon, with some lights from the restaurant, but where he now stood in a small enclave, it was pitch-dark.

Sydney, with Dutch's night glasses, fed him a constant stream of updates on men moving around, coming from boats, a real estate office across the waterway, and the Ketch.

"Nice to see you, Kora."

"Jesus, you scared me," Kora said, stopping and turning toward him.

He studied her expression, searching for some tell he didn't like. Anxiety but not panic. He saw nothing that aroused serious concerns about her attitude in that over-perfect, Nordic face.

"When you didn't answer my calls, that wasn't nice," Marco said. "Got me a little worried."

"I was wiped out. Crashed hard. I'm normally an all-night kind of person to start with. Sorry 'bout that."

She handed the drawings to him. "I did the best I could."

Sydney interrupted him on his earpiece. "Two men coming your way."

"Got it."

Marco reached under his shirt, came out with the Beretta, and laid it against the back of his leg. He pulled Kora back in with him deeper into the narrow space between the building and the storage shed.

"What's wrong?" Kora said in a low, stressed voice.

"Maybe nothing," Marco said quietly. "Don't talk."

The two men in question walked past, talking loud, a little drunk, showing no interest in anything but their conversation.

"You got a trailer," Sydney warned.

The man appeared behind them, out of nowhere. Marco had his weapon halfway up, then realized the man was totally into talking on an earpiece and seemed really upset, hands gesturing, shaking his head. He turned and walked the other way, still talking and gesturing.

Marco tracked him. He was older and not looking like a threat, but he watched the guy for a time.

"He looks okay," he told Sydney. "We clear?"

"Yes."

"You're jumpy," Kora said.

"I live jumpy," Marco said. "It's what keeps me alive." He concealed the Beretta under his shirt. "When are you expected at Thorp's?"

"About this time Friday night," she said. "That's when the party gets going. I'll come back here, then I go Saturday night for the big dinner, and then the party really gets rolling. It'll go all night. Guests will start leaving, but some won't get out until late Sunday."

"Everything okay with you?"

"It could be better."

Marco studied her for a moment. "How's that?"

"I could be getting half the money we find."

"I think we can do that."

"Money buys freedom and the power to do what you want and not what other people want you to do," Kora said. "Besides, these bastards owe me big time for the shit I've had to deal with."

He smiled. "I'm sure." He liked that she was thinking about the payoff. Girls like Kora North spent their whole lives in lies and deception, but he thought he had a pretty good read on her.

"Here's the thing," Kora said. "If any alarms go off, Rouse will get notified instantly on his smartphone. He can pull up cameras and see pretty much every room in his house."

"We'll handle the alarms. If you could find a way to get ahold of that phone, it'd be that much better."

"I don't know. He plays poker all weekend, hardly moves. Gets naps in the rooms off the poker tables. Massages and whatever. There are six little rooms for the poker crowd. I might be able to work something out with one of the girls."

"That would be good," Marco said. "Long as she has no clue what you want it for. We'll be in touch the whole time. I'll text you when I want to know something. So don't sleep without your phone next to you for the next couple days. Okay?"

She nodded.

They waited for a couple to pass. Young love on a balmy summer night in Tahoe. *Nice*, Marco thought.

"Okay," Marco said. "We're set. Everything goes as planned, you're going to get rich."

"I like the sound of that," Kora said.

Marco took out a piece of paper. "This has some call and text codes we'll use. Memorize them."

"I take it Dutch Grimes cooperated?"

"He didn't have a choice, and he didn't look like a guy who could do much resisting."

She smiled. "I bet you aren't easy to deal with."

"I try," Marco said. "Go on back home."

"See you later, cowboy," she said with a sexy little Southern twang.

He watched her walk away. He wondered what she'd do if she got out of here with a ton of money. Probably hook up with some lunatic and end up broke and in a mess soon enough. That type usually did.

When she was out of sight, Marco slipped away, down the side of the dock. He wanted to cross the lake and do a little nighttime recon of the estates. Choose the best place to come in.

47

Kora, knowing Jesup's guy was watching her, tried to walk causally toward the Ketch, letting him enjoy her, yet she half-expected to hear gunshots. Leon in action.

For a brief, intense moment on her way back, she played with some serious doubts. Then reversed herself.

This is what I have to do, she thought. *I've got my hunting dog, and I need to use him.*

With the killer waiting up in her condo, and this Marco guy lurking somewhere nearby, Kora North felt like the walls of her life were closing fast. She took a deep breath to relieve the pressure.

Two outlaws, one goal. I've chosen, she thought. *No backing out now.*

In the end, she figured she really needed a Leon. She had other plans besides money. She needed them both for now to get her to the Promised Land, and nothing was going to stand in her way once she made up her mind. But later, later was a different story. She had a lot of bastards to pay back for what they'd done to her.

She wondered if Marco was doing Jesup. In a way, it made her a little jealous. He had some qualities she liked a lot.

Little love birds on the big caper. Straight-ass cop turned thief planning the biggest heist in the Sierras since the whites stole it from the Indians. She gave Jesup credit. The girl was no shrinking violet, for sure. Kora had developed a respect for the ex-investigator. Lady had some big balls taking on Thorp and his fucking empire.

She also got herself this hardcore dude.

Kora passed the restaurant, people laughing, enjoying their existence, totally oblivious of the sharks circling dangerously beneath the surface. When she reached her condo and went inside, Leon wasn't there. She called his name, but no answer.

"What the hell?" Kora said. But then the door opened behind her and he came in. He'd been outside. Probably watching her the whole time.

"It's like I said—they're serious. They're really going to do it."

Leon's harsh ventriloquist whisper: "Saturday night?"

"Late. Around two Sunday morning."

"Jesup with him?"

"I don't know. He didn't say. He was just there. I don't know if he drove, came by boat, or dropped from the sky. Came up on me like a fucking ghost."

Leon said, "You give him the map?"

"Yes. He wants me to get hold of Tricky Dick's smartphone if I can get it. They got this all figured out. They got the whole security layout from the guy who installed it. I don't know what this Marco's background is, but he seems to know exactly what he's doing."

She told him what Marco had said, and how this was all going to work out. She wasn't sure if she was now going to be killed, now that he had everything he needed and could go back to Thorp and tell him.

But what Leon said in that barely audible voice of his was, "Do what the man wants. We're gonna play their game, take all the marbles. Right now, I'm going to go have them fix my face."

Kora wanted to toast the new relationship. Pour some of the Beringer's 2005 Merlot that a rich prick said was from the Bancroft Ranch vineyard and real quality for the price. She decided to save it until she was by herself.

After Leon slipped out into the night, Kora went out on the small balcony and peered out across the Lake. She realized that she and Sydney Jesup had the same goal of tearing that bastard Thorp down. They were sisters in that. And they both had their Dobermans to assist with the job.

Kora held up her glass and toasted Sydney. She felt sad that she had to betray the woman and her boyfriend. But it was all about survival.

48

After leaving the Keys, Sydney steered the Glastron GX 235 up the middle of the vast lake while Marco used the night glasses to track for Coast Guard boats. They drew closer to Incline, where they could see the activity at Thorp's. They drifted out about a quarter mile.

Sydney's big worry with Kora was her not getting drunk and blowing the whole operation. But Marco seemed pretty convinced she was going to work out.

"Things are happening over there? A couple big tents. Getting ready for the party of the year," Marco said as they drifted a little closer.

They passed the night glasses back and forth, checking out the possible approach, the deck and boathouse, across the corner of the lake past the Cal-Neva to the North Shore, where Thorp and Rouse had their waterfront estates.

At night, the lake had only the light of the moon glazing the water, the surrounding mountains black. Almost no lights were visible on the North Shore. Laws against trimming trees and the lack of streetlights at Incline gave the illusion there was almost no civilization there until you were close enough to see houses.

Marco said, "I used to come out in the middle of the lake with friends and we'd swim. It was really weird because you knew how deep the lake was and it seemed like you were alone in the universe. Really cool at the same time. You think there are all those dead bodies preserved at the bottom, like everyone thinks?"

Sydney said, "Maybe. It's over sixteen hundred feet deep right about where we are now. Tahoe is the second deepest mountain lake in the country. The deepest is Oregon's Crater Lake. It comes in at over nineteen hundred feet. I've been there once. It has no streams feeding it and none coming out. It's fed by snow melt."

"Not as big as Tahoe, though, is it?"

"No. It's about six miles wide, six long or close. Nowhere near as big. Tahoe's twenty-two by twelve miles and has something like forty trillion gallons of water. Enough to flood the entire state of California with over a foot of water."

Closer to the shoreline now, the lights of the Incline estates became barely visible. Marco glassed the Incline estates, tracking from the tents and outdoor party preparations at Thorp's to Rouse's next door.

Marco handed the glasses to her. He drew a sketch on the back of the drawings Kora had given him. The location of the docks, the boathouse, and the tree line, to compare them to Google Earth, get the distances right.

"I like where the dock is from the property east of Rouse's. It has a boathouse, and between them would be a nice place to slip in."

Sydney had them on a slow cruise now. "That looks good."

"Thorp's got four huge tents on the lawns. All of them look like candy-cane color, red and white striped. A band platform is set up. Strings of Christmas lights."

"Looks like it's going to be one hell of a party."

They sat for a time, drifting offshore a few hundred yards. For a time they were silent, drifting in their thoughts. It was one of the few peaceful moments since he picked her up on Sunday.

As they started back, Sydney felt a sense of finality, one way or another, with her long obsession with getting Thorp. Her guilt about getting Marco involved, then his uncle getting killed, was muted somewhat by her feeling that she'd saved Marco from becoming part of the Thorp play against Tahoe.

They talked about the movies that had been filmed in Tahoe. Sydney said that the first movie ever filmed on the lake was *Indian Love Call*.

"I never heard of that," Marco said.

"It'd be a great game-show trivia question. It was some kind of musical back in the '30s."

Marco said the only movie he knew was filmed in Tahoe was *The Godfather*. "And wasn't *Bodyguard*, with Kevin Costner and Whitney Houston?"

She said she thought that was filmed at Fallen Leaf Lake.

Marco said, "Where your girl and her boyfriend were murdered?"

"Yes." Then she said, pointing, "There's a boat coming this way pretty fast. Maybe trouble."

Sydney moved in a half circle and opened the throttle but held off making a fast run until they could make out what they were dealing with. Marco had his weapon out in one hand, the night glasses in the other.

"Looks like kids."

The speedboat turned and headed west toward Tahoe City, rocking them in its wash.

Sydney turned southwest, past the Cal-Neva highlands and then Tahoe City.

***

Back at the Shaws' they stayed up late and intended to do that for the next two nights to get adjusted to pulling an all-nighter Saturday to Sunday morning. They ate from the foods Marco had liberated from the Doc. Linguini, spinach, chicken. A real meal.

They went over and over the maps and drawings, studying the entry point and approach, fighting sleep to acclimate themselves to the night operation. She knew that eventually they would be in bed. That his hands would be all over her and that she'd surrender to him. When it happened, she marveled at the man's ability to turn her aches and pains into something completely opposite.

Afterward, as he was making a predawn check of the perimeter, she lay on the bed feeling utterly fucked, looking forward to a good, long sleep. On the way into that sleep, she went over everything that had happened since Sunday.

She thought about the man whose face she broke with the dumbbell and then shot, his body lying somewhere up in the woods, becoming a feast for whatever creatures got to it first.

49

Ogden Thorp had a difficult time dealing with early guests and party preparations until he finally got word from Rouse that their boy was back. Rouse had him taken to the clinic owned by one of their golf and business associates, Doc Winters.

One in the morning, Thorp finally heard from Rouse that their boy was in the cabin and there was good news. "I'll meet you in the gazebo in ten minutes."

In the gazebo on the water's edge of Thorp's estate, with the work of setting up still going on behind him, Oggie drank scotch and paced as he waited for Rouse to get out of his golf cart and join him. Just getting Rouse to handle the situation when the guy returned had been a major deal. But Oggie had been bogged down with the early arrivals and Rouse had to handle it.

"How's he doing?"

Rouse went for a drink. "The doc said he had a zygomatic fracture. They fixed him up with a mask like a goalie hockey mask. Makes him look like a cross between Hannibal Lector and an alien."

"Well, Kora's okay, right?"

"Yeah. Sit. You'll need to sit."

"None of your drama routines. Just tell me what he found out. Why was she with them? What happened?

Thorp saw in Rouse's face that it was something. "Well, damnit?"

Rouse smiled. He was waiting for this moment. "They're dead. They had Kora, threatening her. Wanted her to lure you out, and she wasn't cooperating. He showed up, killed them both. Kora's right on the water. They took the bodies down to her boat in the middle of the night, wrapped up in blankets. He anchored them with wire and the Kettle balls that Kora works out with. They're at the bottom of the lake swimming, as the Italians like to say, with the fishes."

"Are you serious?"

"Dead serious."

Thorp was dumbstruck for a moment as he looked out at the lake. "Pour me another. Hallelujah. That calls for a toast. Nobody saw them?"

"Not that we've heard."

Finally, Thorp thought. *Finally that bitch is gone.*

"Our boy is something else," Thorp said. "He goes over there with his goddamn face broken and does the job. Jesus, that's a real soldier."

They toasted to their boy.

"I worry," Rouse said. "He's killed four people. That's a lot of dead. They haven't even found Corbin. Maybe we should send somebody over to get rid of the body."

"Cillo's was an accident. Corbin committed suicide or something. Who cares? Don't go anywhere near that. And Cruz ran off to places unknown with his new girlfriend. Don't worry so damn much. We own the right people and means, we get to decide what the truth is. And that, my friend, being a lawyer, you should know is the greatest power of all."

They clinked glasses. Behind them, the party crews below were putting up the finishing touches for the big striped tents, outdoor dance floor, stage, and the movie screen behind the stage that would play, silently, over and over all night, the movie version of *The Great Gatsby.*

Thorp was buoyant, thrilled, in love with his hired gun. Getting rid of Jesup was a big relief, a huge weight off of him. He couldn't wait to see Kora and find out the details of what those bastards had wanted her to do.

***

Friday night, when the festivities got underway, Thorp was in for another surprise.

"She's at the Cal-Neva," Rouse said, coming out on the veranda. "She's coming over in a limo with, she says, the mystery guest."

"What?"

***

From the moment they exited the limo, Kora and her masked

mystery guest were something of a sensation. Kora, decked out in her white Daisy outfit, Leon in a black suit, black mask, perfect beside her. Thorp and Rouse met and escorted them up to his office, its deck overlooking the party and the lake.

They listened, enraptured, as Kora told them told them this wild story about how Corbin was blackmailing her and how she was kidnapped by Jesup and Marco Cruz and how they were going to use her to get to them and kill him.

"If Leon hadn't shown up when he did, killed them both, you might be the ones dead."

Kora seemed very different in some way. Beautiful and bold as he'd never seen her. And brilliant.

Touching Leon's arm, she said, "You need to offer a big prize for anyone who can guess who he is. Not that they will, but it'll be a lot of fun. Offer half a million or something. It'll be really cool."

It took a bit for Thorp to buy into it, but Kora proved right. Friday night was a winner all around. And it was just the opening act. The warm-up as people continued to stream in from Hollywood, Vegas, Silicon Valley, Texas.

The whole mystery-guest thing got bigger and bigger. Word went around of the half million to the winner. People came up to Thorp with their guesses. Saturday, it grew until the mystery guest was almost the centerpiece of the event.

And the pro played it to the hilt. He seemed to love the whole thing.

Rouse, as usual, wasn't happy, especially when he learned from Kora that the pro decided he might take Thorp up on the idea of becoming a permanent part of the new world Thorp and his investors were planning. Rouse looked petrified at the idea. They watched as Leon walked among the guests.

"He's great," Kora said. "He'll be a great addition. He can run all the security operations. And deal with problems."

"Why don't we just make him a *Tonka* overseer to senior management," Rouse said with disgust.

Thorp and Kora both laughed.

The band was in full throat. Servers in their elegant outfits were carrying trays of drinks. The lakefront, gazebo, and dance floor festooned with lights.

Thorp said, "Daisy, this mystery guest is genius. It'll be talked about and guessed at for years because we'll never reveal who he is. Hell, I even had one drunk woman suggest it was Obama with his skin deliberately whitened for the occasion."

Rouse, not amused, left, heading for the poker room. Kora watched him go. "Well, that'll probably be the last we see him until Sunday afternoon."

Thorp put his arm around Kora and escorted her into the crowd, calling people *old sport* and acting like he was king of the universe.

Enjoy it, Kora thought, *it won't last all that long.* Thorp, thinking he had the world in the palm of his hand, King of the Sierras on his throne, had no idea what was going on. He was in for a big shock.

He loved to brag how his ancestors had cleared the Indians from this land, housed and fed gold seekers, hung a few, brought Chinese coolies to help build the railroads. This was his land, his heritage.

Not for much longer, asshole, Kora thought, as she smiled at admiring guests. Somebody was insisting it was Brad Pitt.

"He's better looking and more available than Brad," Kora said, drawing laughter.

Kora needed to break free and go text Marco Cruz, so she whispered to Thorp she needed to take a pee, and then kissed him on the ear, thinking that would be a nice place to put a bullet.

She needed to know if they had anyone else on the inside. If they did, explaining the mystery guest might be a problem. She hadn't thought about that.

But when she contacted Jesup and Cruz, it seemed she was their only inside girl. "So far, so good," Kora told Leon when she met him out by the gazebo.

50

The communication with Kora had gone well. Her head, as Marco had predicted, was very much in the game. They learned from Kora that the party was a huge success. So far, Kora knew nothing about what happened to the guy who'd killed Corbin.

Sydney kept tabs through her police-reporter friend on what was going on, and Corbin's body hadn't yet been found. He apparently had no friends coming over to see what he was up to.

Saturday night, Sydney, feeling the butterflies of excited tension, helped Marco get everything into the boat they would need. Marco had two escape plans in case everything went to hell. Sydney didn't want to get into negative thinking, so she left that up to him. In her mind, if something went wrong, escape might be all but impossible given the security Thorp had roaming around his estate. Fortunately, they weren't going anywhere near his party or his grounds.

It had been a week since the incident at the hatchery and for the first time, Sydney felt good physically. The wounds had enjoyed a few days without further trauma and were beginning to heal nicely.

That night, they ate a good meal, rested, then left in the boat at two in the morning. It was warm. A balmy, beautiful night on the empty, vast waters of the lake. They were both dressed in black, camouflage under their eyes, ball caps. Marco carried Dutch's equipment. She brought Kora's tapes and pics in a shoulder bag along with nylon rope, cutters, backup batteries.

Sydney drove the boat toward Brockway, leaving Tahoe City behind to the west, then past Carnelian Bay and Kings beach on the eastern side of the lake, where they crossed that invisible line that separated California and Nevada. They approached Incline east of the Cal Neva Highlands and entered Crystal Bay without encountering any other craft on the lake, since it was so late at night.

The denizens of Incline, usually in total darkness at night from any distance out on the lake, had a brightness this night. One big splash of colorful Christmas-style lights ringed the Thorp estate.

"I've been dreaming about this night for a long time," Sydney said.

"Let's hope it's a dream come true," Marco said. "This equipment works, Kora keeps it together, the lawyer doesn't check his place every fifteen minutes, we'll get into the house. Then, of course, we need to get into the office and then, if the safe is too much, we're going to need some help."

They discussed this possibility and decided at that point, Kora was going to have to find a way to bring Rouse over. They hoped that wasn't necessary.

The closer they came, the more they could make out the lanterns and colored strings of lights. The band had a giant movie screen behind it. The tents and outdoor dance floor swarmed with what looked like hundreds of people having a riotous time.

Marco trained the night glasses on the party. "It's in high gear," he said. "Won't be many sober folks around."

"If they get their way," she said, "that's what the whole lake will look like every night. The Vegas Strip wrapped around from one end to the other like a big neon necklace. Okay in the desert maybe, but not here."

She then drove the boat past Thorp's and Rouse's, turned, and moved in toward shore at Incline beach. They came in quiet as a shark slicing across the calm water, the boat engine's hum silenced by the background big-band noise. Two hundred yards out, she slowed and took the binoculars. The party was in full throat, the guests in their Roaring '20s finest.

"I never get invited to these kinds of parties," Marco said. "I bet you don't either."

"My invitations always get lost in the mail."

The grounds were swarming with Mexican frijoleros in their waiter outfits. The ladies in their flapper dresses and hats out on the open-air dance floor, Lindy hopping all over the place.

"But look at the bright side—we're both invited to this one," Sydney said.

As they drew closer, they could see the big screen behind the band stage, the movie showing Nick Carraway losing his hat from the boat. The beginning? She couldn't remember but thought so. The movie probably played nonstop, over and over. No way, if there was sound, anybody could hear anything with that big band.

The boat bobbing gently in the water, Sydney sent a text to Kora North and waited for her reply. With the party lights sucking up visibility, and dark mountains behind them, they were virtually invisible to anyone farther than fifty yards away. Rouse's estate was dark except for ground-level Malibu lights along the walkways through his gardens.

"C'mon, Kora, respond," Sydney said anxiously.

Finally, they got the text they were waiting for. Kora was ready per the plan. She had Rouse under close surveillance with the help of two girls who were working the gaming.

51

Kora went back outside after her last text. She found Leon in the middle of a small group trying to guess his identity. The reward was now rumored to be a cool million dollars.

Thorp, all decked out in a white suit exactly as Redford, came over to Kora. "The fountain swim is in about an hour. Get the girls together. This will be the icing on the cake."

"We'll be ready," Kora said. Somebody called Thorp, and he went off to join some of his big investors.

Kora smiled when Leon came over to her followed by a couple of drunk girls all leggy and excited, dancing on the grass, shaking their booties, each with a colorful headband. Part of the girls-gone-wild-naked-in-the-fountain routine to cap off the party.

"I like this," Leon said, his voice a little clearer now that he'd learned some ventriloquist tricks. "I like this a lot."

"It's not hard to get used to, old sport," Thorp said, putting a hand on Leon's shoulder. "You're gonna like being the man in my organization. This place will grow on you. I need to go see some people. You enjoy." He patted Leon on the arm, then left the two of them to go meet some new arrivals.

Kora gestured at the movie playing silently behind the band, the circus lights, the red and white striped tents. Food, waiters everywhere.

"Money, power, and mystery," she said. "It's all there for the taking." She handed him a drink with a straw, then kissed him on the side of his mask. "They fucking love you."

"Our friends here yet?"

"They'll be getting here soon. We need that smartphone of Rouse's."

"You … tell him … come." Tell him it's important. He doesn't want me to come down to the poker room to get him."

***

After Daisy left to get the lawyer, Leon stared out over the party to the lake. He hadn't decided how he would do this. Kora had convinced him they were essential to making it all work. "They'll be our shield," she had said. If he wanted to kill them, he'd have to do it later.

He had agreed with her plan. Still, he wanted to hurt them. It would be hard to wait.

This is what it's all about, he thought. *You're either royalty or you're a peasant.*

Leon went up into the house. He saw Daisy and the lawyer. They went up into the office, the lawyer moaning and groaning about something.

"What do you want?" he said to Leon.

"Your smartphone," Leon whispered.

"You can't have it. What the hell do you want my phone for? You pulled me out of the game—"

Leon grabbed him by the arms, slammed him up against the wall, and pulled a pocketknife out of his jacket. He flipped the blade open and pressed it near the lawyer's eye. "You give me grief, you little piss ant, I'll cut your eye out, put it in a martini glass, make you drink from it, and then I'll make you eat that little olive. Give me the phone. Kora's gonna show me all the cool stuff you have, and we don't want you spying on us."

"You don't need the phone. I can open—"

Leon smiled and said, "I don't want you looking because I might fuck her there. You know how it is."

Rouse, shaking, carefully reached in his pocket and then handed the phone to Leon.

"Don't tell anyone," Leon said. "They might get jealous. You even tell Thorp, I'll come for you. Cut both eyes out. Go back to your game. Win some money, counselor."

"I need the keycard to the tunnel doors," Kora said.

Rouse took a keycard from his pocket, then, with a glance at Leon, he backed away and left.

Kora smiled and said, "You're so mean to that poor man."

She came up and encircled him, a light, sexy laugh, pulling him back out of view. Gave him a kiss on his ear. "Who says some masked bandit is gonna fuck me?"

"That would be the masked man himself." Leon made a little chuckling sound. Mia Farrow on her best day couldn't come close to this girl.

She used the keycard to get into a back office. They passed a bank of monitors. He paused. One of the cameras showed a threesome, two girls and a fat ass.

"That dude is a congressman from Nevada. He's one of the key players in getting some land rules changed. Can't make up his mind if he likes girls or boys. Likes both at the same time. You wouldn't believe some of the shit some of these guys are into."

On another camera, they saw Rouse re-enter the poker room. "Like they say, the worst offenders of a society's creeds are its rulers."

Kora used the card to get through a door that led down a staircase into a stone corridor lit by faux torchlights. It was like something from the Middle Ages. She led him along the tunnel, their shadows sliding like ghosts along the walls lit with fake torches. Leon, wired up on OxyContin and a few drinks, but not too much, felt relaxed and fine. They went down the corridor, to a cage off to the left.

"That's George," she said, pointing to a huge lion sitting on a flat rock on the other side of a small pond.

"Damn prisoner," Leon said. "I got a feeling the lion ain't gonna sleep tonight."

"Any more than we are," Kora said.

He said, "I don't like seeing lions in cages. I used to get locked up when I was a kid. Days at a time. I got a thing about that."

The massive, yellow-eyed king of beasts trapped in his dungeon. Leon hated human beings who did that.

"Solitary confinement. I don't believe in cages for predators. It's a contradiction of their nature. Cruel and unusual punishment. They need to be free to hunt. They need the kill. The taste of fresh, warm blood."

Kora said, "I agree. The closest George has been to hunting anything was when Thorp put this drunk in there once. He was doing it because that's what his idol, the guy he named the lion after, used to do."

"What happened?"

"The guy was lucky. George had been fed and didn't do anything. He's an old circus lion, so they don't have the same aggression. But it scared hell out of the guy. He sold his company to Thorp, left town, and has never been back. But here's the thing: George Whittell— that's Thorp's hero—he'd take his lion out all the time. Drove him around. Let him see the world. Thorp never even does that. It's illegal, and these days, people would shit seeing a lion in the front seat."

The made their way up to the door leading to Rouse's.

"Why is Thorp so obsessed with this Whittell guy?" Leon asked. "That's pretty weird."

"Their families go way back. They both lived in San Francisco. Summered here. I guess Oggie grew up hearing all the great stories about card games with Howard Hughes, Pretty Boy Floyd. The guy supposedly sparred with Jack Dempsey. His parties were legend. Big game hunter. Ogden thinks he's the incarnation of George Whittell. He couldn't clean Whittell's piss bucket."

"Maybe one day he'll wake up in the lion's cage. See what it's like. Maybe tonight. Maybe we'll invite the bastard to his own party."

Kora smiled. "You're something else, dude."

52

"Here we go," Sydney said as she drove in close to the Incline Village beaches. Past Ski Beach with the boat-launch facility, Incline Beach, and then Burnt Cedar. Marco worked the binoculars. She angled toward the estates to the west, getting that familiar mix of excitement and apprehension.

It's time. This is for Karen.

You wait, plot, investigate, fantasize, despise, and then, one day, that hour you've been longing for finally arrives, she thought. *The hour of retribution.*

She eased the boat slowly past the beaches, then an outcrop of rock, keeping out of the orb of light from the party as she steered into an empty slip beside a small dock. The only lights at the Rouse estate were some Malibu lights on the walkways.

"We have company," Marco said.

Where they pulled in between two other boats, it was obvious one had occupants in the boat's cabin. In spite of the noise from the party, they heard a sharp giggle. A laugh. Somebody getting some action.

Marco texted Kora North again and this time got what they wanted. *GTG:* good to go. She was at the party playing her Daisy role.

"Good girl," Marco said quietly. He turned to Sydney. "You ready?"

"Let's move back away from these guys, just in case. Wouldn't want company right now."

She backed out and moved further away, putting the boathouse between them and the lovers. She edged into shore, to the copse of trees that separated Rouse's place from the neighbor's.

Marco glanced up at the faint moon. "That a good moon, or a bad moon?"

"We're gonna find out," Sydney said.

He grabbed the dock with one hand, then, using the heavy-duty climber clasps the Shaws kept onboard, he secured the boat to the dock cleat, then grabbed his bags and dropped them on the dock as Sydney climbed out. They slipped ashore stealthy as a couple of big cats and headed into the trees, toward the lights and noise of the party on the other side of the lawyer's estate.

The night filled with the high-pitched laughter of female flappers kicking up a storm to the Lindy Hop while somebody on a mic amped up the crowd. Sydney couldn't help fearing that security guys could jump out of the bushes at any moment and gun them down.

When they were close to the lawyer's property line, Marco stopped. He worked the grounds with the night glasses—the perimeter, the gardens, the fishpond, and the house. "Clear as far as I can make out."

Marco looked back at the boat with the couple. "It's a good moon for somebody."

They moved closer to the property line.

"Looks quiet," Marco said as he handed her the night glasses.

He put the heavy bag with the equipment down. She did the same.

Sydney said, "The perimeter should be just this side of those lights if Dutch's map is good."

After scanning the area, she squatted next to Marco to help him.

He said quietly, "At what point did you know you had me?"

"I was never really comfortable with that until the guy came into the back hall and tried to kill you."

He nodded but didn't say anything as he went to work.

***

I got me a real sweet girl, Leon thought as they moved through Rouse's house, down a long hallway. It was pitch-black until they moved to a front room, and the lights from the party spilled through the windows.

He felt all aglow just looking at Kora, in her Daisy outfit, all excited over what they were doing. It made her all the more sexy to Leon.

Fantasies ran through his mind about how all this was going to play. The future. All the places they'd go and hang out. The world's best beaches. Hotels. He'd never really had fun. It was always the hunt, and then the next one. They weren't fun in the same way he now envisioned. Kora had changed all that.

"How many people have you killed?" Kora asked, touching his arm as they stared out across the veranda to the lake.

"In my career, counting the two here, eighteen. That doesn't sound like much, but I'm not all that old. And I don't take crap jobs."

Kora, smiling, said, "You want to up the numbers, I can think of some really good candidates."

He emitted a gruff chuckle. That this girl liked what he did for a living was crazy-great. No woman had ever reacted to him this way before.

How outstanding, Leon thought. He was seeing himself as a James Bond of the dark world, and now he had his Bond girl.

They came up in a small, empty room, then continued on into the lawyer's house. The place was open and polished—everything looked like top dollar. Style-wise, it was the opposite of Thorp's.

"Tricky Dick is into chrome and glass. He's a clean freak."

Kora showed him where the panic-office-vault-room was down a hall from the great room. The walls were lined with pictures of celebrities and stupid Roman statues.

Leon studied the vault and knew quickly this wasn't something he—or anybody but a serious B&E guy with the right tools—could get into easy. He hoped their boy came prepared.

"What the hell is this?" Leon said.

On a shelf above a bar were two stuffed birds, a lion's head was mounted over the doorway, and in the corner, huge elk posed, their antlers reaching halfway across the room.

Kora said, "He brings girls in here. Likes to have sex with all this hunting stuff around. Maybe needs that to get it up. It's his Hemingway complex."

"How weird are these guys?" he asked.

"Tricky Dick fucks girls while he's telling them about these animals. I hear it all from them later. They pretty much hate the guy."

"Those birds," Leon said, pointing to a couple of falcons on a platform above the door into the great room. "They're peregrine falcons. Great hunters. They can hit dive speeds well over two hundred miles an hour."

"You serious?" Kora said. "That is fast. I didn't know any animal had that kind of speed."

"They're like missiles. They create the coolest flight. Graceful and fast. Nothing maneuvers like they do with those deep wing beats. They can see a mouse on the ground a mile away. The Air Force Academy in Colorado is big on falcons. They call peregrines Mach ones because of their speed. Having them stuffed is a crime."

Kora got a text message. "They're here." She gave Leon a kiss on the side of his face mask. "Time to party hearty, mate."

Leon, looking at the excitement on Kora's face, felt a rush of blood to his loins. *God, I love this girl,* he thought.

53

As this most successful of his Gatsby Galas rolled on toward dawn, high on coke and alcohol, Ogden Thorp, felt great. "Superb, old sport," he said to one of the guests as they clinked glasses in passing.

There was a gathering by the fountain he'd had built. They knew the scene was coming where Daisy and some other girls were going to rip off their clothes and jump in.

Where the hell are you, Daisy? Getting time.

It was a magnificent party. His coming out party, joining the top dogs. He'd stop people here and there to raise a toast to success, to the "death of the witch." They didn't know what he was referring to and didn't care. A toast was a toast. And they'd throw more mystery-man guesses at him.

Thorp moved over, out by the fountain, where some guests— one a banker's wife he'd like to bed down—were drinking and talking.

There were moments, and this was one, when Thorp believed wholeheartedly in a semi-feudalistic world where you did good by your peasants but kept the peasants in line, and where you had parties like this and the smart people controlled the world because that was what nature demanded. And with the end of the middle class, it was back to normal. A world he was creating in Tahoe. One he understood. And one he believed was his birthright.

He'd even gotten into a "green" discussion. He went on about how the forest service was the real culprit behind the pollution of the lake.

"Nobody has the balls to admit that," Thorp thundered. "Hell, according to scientists in Reno, clear-cutting and debris reduction that was done to supposedly prevent wildfires had the unintended consequence of reducing the habitat for aerator ants, and that was the cause of all the problems. Those forest-service people should be in prison."

Then Thorp raised his glass. "The witch is dead. Long live the aerator ants."

He got a round of laughs and applause.

Thorp liked the sound of his voice, of the authority in it. He held sway, feeling better and better at the sound of his own voice until somebody asked where Daisy and the mystery man he'd promised were. It was time for the girls to jump in the fountain.

Thorp was irritated. He couldn't get her on his phone. "I'll be back with her," he assured them.

"Zac Efron," the banker offered as a guess of the mystery man as Thorp was leaving.

"Not even close."

Other names jumped out of the crowd.

Shia LaBeouf.

Bruno Mars.

Joseph Gordon-Levitt.

Half of the names he heard, Thorp didn't even know who they were. He assumed all of them were Hollywood types.

"Obama," somebody yelled. Everyone laughed.

"He couldn't get permission from his wife to come," Thorp said, getting big laughs.

"Charlie Sheen," someone shouted as he was walking away.

"Close," Thorp yelled back. "Charlie and the masked man have a lot in common, as a matter of fact."

More laughter from the drunk crowd.

He walked back between the large tents to the house, greeting and being greeted along the way. He didn't find them anywhere in the open rooms or up in the front office, and none of the servants had seen them either. Now he was getting angry. He went down into the poker room to find Rouse.

The attorney's stack had shrunk by a lot since he'd last looked in. Going down like the Titanic.

"Take a break, old sport, and come have a celebratory drink with me. Where the hell's Daisy?"

There were plenty of big boys there from Vegas, some involved in the poker room while some were with the women of their choice in other rooms.

"What's going on?" Rouse asked, irritated he had to leave his sinking ship.

"I ask a question and get one in return," Thorp said as they moved toward the staircase leading up to the office and the balcony. "Get your smartphone. I want to see the grounds, the rooms, and the tunnel."

Thorp glanced at the movie playing silently on the screen behind the now empty stage—Gatsby in swimming trunks on the raft in his pool, looking back behind him as the curtains to the pool entrance flapped in the breeze.

"Why are you taking me away from the game?"

"It's time for the girls to follow Daisy into the fountain. The finale. Where the hell is that woman and where the hell is my mystery guest? Well, get your damn phone out."

"I don't have it."

"You always have it. Where the hell is it?"

"He's got her," Rouse said, "and my phone."

"What are you talking about?"

"They're fucking on my furniture, that's why. I hate that guy," Rouse said.

"You gave him your phone?"

"I didn't give it to him. He took it and threatened to gouge my eyes out with a knife. He's nuts. She didn't seem all that upset, I'll tell you that. So, yeah, he took my smartphone. Afraid I'd watch them. He wanted to go over there. Those two are love irds, if you can believe that. A killer and a whore. Hopefully they won't propagate."

Thorp didn't know how to react. They had done him a huge favor. But at the same time, they were employees. They'd both abandoned their jobs at the party of all parties.

"Why the hell did they have to go to your house? We have a dozen bedrooms right here. She's supposed to be entertaining guests, not that lunatic."

"How the hell do I know?"

Thorp stared at Rouse. "Why didn't you tell me earlier?"

"He said I better keep my mouth shut. He's a scary bastard. No way you want him on permanent. And don't tell him I said anything."

Thorp's mood danced around looking for somewhere to land and get back to something fun. He looked over through the trees to the dark outline of Rouse's place.

The killer certainly deserved a reward, and Kora was any man's reward, to be sure. But, in the back of his mind, he didn't like that his two most prominent party employees had abandoned him. And he still couldn't fathom why they wanted to go to Rouse's. Thorp's celebratory mood took a tumble. He was getting very pissed off at the two. He wanted to forgive them their moment but couldn't. They were his employees.

I won't stand for it, he thought angrily. "Everybody is waiting for the girls to strip and get in the goddamn fountain. I paid a fortune for that damn fountain. You're going to have to go over and get them."

"The hell I am."

54

Sydney fixed the glasses on the party and the dance stage partially visible through the trees. Now she was looking for the exulted one among the movers and shakers. She and Marco were between two huge boulders, just in front of a copse of lodgepole pine.

From where they were, she could clearly see the outdoor movie screen that Thorp had set up behind the dance floor and band. It was the scene where Nick Carraway and Gatsby talk after the party...and the famous line of Redford's Gatsby. Though she couldn't hear the line, she knew it. *"Can't repeat the past? Of course you can."*

"Where are you, Thorp, you miserable bastard?" Sydney asked quietly.

She turned back to Marco, who was working on both a small laptop and an iPad. "How's it going?"

"So far, so good," Marco said. "I'm going to bring down the entire system. You need to contact our girl, see if she can get away and meet us. I'm bringing the systems down in a few minutes. Hopefully."

Sydney sent Kora a text. While waiting for a response, she watched Marco. He worked fast and sure, like he'd done this many times before. She wondered if it hadn't been for her, if he had gone to his uncle's without running into her, if he would be with them right now. If, given his background, what he'd gone through in Mexico, that working on the other side of the law was just as easy for him.

It always amazed her when she ran into intelligent, hardworking criminals. Something in their childhoods maybe sent them off on the wrong track. All that energy and brains could as easily have gone into legitimate professions.

This guy was different. He'd had legitimate ambitions and experience and had gotten sidetracked by the murder of a colleague, just as she'd gotten sidetracked by corruption and the murder of two potential witnesses. That line she'd never anticipated crossing even for a moment had been crossed. And what was scary was how easy it was as long as there was some powerful motive.

"This program," he said with a note of satisfaction, "isn't readily available on the market. You need someone like Dutch, who has connections, to get one of these. I've seen it used. It'll pick up signals, run them through the mill, find out what they are, what they do, and then we'll kidnap the whole system. Basically, you ride the signals to their destination and then you're operating like any good hacker."

"You're in?"

"Yeah. I've co-opted the program. Thanks to Dutch, we've already gotten all the security protocols in the system. Something went wrong, he could get in and fix it without having to reinvent its brain. But that's the one big vulnerable spot. Somebody gets to Dutch, they get to the system. We did, and we have the access ID program that can capture and compromise the system without triggering an alarm."

"How fast?"

"Superfast."

"This works, you can have your way with me later."

He smiled at her. "Didn't I already have that pleasure?"

"That was just a little foreplay to the main event."

"Sounds scary."

Sydney smiled. "Be afraid. Be very afraid."

He pulled her over and kissed her hard on the mouth. "I am." Then he said, "Let's do this."

55

Leon stared at the blank screen on the smartphone. One minute he was running his finger across the screen bringing up every room, every outside nook and cranny, and the next, he had nothing.

"Sonofabitch did it, brought it down," Leon said. "He's good."

Kora said, "We're getting close."

Leon slipped out on the side of the veranda, rested the night scope in the opening of a latticed panel, and tracked along the shoreline, working up to the trees.

He finally found them—white figures in a greenish soup. The boy and his girl doing their thing. Nice. It passed through his mind to kill the bastard and Jesup, then go back to the clients and play it all off as a neat little setup.

But then he figured it was just a throwback thought. He resisted it. Chastised himself. He was moving on. *Keep focused,* he told himself. He never liked second-guessing himself and rarely did, but this whole situation in Tahoe was a brand new ball game. He'd never turned against clients before. Never even considered it.

He looked at Kora, his girl, his little schemer, and what he saw was excitement in her eyes and a slight grin on her mouth.

"What?" Kora asked, seeing his look.

"You made me think of Xenia the Janus agent, the chick in James Bond's *Goldeneye* who liked to squeeze her adversaries to death with her powerful legs, and in so doing would have orgasms."

She laughed. "Better watch out, dude."

He chuckled. "Here they come. Man is gonna get a bit of a surprise."

"He's going to be pissed, for sure," Kora said. "Just don't kill him. We need his skills. We're only halfway there."

He watched the thieves all cool and confident.

Twenty million and Kora. And a new life. Could buy a fucking island. Maybe he'd get one of those manmade deals the Arabs built in Dubai that looked like a palm tree in the water. They were going cheap with the economic mess the world was in. He could live like a Sultan. Hunt when the mood came over him, or when somebody in the world pissed him off enough. Be his own man, his own boss.

Then, when he went hunting, it would be solely because some asshole somewhere was being too stupid to live.

Leon the Professional felt blissful. It was one of the happiest feelings he could remember. He had a girl. He'd soon have millions. It was like a whole new world had opened up and blessed him.

Still, he really wanted to kill these two for breaking his face, humiliating him, causing him all this misery. It was going to be difficult restraining himself. If he succeeded in that restraint, it wouldn't be for the money, it would be for his sweet, knockout little Xenia.

56

Sydney followed Marco between sumptuous flower gardens and fishponds, around a sand trap, and headed for the side of the Rouse house, accompanied along the way by the band doing a Duke Ellington number. They paused. A hundred yards away, they could see Mia Farrow and Robert Redford, Daisy and Gatsby, talking on the giant movie screen behind the band stage, the last couples standing attempting to dance the night away.

Sydney took the glasses and scanned the dancers, the crowd in front of the platform, then on past the tents to the gazebo, and up on the long, second-floor balcony. That's where she found Thorp and Rouse. "I hope you bastards are enjoying your party," she said quietly. "I get my way, it'll be your last big celebration."

They continued toward the lawyer's house—two stories of marble and sandstone and vast windows. Marco approached the side door, the B&E bags bumping against his sides. He stopped, with Sydney just off his left shoulder with the other bag and equipment.

Marco made quick work of the side door by breaking through the long window using tape and a glass cutter.

"We're in," he said quietly.

They didn't get more than three steps into the room when a female voice in the dark said, "Nice work."

"Kora?" Sydney said.

"It is I," she said.

Why didn't she open the door, let us know she was there? Sydney wondered.

Kora emerged from behind a massive statue of a Roman soldier that stood at one side of the entrance to the next room, a naked statue of a woman on the other side, both over six feet tall. Sydney didn't like something in Kora's demeanor, maybe the inflection ion in her voice, the way she stayed back, still partially behind the statue. Something felt very wrong.

Then a man emerged from the dark into the faint light of this outer room. He wore a plastic mask and had a weapon in each hand, one pointed at her, the other at Marco.

"The thing is," a raspy, strained voice emanating from behind the mask said, "I wanted to kill you, you'd be dead. But you aren't dead, which means this is your lucky day. We need to work together."

Kora, now fully out into the open, also had a gun.

Sydney realized with shock that the man in the mask was the one they had fought. He was not only alive, stunningly enough, he had hooked up with Kora North. How in hell had that happened?

The idea that Thorp had orchestrated this trap was difficult for Sydney to accept. Yet here they were. She expected Thorp to emerge from the room next.

"Welcome to the Bank of Rouse," Kora said, moving closer. She was dressed in white, a little hat perched on her head, lipstick bright red, hair cropped. A hot Daisy. "Leon here made me an offer I couldn't refuse. Isn't that right, baby?"

Her new friend whispered hoarsely, "That's right, Daisy, my little sweet pea. Man knows when he's met his match."

Kora smiled, teeth gleaming from the refracted light coming from the party next door. She looked magnificently evil.

"Sorry," she said, "but a girl's gotta do...and don't worry, this is going to be a win-win situation. We're all going to get what we want. Isn't that right, baby?"

"That's right, Daisy, win-win. Let's go get into Tricky Dick's bank and see what's for Christmas."

Sydney now began to see a different picture. This wasn't Thorp. This was the two of *them*!

She sensed Marco wanted to make a move but now wasn't the time. She gave him a look.

"Do everything nice and slow and careful," Kora said, apparently seeing what Sydney was seeing in Marco. "We don't want to kill you, right Leon?"

"That's right, we don't want to kill the golden goose who's gonna bring us the golden eggs," Leon muttered. "They make any moves, they'll die, and that'll be too bad. I see your shoulders getting tight, which means you got some Rambo shit in your brain. Best back down. Daisy sweet, if he makes some dead-hero move, I'll do him and you do his lady."

"Be my sad pleasure," Kora said, bringing her weapon to bear on Sydney's face. "But they're gonna see the smart thing to do. We're not here to shoot you guys. We have a proposition you can't refuse, believe me. My good friend Leon has decided that it's time make a change. A little revolution in which the workers take over and the rich assholes get what they got coming to them, right baby?"

"Socialism for two."

Kora chuckled. This was fun and games to her.

Marco said, "Sounds like it should be for four."

"It will be, if you play along," Kora said with a smile.

"Now that we all understand each other," the guy she'd called Leon said, "let's remove weapons. Then we can take a look at the office."

They stood there for a tense moment.

"How many weapons you got between you?" Leon asked. "Be honest. I hate people lying to me. Makes me do bad things."

With great reluctance in his voice, Marco said, "Three."

"Well, let's get you disarmed. We don't want any failure to communicate, as Newman put it in *Cool Hand Luke*."

Sydney didn't know what the hell the deal was, but obviously these two had formed some sort of sociopathic bond. They were working like a couple with a very good sense of each other. How in hell had that happened?

Leon told Kora how he wanted her to remove their weapons. He made them get down on their knees, hands behind their heads.

Marco had his gun belt-holstered in the front under his shirt. Kora reached around and took it, and in the process felt him up, chuckling like a kid. She took his two, then came over and removed Sydney's. "We'll work this out," she said.

Then Kora, having removed all three weapons, went through the bags looking for more weapons. She didn't find any. "They're clean," she said. Then she turned to Sydney. "You brought what I wanted?"

"Yes."

Leon said, "Let's go, folks, we have work to do. Money to make. Places to go. Right, sweet pea?"

"You are right, old sport."

57

L eon isn't a break-in artist on your level," Kora said to Marco. "He might get into the office, but no way could he get into that safe. Isn't that right, Leon?"

"That's right."

"Leon isn't his real name," Kora said. "He took that from a movie. I'm thinking of changing my name as well."

"I think she should call herself Xenia," the masked killer said.

Chatty couple. Having fun. *Who's really running the show?* Sydney wondered. They had really underestimated and misread Kora North.

They were ushered at gunpoint into the vastness of the great room. She feared the killer wanted his revenge, and might take it at any moment, but was forced to delay until he had what they came for. At least it might buy them some time.

They paused under the vaulted ceilings, moon shadows spilling across the tiled floor, a cut of light on the grand piano. The rooms of the house had low nightlights. Statues from Asia and some Italian stuff. Paintings looked like they belonged in a museum. Stuffed animals in the adjoining room.

"Here's how this works," the smothered voice from the mask said. "Kora here has convinced me of a new plan. See, the thing is, I'm not all that fond of my clients. Right, Kora?"

"That's right, baby. Leon doesn't like Thorp or his lawyer much at all."

"So," Leon said with muffled exuberance that resembled a cartoon character, "we're going to work something out. I wanted to kill the two of you for breaking my face, but Kora came up with a way you can pay me back. And pay me big time, right Kora?"

"That's right," Kora affirmed. "That's exactly right."

Aren't they the cutest couple outside of a fucking asylum? Sydney thought.

"Turns out," Leon said, "we're all on the same side of this."

A strung-out killer and whacked-out hooker taking over the

world. Gonna pull off the robbery of the century."

Sydney said, "How is it we come out ahead?"

Kora said, "Relax. We get the money and enough dirt on these guys to protect us, and you get enough to destroy them. That's your end. Everybody gets what they want. Everyone goes home happy. So let's quit wasting time and get in that office and see what we have."

Kora North was definitely running the show, Sydney decided.

Marco answered Leon's garbled questions as he went along. How he used the density meter, and then methodically studied the framing. Leon kept back so Marco would have no chance if he decided to try something.

At the safe, it was quickly clear that the door, covered in a fine mahogany veneer, had beneath it high-grade plated steels with "engineer only" removable fixings. The locking mechanism had a punch-code lock. That was definitely the way to go.

"The lawyer isn't big on trust," Marco said.

He went into his bag, showed Leon the sequencer and the black light. "This code sequencer should give the numbers up pretty quick. Runs a thousand a second."

"I've seen that in a movie," Kora said. "He doesn't have the iris reader or a fingerprint thingy."

"Not on this door," Marco said. "You said this was just the outside door, right?"

"Yeah, there's a big metal door to the main office door."

Marco studied the keys with the light and then went about fixing the box over the keypad.

"Here we go." He pushed the ON button on the sequencer.

Leon, showing student-like curiosity, fired questions at him the whole time he worked. Like he was learning for future reference. Sydney appreciated how Marco entertained the guy, getting him involved, telling him all about the design, how they got ahold of it through a contact in the high-tech security world, keeping him focused and distracted. She wondered if he had a plan or if he was just trying to keep the guy interested.

"It's designed to fit the universal punch codes. It could be set to any three, four, or five keys. It should find the unlocking sequence in about one to three minutes."

"You got that from Dutch?" Kora asked.

"He's a man with resources. If Rouse had a retina or fingerprint scan, we'd have no choice but to do a hot caesarian."

"Which is?" Kora asked.

"Torch cut."

The outer door opened with no problem. But that was just the veneer. The real door was next, down a short hall. Marco grabbed his bag and Leon moved back. They reset their physical relationship, but Marco kept right on talking.

"Acetylene torches only reach six thousand degrees, and when you were working steel-reinforced concrete and solid-steel fixtures, you need thermic power in the eight-thousand-degree range. You need to handle different consistencies in the pour matter."

"Why would they be so different?" the killer asked. "It's cement."

"Cement mixture is vibrated to get rid of air pockets to create a zero slump," Marco said. "The only effective and fast way to get around dual-control and time locks is with a combination of torch and blast. But this locking mechanism doesn't need a blast. It's not that heavy. You're always dealing with the endless escalation of technology. A thief has to be on the cutting edge. Crime is an arms race."

Leon emitted a chuckle.

Marco, working intently, talked nonstop, telling Leon that it started during the Gold Rush days, all that robbing going on. Banks started using safes and then the robbers brought in the pickaxe and hammer to break in at night and steal the safes, taking them somewhere in the hills to break them open.

"So the banks built bigger and heavier safes with heavy doors that had to be blasted open. That proved easy enough to do, so the combination lock was invented to thwart blasting. So the robbers developed the technique of drilling and using a mirror shoved inside to see the slots on the combination wheel."

"It's nice to see you boys enjoying your work," Kora said, "but let's get this done."

"He's doing his job," Leon said. "Let the man work. He can talk while he works, can't he?"

"He can, but not if it slows him down. Which he might do purposely."

"I can only go as fast as the technology allows," Marco said. Then he added, "The next escalation of defense was time locks." He drew cut lines on the wall. "That led to kidnapping bank employees. They always tried to keep a step ahead. Now it's all about using the Internet. The only people going directly after banks are bankers getting rich off toxic assets."

Sydney tried to catch Marco's eye, to see if he had something else behind all the chatter, but he didn't look her way.

"There," Marco said. "The cut line is prepped."

Marco donned welding glasses, still talking nonstop about the changes while he prepared the torch.

"Got to hit this hard with the gas-axe," Marco said. "Best stand back a little."

Sydney noticed how Leon seemed to like Marco's knowledge, his attitude, which is what Marco appeared to be after. A little bonding between criminals. At some point Sydney figured she'd have to find a way to do with same with Kora.

He fired the torch and they all took another step back.

Marco directed it at the surface of the cut. "Got to get the iron oxide moving, knock slag aside, and get the heat through the cherry red to the white heat."

He quickly burned his way through, and it wasn't long before he had the door open and they were inside Tricky Dick's inner sanctum.

"You're good," the killer said. "Damn good. You ever find any box you couldn't open?"

Marco removed the welding glasses. "Well, there was this really cute little lesbian…"

Leon broke out in a stammered, bizarre laugh so abrupt and hard it appeared to hurt him, and he stopped as fast as it had come.

Sydney now saw how Marco was going to work this guy. Become his friend. Bond. Wait until the moment was right.

58

Sydney, excited, followed the men through the door. The lawyer had a massive executive teak desk behind which sat this cushy, red-leather chair. He had some really expensive-looking artwork on the walls. Plants, exotic fish in a massive tank. File cabinets, computers, a wall of TV screens displaying every inch of the house inside and out. And a five-foot-high safe taking up most of the far wall.

"Man's got himself a plush bunker and war room," Marco said.

"You really can open the safe?" Kora asked.

Marco went to the safe embedded in the wall. He checked the locking mechanism and shook his head. "This is a big damn problem. This baby has serious defenses and a bank-style time lock."

Kora came over. "Dutch didn't give you the combination?"

"Not for this baby. This isn't the safe he thought was in here."

Sydney liked this play. It was, in fact, the safe that Dutch had put in, but Kora and the killer didn't know that.

"You can't crack that?" Leon asked in a hiss of a voice. "'Cause if you can't crack that, you got nothing to trade your life for."

"This is state of the art," Marco said. "You want inside this thing before tomorrow afternoon, the only thing you can do is get the lawyer over here. Let him open the thing for us."

Leon turned to Kora as if she had the answer.

She said, "If that's what we need to do, that's what we'll do. I'll call Oggie and have him send Rouse over. Tell him we broke something. He'll come on the run."

Leon said, "You sure they won't send a bunch of goons over here?"

"Hell, no," Kora said. "Everything in here stinks of some kind of fraud or another. Most of those guys are cops."

Kora turned to Marco. "Can you bring the cameras back up so we can see who's coming?"

Marco said he could. Within a minute, he had the cameras back online so they could get pictures on Rouse's smartphone and on the cameras in the office.

Kora then took out the smartphone. "Thorp is gonna be a little pissed, but he'll do the right thing."

"You aren't calling Rouse?" Sydney said.

"Can't. This is his phone. Oggie will send him over."

***

Thorp was already in a highly agitated state, his imagination all over the place about what was going on with Kora and the pro, when his cell buzzed. It was Kora.

"About time, Kora. We're waiting for the fountain scene. Where the hell—"

"Get Rouse over to his house right now," Kora said. "We broke something that might be important. Have him come through the tunnel so he doesn't set off a bunch of alarms."

"Kora, damnit, what are you—"

"Right now. It's kinda a big problem and he's gonna be pissed. But he needs to deal with it right now," she said, and then the bitch promptly hung up on him and wouldn't answer when he called back.

Thorp pulled Rouse out of the game again. He was getting killed anyway.

"What, goddamnit? I need to get back in there. There's only a couple hours left."

"They broke something. Kora and Leon. Something valuable."

Rouse, stared at him, a drink in his hand, and said, "I knew it. Jesus!"

"Just get your ass over there. I want Kora back here now. Everybody's waiting for her to get naked and jump into the goddamn fountain with her girls."

"Fuck that, Oggie, I'm not going over there. You need to send some security guys over there. No way I'm going—"

"It's your house and you gave them your phone. You let them do it without telling me. You damn fool, you really want me to send security? Most of them are moonlighting sheriff's deputies. You want them to arrest Kora and Leon, or whatever the hell his name is? Wouldn't that be nice?"

"Why is she with him, anyway?"

"Women love killers," Thorp said. "C'mon. Faster you deal with this, the faster you can get back to losing your ass."

"I'm not going over there alone. No way. You're coming with me."

"Take this," Thorp said. He took out the Derringer.

"I'm not shooting anybody. That thing would probably blow up and kill me. You want me to go over there, you're coming with me."

Thorp swore under his breath. He looked out over the crowd gathered around the fountain.

"Alright, let's get moving," Thorp said, shaking his head. He put the gun away and led his reluctant friend through the office and down into the tunnel.

Thorp stopped at George's cage. "He hasn't been fed in a while. Go on. I'll take care of George. You go see what's going on. What they broke. I want all of you back here in about five minutes."

"I don't like this. This guy—"

"I don't care if you like it. Go. Tell Kora I want to see her now. If there's a mess, you clean it up. It's your fucking house."

"You're coming with me."

"I'm feeding George." Thorp pulled out the Derringer. "I'll shoot you. Don't think I won't. You're such a pussy."

The big old lion grumbled.

Rouse went off, mumbling incoherently.

The old lion, lying on a flat rock across the pool, made another deep-throated growl. Thorp liked to believe he had a special bond with George. That he and the old lion had an instinctual connection on some primal level. "We're going to have us a little party for you one of these days, old sport. How would you like that?"

The big cat stared at him. "You and me, my friend, are the kings. We're the ones nature made to rule."

The big cat again responded with a stunted growl.

Thorp, when he was drunk, liked to come down and talk with George, and he thought George talked back to him in some special way. They had an understanding, like Willett had possessed with his lion.

He stared at the old lion lying on the rock, the lion staring back, the dim light on the ceiling of the cage casting a shadow on the lion's face, heightening the golden hue of his eyes, and the ragged state of his thick, dark mane. Somewhere in the back of his mind, Thorp remembered some animal guy telling him that the mane was what females looked at to see if the guy was healthy and strong. As did the lion's would-be male opponents. But, the animal guy had said, big manes were going to go away because of global warming. In places where it was really hot, the manes were shorter and less attractive to females, as well as less intimidating.

"You still got that big mane," Thorp said to George. "Scare the hell out of anybody."

Thorp laughed. He assumed the big cat agreed.

59

Looking at the large-screen monitor, using the gun as a pointer, Kora said, "There they are in the tunnel. Mutt and Jeff. But looks like Mutt is the only one coming. Old sport is talking to his lion."

She turned to Leon, handing him the smartphone. "You two go intercept our boy. Me and Sydney are gonna talk, look at files, and see what old Tricky Dick has on the world."

Sydney wasn't sure how to interpret this, but she did appreciate the time alone to deal with Kora, find out what the girl was really thinking.

As the men started to leave, Kora said, "Careful, Leon, alcohol and pain pills—"

"I'm good," Leon said.

When the men were gone, Sydney said, "I gotta hand it to you, you got that boy wrapped around your little finger."

Kora sat behind Rouse's desk, gun on the lap of her white Daisy dress. "He's a sweetheart once you get to know him. We girls both got our Dobermans. Now we just need to get into that damn safe and get the hell out of here. Let's take a look at what we have in all these files and maybe you can get into the computer."

"So, what are you and your stud thief gonna do once this plays out? If you get what you came for, bring them down."

"We're thinking of Rio," Sydney said.

Kora studied her for a moment. "I guess it's true what they say about cops, that if you scratch the surface, you'll find a criminal waiting to get out."

Sydney smiled. "I guess so. Where are you going once you leave here with all that money?"

"Around the world in style, for sure."

"With Leon?"

Kora smiled. "We'll see."

"When you leave," Sydney said, "just remember the mistake the turtle made giving the scorpion a ride across the river."

Kora chuckled. "The river of no return. Don't worry about me. I got a hard shell, but I'm no turtle."

Sydney smiled and nodded. On some level, she had no doubt that beneath all that sex kitten stuff, there lay a very dangerous woman.

***

Leon and Marco went into a room that had a huge bar. The only light came from a wine cabinet and two dim lights from somewhere behind the bar below a massive, etched mirror. The bar itself was made of leather and wood with ivory railings. Marco figured it had to cost a fortune.

Leon put the smartphone down on the bar. "Puttin' a lion in an underground cage. That's a crime against nature."

"You're right about that," Marco said, looking to agree with this guy as much as possible. Find some way to get at this crazy killer, get him to relax and get careless.

"Take a load off," Leon said pointing to one of the small tables. "What can I get you?"

"Beer's fine," Marco said. "If he has beer?"

Leon reached under the bar yet never took his eyes off Marco for more than a second. "The lawyer's got three different little refrigerators under here. Here we go—door number two. Man's stocked up for all types. Let me choose for you."

Leon put a beer bottle down on the table. He went back behind the bar and rooted around for a time, broke the glass of a locked cabinet, and then came up with a bottle. "Glenfiddich."

"Never heard of it."

"Me either. But it looks like expensive whisky. Must be if he has to keep it locked up in his own house."

He opened the bottle, then took out a bottle of pills and got one in his mouth. He poured some of the amber liquid into a glass and then found a straw. He took a swallow and got the pill down. Then he said, "Better."

He laid his gun on the counter, eyes behind his mask watching Marco. Unfortunately, it was too dark for them to reveal anything about what the killer was thinking or planning.

He said, "You and your girl messed me up bad."

"We didn't have a lot of choice; we didn't want to end up like Corbin. We thought you died up there in the woods. That a couple bullets got you."

"I'm not that easy to kill." Leon made a sound something like a wry chuckle, the light from the wine cabinet behind the bar reflecting on his black plastic face mask.

"I'll tell you what," Marco said. "We broke your face. You killed my uncle and then ended up with the most beautiful lady on the lake. On top of that, we're gonna make you rich and then, we get the dirt we're after, we'll shield you. You'll be home free. I'd call it about even, don't you think?"

Leon leaned on the bar. He thought about that for a time. "Yeah. Why not? Cillo was a tough old bird, I'll give him that. I wanted to stage it as a simple suicide, but he fought like goddamn angry gator in that pool." He paused. "Okay, we're even. And I got rid of the idiot who shot your girl. She should be happy about that."

"She is."

Leon nodded. "Those aren't your average chicks for sure, my man."

Marco agreed. "They're the kind can get a man to change course in midstream. We're both in that situation."

Leon settled catty-corner at one small bar table over from Marco, where the killer had a view of anyone coming.

This how it was with Shaun Corbin? Marco wondered. *Sit, talk, get friendly, then a bullet to the brain?* He had no move but to sit there and drink his beer and wait for something to develop he could use.

Even with a straw, Leon had a hard time drinking with the face mask, so he took it off. Marco tried not to show the shock he felt seeing the mess of purple and pink swelling on the side of the guy's face.

"Ain't real pretty, is it?"

"You'll get back to being the handsome guy you were soon as the swelling goes down."

Leon said, "You're a funny guy. I amuse you? I make you laugh?"

"*Goodfellas,* right? Joe Pesci."

"That's right," Leon said. "You like that movie?"

"One of the greatest ever," Marco said, thinking, when dealing with a sociopath, be one.

Marco took a swig of beer, then said, "You should see how things are south of the border. No damn discipline. These *Sicario* Juarez hitters, they just shoot up everything. It's O.K. Corral day every goddamn day. It's chaos."

"You do damage?" Leon asked.

"Time to time. Like this family I had to talk to. I walk in, there's this guy sitting back against the wall smoking his last cigarette, wasn't his turn to die. But he forgot to check if everyone was really dead. Got himself shot. Still, he wanted to die like a man. But he was just a kid, and he'd messed it up good. It's not about the job to them. They never even know why. And they paint the whole fucking neighborhood."

"You put that boy out of his misery?"

"Yeah," Marco lied, and did so with effect. "I give him credit. He's facing it, and he's swearing at me like some street-corner badass. His last words: *Me cago en la leche de tu puta madres!* You goddamn motherfucker. I got a neat *coup de grâce*. Not quite as perfect as you did with Corbin. How the hell close were you, you took out that ugly mole?"

Another partial smile formed on that ruined face. He liked this—Marco making stuff up that fit into this guy's wheelhouse, maybe got them bonding a little more.

"I hear about all those crazy mothers down there," Leon agreed. "Fucking Mexicans, no offense, are trying to take back California, New Mexico, and Arizona. Latinos already own Florida. We ain't gonna lose the country to the fucking al-Qaedas. While we're fighting stupid wars over there, your relatives are coming in by the millions to take it over."

"I'm half-wetback and half-wop. The wops been here awhile, and the Mexicans used to own it. So I'm in the best of both worlds," Marco said with a grin.

"True. Badass on both sides."

"You're getting ahead of the game working with me." Marco smiled. The killer seemed to like that. Then he added, "You and Kora North seem to have a real connection. Guys in our businesses sometimes have a hard time finding women who can fit in."

"Ain't that the truth," he said, then looked at the smartphone. "He's coming up into the back room."

"How'd you get into the trade?" Marco asked.

"Not like you might imagine," Leon said. "Happened by accident. I'd killed my mother's crazy boyfriend. But I knew right off I was a true hunter. Then later on, this rich kid came to me. I had a rep by the time I got out of high school. In and out of juvie. I don't know how he knew about me, but he had a problem with somebody trashing him on the Internet."

"Happens a lot these days," Marco said.

"Yeah. Making up shit about him. Nasty stuff. How he was this fag and did all these things. He wanted the bastard located and killed. But he wanted it done so nobody would do any investigation. Paid me more for it than I'd earn in a couple years. I did the job, my second suicide. No links. And two years later, he finds me again. He's got this friend who needs help. Before you know it, I'm in business. Been booming ever since."

He checked the smartphone again. "What the hell's taking this guy so long? He's walking like something's gonna jump out at him."

Marco said. "A suicide specialist is a pretty unique and cool profession."

"Hell, I turn down five for every job I take," Leon said. "First of all, I won't do certain kinds of jobs. You do, you get sloppy. Thing is, the usual guys aren't in business so much anymore. Mob types. So now what you got is freelancers. Some of them come out of the military. Can't find legit work. Try these contractor companies and then get tired of that and somebody contacts them, makes an offer, and the rest is history. It's a new world, my friend. But then, good for guys like us. You aren't an old-school, second-story guy either, all that high tech. It's a new age."

Leon seemed to be feeling good now, sucking down the whisky, chatting, watching the lawyer make his way through his mansion, the killer talking about his kills. Next talking about his last job in New York. How the guy wanted to die. Hardly needed Leon, except he wasn't man enough to do himself.

Marco wished they had a little longer. Get the guy drunk. But it didn't work out that way.

Leon put his mask back on. Then he got up and looked down the hall. "Our boy has arrived."

He waited a moment, then, his voice amped up a bit, "Well, if it isn't the man of the hour."

Rouse came across the great room, the lawyer abruptly stopping, unsure what he was walking into, making Marco think of a virgin boy in a brothel, eyes wide.

"C'mon, counselor," Leon said, "get your butt over here."

Rouse remained tightly rooted to the spot, shocked, like he was considering which way to run.

"Goddamn, dude, don't hold up the party," Leon said in an exasperated voice. "I got to drag you over here? Nobody gonna bite you."

Looking at Marco, Rouse said, "Who is this?"

"Friend of mine."

"I've been hearing a lot about you," Marco said. "None of it good. Best do like the man says."

Rouse struggled to gather himself. "What the hell's going on here?"

"Been a little change in plans, counselor," Leon said. "Got somebody I want you to meet."

Rouse glanced at Marco. "What's going on. We need to get back to the party. You break something?"

Leon stared at him.

Suddenly Rouse saw the bottle of whisky. "That's a sixteen-thousand-dollar bottle!"

"It ain't bad," Leon said. "Little overpriced, if you ask me. I see old sport is waiting at the lion's den. What's he doing?"

"He wants me to send Daisy. He's angry you guys aren't at the party."

"Tell old sport she'll be down shortly," Leon said. "Don't elaborate."

Leon handed the phone to Rouse and the lawyer made the call. Before he could say anything else, Leon grabbed the phone back. "Let's go to your office."

"How the hell did you get into my office?" The lawyer didn't seem to want to believe that they were really in his office. Or much of anything that was going on.

"Have a sixteen-thousand-dollar drink," Leon said. "A double. I think you're going to need it."

Rouse seemed unable to come to grips with the situation, let alone a drink.

Leon just shrugged. "Well, let's go to the office, work out

something. Our prenup has to be changed." Then he said, looking at the smartphone, "Thorp's talking to his lion. Man's a little nuts. C'mon, move it."

Marco wanted to make a move, but not with Sydney out of his sight and under Kora's control.

60

When the three of them entered the office, Rouse followed by Marco and then Leon, Sydney felt a little sense of relief. She'd feared the two men might not get along, end up in a battle, and bring the whole thing down with them. She turned her attention to Rouse.

"Well, well, if it isn't Tricky Dick," Sydney said.

Rouse looked like he was on the verge of a stroke or heart attack, his face white, his eyes bugged out. He stared at Sydney as if she'd arisen from the graveyard before his eyes.

"You find anything interesting?" Leon asked Kora.

"You wouldn't believe the shit this pervert has on people," Kora said. "He takes voyeurism to a new level. He's got surveillance tapes on everybody and their mother, and we haven't even gotten into the safe. Can't wait to see what's in there."

Kora looked at Rouse. "Oh, and Sydney needs your various passwords."

Rouse, as if trying to wake from his nightmare, seemed for the moment incapable of movement or speech. It was hard to tell if he was petrified or so stoned he couldn't get his brain in order, or just in extreme shock.

Leon encouraged him with the business end of his automatic's silencer pressed against the lawyer's ear.

Kora said, "If you're going to shoot him, back up a little so we don't get splatter all over us." She said it with a small, cold grin.

Rouse wrote down his passwords on a desk tablet without further encouragement.

"Now let's get that safe open," Leon said. "See what kind of goodies you got in there." Leon checked the smartphone. "Thorp is still down there talking to his lion. Bet that's a conversation."

Rouse went to the safe and began the process of opening it.

"You can rob us," he said in a hushed, tight voice. "You can kill us. But it'll trigger the biggest manhunt ever."

Kora said, "He opens his mouth again, shoot him. Then we'll bring Thorp up here and see if he can't open it. I'm sure he knows the combinations and how to change the time-lock sequence or whatever."

"She's not kiddin', dude. Woman doesn't like you much," Leon said. "Not much at all."

Rouse sucked air like a landed fish, the veins on his neck popping. He spun the dial.

Kora chuckled. "We've been your little slave girls for the past couple years, Dicky. Now we're gonna see how you like it, you disgusting freak. You and that tiny little prick of yours that needs drugs to keep it propped up. One of the girls says you make clucking sounds when you fuck, sounding like a sick chicken."

Leon laughed as best he could. "He don't get this safe open pretty quick, he's looking to become Tricky Dickless."

Rouse's hands were shaking violently. Everything he did with the combination, the wheel, had to be repeated.

Finally, a gun against the back of his head, he got himself under control and opened the wall safe.

"Holy shit," Kora exclaimed.

There were three shelves piled with stacks of money. Open boxes that appeared to have stocks and bonds. They had Rouse bring out those and other boxes that contained gold, jewelry, and various bonds and certificates of deposit.

"The mother lode," Kora said, opening a box and pulling out a handful of jewelry.

Leon looked at Rouse's cell when it buzzed. "That's your boss," Leon said, handing him the phone. "Tell him everything's cool. Tell him we're on our way down with Daisy. And talk normal. I even think there's a hint of a signal, you're dead."

Rouse did as he was told, and then Leon took the phone from him, adding, "We're on our way, boss."

He hung up.

Kora said, "I stay with Tricky Dick here. Find out some things, like where else he's got secrets hidden. And he can help me pack some money and stuff. I don't want to hang around. You go deal with Thorp."

Motioning to Sydney and Marco, Leon said, "Let's go down and see old sport, get him on the program."

This can't go well, Sydney thought as they left Kora and Rouse in the office and headed back into the hall.

Sydney was in the lead, followed by Marco and then the killer. She was edgy. Leon was unpredictable, and how much power Kora had over him—and how long it would last—was the question. Plus the guy was on some powerful drugs and drinking, by the smell of him.

She saw no good end with Thorp once he realized what was going on. Or maybe Leon and Kora had another game up their sleeve. Maybe an ultimate betrayal was still coming.

They were ushered through the great room, then down another hall filled with paintings, mostly of what looked like French and Italian scenes. Then they walked into a back room that led to the tunnel.

She heard Marco say from behind her, "I'm thinking, after this, you get bored down the road, we might work together again. This is turning out to be interesting."

Sydney liked how Marco was playing this guy, trying to get the guy thinking ahead. But that might not mean anything in the end. Outthinking a sociopath was impossible.

"The world is ripe for the taking," Leon said.

Based on logic and Sydney's experience, either the client was going to be killed, or they were.

They reached the tunnel. Ogden Thorp waited, standing by the cage door.

They passed under the faux torchlights on the medieval stone walls.

"What took you so—" He stopped and appeared to be trying to make sense of what he was seeing.

"I got a present for you," Leon said. "They aren't dead. I was just fooling you. Setting you up for the big shockaroo. It's something I wanted to surprise you with."

Sydney's gut tightened. Maybe he was always, in the end, going to hand them over to Thorp and his lion.

"What the hell?" Thorp said, confused, looking a little drunk and definitely shocked.

"Alive and well," Leon said.

Thorp didn't seem to know how to react but chose to be positive. He smiled. "I'll be damned. You're just full of surprises."

"Life's all about surprises," Leon said.

Thorp said, "Sydney Jesup, I thought you were dancing at the bottom of the lake. But I'm actually glad to see you. I have someone I want you to meet."

"I'm sure you do," Sydney said, looking at the big old lion sitting on the slab across the pool, under a dim ceiling light, his yellowish eyes watching them, a massive wreath of fur exploding around his neck. Behind him, a cave, more rocks.

She figured the moment of truth had arrived. But she had no idea which way it was going.

61

"Easy, boy," she heard Leon say to Marco, who was no doubt poised to make some kind of desperate move.

"Marco, we're good," Sydney said. "Right, Leon?"

"That's right," Leon said in that muted drone of his.

They had gone from trusting Kora and getting betrayed to now hoping the killer was under Kora's control and would follow the plan.

Sydney thought Thorp looked like some mad fool pacing around in his white suit with his English racing cap. He pushed open the iron cage door, saying, "George has been waiting, haven't you, old sport? Didn't get fed yet today."

He turned to Leon. "Where's Daisy and Rouse? They don't want to miss the big show."

"We made a mess," Leon said. "They're cleaning it up. Maybe we'll go up, help them."

Thorp said, "I got something here I want to show you." He pulled a small Derringer from his pocket. "Jesup, come on over here." He pointed the small gun at her. "You and me need to conclude our business."

Thorp said to Leon, "This is the woman who busted your face and nearly destroyed the greatest project in the history of Lake Tahoe." Then he turned back to Sydney. "You've been a royal pain in the ass. I've dreamed about this moment. You and your boyfriend here like to fight, well, you're gonna have a real fight on your hands."

"First we need to talk about some things," Leon said.

"Later," Thorp said, almost yelling. "I'm gonna hire you permanent. You did one hell of a job and you're going to get a very big reward. A payday you'll love."

Thorp motioned to Sydney with the Derringer. "George has been dying to make your acquaintance, right George?" he said, glancing back at the old lion.

"Damn, that's a pretty gun," Leon said. "Never seen one like that."

"A piece of history," Thorp said with drunken pride. "Two guns were made and one of them John Wilkes Booth used to kill Lincoln. This is the brother to it. A real piece of history."

"You're bullshitting," Leon said.

"I certainly am not. This is the real thing."

"Let me see that," Leon said. "I love the history of guns. Marco, move over there along the wall under the light."

Marco went to the wall under one of the torchlights. Sydney exchanged looks with him. He was tight, coiled. Leon was well aware of his demeanor and didn't want him close.

Leon moved Sydney ahead of him and then reached out for the gun. Thorp didn't look like he wanted to put his prize in Leon's hands, but he surrendered it, given Leon had a much bigger weapon in his hand.

Leon, a gun in each hand, brought the Derringer up where he could get a good look in the dim light. "Boy, that is a beauty. You have this tested or something? Make sure it wasn't some fake replica?"

"Everything was checked out," Thorp said. "I'd like to give it to you, but I can't do that."

"I love old guns," Leon said. "But nothing in my collection matches the history of this baby. Consider it a gift for a job well done."

"We'll see about that later," Thorp said. "First things first." He made a sudden move, grabbing Sydney by one arm and her hair. He jerked her against the door and then into the cage with such violence she was thrown off balance as he yelled, "George, got something for you."

It happened so fast, Sydney found herself falling backwards toward the pond, but she twisted around, reversing the momentum. Thorp lost his balance when she twisted. He started falling and had to let go of her. Sydney jumped back.

Thorp tripped, struggled to get his footing, and kept staggering back toward the pond with a cartoon-like struggle to regain his footing. His attempts failed and he went down on his butt at the edge of the water.

The old lion—roused by all the commotion, his primal instincts kicking in—suddenly rose and came across the small pond in a single bound. The big old cat hit Thorp with the impact of a three-hundred-pound linebacker coming full speed.

Thorp never had a chance. His racing cap flew all the way back to the door. The old lion grabbed him around his head and neck and began to drag him away.

At first it looked like Leon was going in to help him, but instead, he went in for the racing cap, never, as he moved, taking his eyes off Marco or her.

"Back out," he said.

She retreated to the tunnel corridor.

Leon came out with the cap and shut the cage door behind him.

The big cat dragged Thorp across the concrete floor around the pond and disappeared with his catch into his den. At first, Thorp's legs had kicked and his arms flailed, but by the time he was dragged around the pond, he stopped all resistance.

One shoe had come off. He had on white socks that looked to be held up by garters. He never even got out a scream. The big cat had knocked the wind out of him, then dragged him by the head. A wing-tipped shoe floated in the pond.

"You see how fast that bastard came across that water?" Leon said, all excited. He put the racing cap on, like a bowl atop the face mask. "How do I look?"

"Smashing," Sydney said. "You look like you were born to drive a Jaguar convertible across the English countryside."

Leon laughed. He kept the cap on and then backed off and told Marco to secure the iron cage door. The sound of metal on metal echoed down the tunnel like a cannon shot.

To Marco, Leon said, "You did good not making a move. I'd hate to have had to shoot you."

"We're gonna work together," Marco said. "Never entered my mind to mess things up. Far as I'm concerned, we're partners."

Leon stared at Marco for a moment. Then he turned to Sydney, "If someone put this scene on the Internet, it'd get a billion damn hits."

Leon chuckled. The mask and the English cap gave him a comedic and completely insane look. He then said, "Well, let's go get paid for our hard work. Been one hell of a night. Can't remember when I've had so much fun." He held up the Derringer. "I'd of loved to know how many people back in the day took a bullet from these little babies."

"There was only one that really counted," Sydney said.

"I guess you're right about that," Leon said. "Too bad I can't use this on some future project. Drive the CI guys crazy. But I'd have to give the gun up, and I have a better use for it."

Sydney and Marco exchanged looks. *This isn't over*, Sydney thought. *This guy is orbiting a planet we've never visited.*

As they started to leave, Sydney glanced back at the cage. She had no sympathy for Thorp. He'd gotten what he deserved.

62

When they retraced their steps and returned to the office, Kora and Rouse were talking about something intense. Kora played with her pistol on the desk, the big briefcases from the vault in front of her. Rouse sat in the chair, looking very frightened.

Kora turned as they walked in, a strange, almost ecstatic look on her face. She said, "We watched on the monitor. That lion...Jesus, that was the coolest thing ever."

"You liked that?" Sydney asked, thinking this girl was really, truly sociopathic material.

"Loved it," Kora said. "That video is going with me. I want to have it for whenever I'm depressed. I can watch that bastard meet George over and over. Me and Dicky, here, had a ringside seat."

Leon smiled and said, "I got a little present for you, sweet pea. The twin brother Derringer to the one that killed Lincoln."

He handed her the gun.

"You lie. No way this is the real thing," Kora said, looking the gun over.

"It is. Thorp told us all about it."

She turned to Rouse. "Is that the truth?" Rouse nodded that it was.

"How awesomely cool as shit is this?" Kora said, beaming as she checked the small weapon out. "Damn. Thanks, babe. This is, like, the coolest present ever. It's so pretty. It's like jewelry."

"And it's yours," Leon said, beaming back at her. It was like he was giving the girl of his dreams an engagement ring to beat all engagement rings. "Careful, it's loaded."

"No way."

"For sure."

She pointed it at Rouse and for a moment, Sydney thought she was going to shoot the lawyer, who looked like he also expected a bullet in the face.

"We need him," Sydney cautioned. "He's going to be the only one who can close down the party, make the death of Thorp an accident that'll be discovered long after you guys are gone."

She watched as Kora backed off, glad she was smart enough to know they needed Rouse if all of them didn't want to end up on the run from every law enforcement agency in the country.

"What's the take?" Leon asked.

Kora turned to him. "Rouse says it's about sixteen mil. Couple more in the jewelry and gold and bonds. All in nice cases. Like he was gonna be ready to run to the Caymans if it came to that. Which makes it easy for us." She held up some of the jewelry from one of the four matching briefcases that were out on the big teak desk.

"Of course," Leon said, waving his weapon at Marco, Sydney, and Rouse, "I could just kill all three of them and stage it like they killed each other."

"No, sweetness," Kora said. "We have a bargain and we're going to keep it. And it's important that this end is in good hands. Nobody's going to believe that if I just up and vanish with the mystery man. Sydney will cover us. I know what she wants, and that makes us safe. I have no interest in becoming the most hunted couple since Bonnie and Clyde. Look how that turned out."

"You're right."

"Besides, don't you and Marco want to work together sometime in the future? You make a great team. Oh, and I want to thank Tricky Dick here. He was nice enough to sign his car over to me." She waved the pink slip. "He's such a sweetheart when you get to know him."

Sydney said, "Listen to your lady. She's smart. Rouse will tell the world when they find Thorp's body that the fool went in to have a drunken conversation with George and George didn't like what he had to say."

Leon chuckled. "Alright, then, let's get on out of here. We have a world waiting for us."

Kora told him to take the briefcases to the car. When he came back, it was time to leave. Already, dawn threatened. The party next door was coming to its final moments. The poker game would soon end.

"Be careful driving with all that money in the trunk," Sydney said. "And watch out for scorpions."

"I will," Kora assured her, smiling back at her like they were old chums.

The cute couple, Daisy and the masked man, left on whatever honeymoon awaited.

Moments later, Sydney, Rouse, and Marco watched on the monitor as a black Mercedes exited the garage and headed down the feeder road to Lakeshore Boulevard. Then Marco got a suitcase from Rouse's bedroom and they spent an hour filling it with tapes, pictures, hard drives, and notebooks.

Sydney turned to Rouse. She explained to him how it was going to work.

Marco left with the suitcase.

"He'll be back in an hour or so, when the suitcase is secure," she explained. "Then you're going to go over and end this party with apologies. You don't know where Daisy and Thorp disappeared to. Everyone will smile knowingly and that will be that. You make a mistake, decide to do something stupid, everything we have on you will go public very fast. It will get ugly for you."

He stared at her.

"When things settle, after Thorp's tragic accident is discovered, you'll cancel the deals you made, have a nice big funeral, and then you'll do exactly what George Whittell did: Turn into Lake Tahoe's greatest defender. No Taj Mahals, no Vegas North. One day, you'll win awards."

Rouse said, "You aren't going to go to the FBI or any authority?"

"No. By the way, I hear you make a mean Hangtown fry just like they used to do in the old days. Really nasty food. Oysters, eggs, bacon. I think I'd like to try it. You have the ingredients?"

He nodded.

Sydney said, "Good. Go shut the party down. Then, when Marco comes back, we'll have a nice brunch, talk some more about the future."

63

Leon felt strange as they tore down the highway, Kora driving. He'd taken more pills, but things weren't right in his head and he wanted to get back to what he'd been feeling.

He thought about the dead client, the others, the whole deal that had taken place in Tahoe.

Suddenly, shockingly, he turned against everything that had happened. *I hate her,* Leon thought, glancing at Kora, at the woman he now thought had destroyed him.

He tried to fight the feelings. The change came over him with the force of a tsunami. It washed him away from the emotions he'd been feeling and brought him back to himself. The self he'd constructed so carefully over the years.

I have to kill the bitch.

It was a devastating notion. It happened so fast, this negative reversal of feelings, this conflict in his soul. It began within an hour of Tahoe, the sun coming up, the heat rising, his head swelling again. He took off the mask.

He felt confused. He grew angry and couldn't understand it. Beautiful woman, millions, freedom. What was wrong?

As the distance away from Tahoe grew, the desert rolled under them mile after mile, hour after hour, and things began to change in the deepest regions of Leon's brain. The change in topography, in circumstance, seemed to be having a profound effect upon him. For a short time, the strange high that had driven him over the past days looked like it would return. But then it began to dissipate. Like a man coming off an excess of partying.

His face resumed aching. His mindset deteriorated. The binge melted away in the hot sun, leaving behind growing distress.

It became conscious to him—the feeling, the angst—first in Virginia City. His face began to throb again while he was waiting outside a store for Kora to buy whatever crap she was shopping for.

The feeling of being out of sorts—disconnected from his real self, his authenticity—continued to build from there as they ate up the long empty roads across the desolate Nevada desert toward Vegas. He didn't want to go anywhere near Vegas, but Kora had insisted.

He glanced frequently at Kora as she drove. She appeared to be in a great mood, and that only irritated and bothered him all the more.

Leon realized with a poignant shock that everything that had happened to him since arriving in Tahoe was crazy. It simply couldn't go on. He had lost himself. He was living in violation of all his principles, of his personal code. As if he'd been led by this whore and thief down a terribly wrong path.

The party of parties was truly over. What had happened in Tahoe, the whole insanity of it, now hit him full force.

He took more OxyContin, thinking maybe he'd get his good feelings back. He didn't. Having a couple drinks at dinner didn't either. The truth was right there, and it was a truth he couldn't ignore. He had sinned against himself in a bad way. And now he had to purge himself of this whole sordid affair, reclaim his truth. And to do that, the first thing was to get rid of this crazy, wild child of a hooker he'd gotten himself involved with. Love had ruined him.

Leon lamented his fall with sickening awareness of how he'd been deceived by evil. He knew he was lost. Between Thorp and this hooker and those two back there, he'd completely relinquished his sense of self. He'd caved to pleasure, to consumption, to the rot of civilization. Like that goddamn wolf-dog of Cillo's…you're either one, or you're the other.

That was Leon's problem. He felt like a man out of control. The feeling grew stronger and stronger until he couldn't stand it. He had to kill her and go back and fix things. Maybe it all was because of the blows to his head.

Go back, he ordered himself. *Go back and kill the other three.* He didn't care about the money. Being rich. Living on some damn beach. He wanted his dignity back. He was a hunter. Predation was his calling.

Get rid of the bitch now, he thought. Like a rattlesnake shedding its skin, he had to shed her. No way in hell he could get his life back with this bitch telling him what to do every damn minute like he was her fucking lapdog. He couldn't believe what he'd become in so short a period of time. From the minute he'd looked at her nude shots, he'd simply lost his mind.

Finally, as evening approached and they crested the mountain, in the distance, the lights of Vegas came into view. He asked her to pull off the road.

"You just took a leak twenty minutes ago," she said.

"Pull off there. I need to stretch, and I want to remember this. Vegas out there, what's behind us, and what we have together. Let's stand out there for a minute on the top of this mountain and fix it in our memories. This is special."

Leon, feeling at the end of it now, full of dark fury, took out the CD she'd been playing that Rouse had left in the slot: *From the Rockies to the Redwoods*. He was sick to death of it. Sick of it and this new thing, this new connection.

She parked and got out.

This is the place, Leon thought. No traffic coming into Vegas from this way on a Sunday night. Throw her body down into the canyon. Be years before anyone would stumble on the bleached bones. If ever.

When he got out of the car, Kora was already up on the overhang waiting. She said, "It is a cool view. Like being on some weird planet. Like we landed in a spaceship and that's the galactic empire's capital city or something. Come here, Leon."

A man like me cannot have a partner, for there are not partners adequate, none that understand.

He was a loner for a reason. He was a professional, not some lapdog for a hooker who had him wait on her while she went on a fucking shopping spree, buying crappy Indian jewelry. Fuck all that.

Still yapping away, she continued. "Come here, Leon. Stand with me. Our moment of my liberation."

It'll be your liberation, alright. And mine.

She turned, saying, "It's really spectacular. Come here, sweet love. What are you doing?"

He made his way toward her, the whore yammering away. The woman just could not shut the fuck up.

She stood in the brilliant effusive glow of the great neon metropolis, sin city, the drugged desert flower. A slut like all the rest of them. Only this one was the greatest threat he'd ever faced. She would destroy him. He had no defenses against the sexual force that she possessed.

This was just wrong and it was all her fault. From the moment he'd seen her pictures and hung around to meet her, it went wrong.

Leon the Professional walked up to Kora North, and as he did so, his hand slipped under his shirt, his fingers wrapped around the butt of his weapon as he considered where to put the first bullet. He had to blow that beautiful face away. Wipe it out. Wipe out every corrupting thing about her.

This is how it has to be, Leon told himself.

He said, "Great view, sweets."

As he began to pull the automatic from behind his leg, Kora smiled at him. Such a beautiful, evil face.

Then, as he was raising his weapon to end the life of this danger, this evil destroyer, he saw something in her hand.

Small.

He had forgotten.

Next thing, he heard a bang and saw a flash. A flash that was partially obscured by the bright glow of the midnight sun that was Vegas behind her.

The bullet from the Derringer slammed into his chest with shocking force. And he thought with bewilderment, *The bitch shot me with my present!*

The icy smile stayed on her face, and the words that came out of her mouth slapped him as he sank slowly, stunned, to his knees, his weapon slipping from his fingers.

Kora said, "You nasty little scorpion. You were going to shoot the one you love, you psycho piece of trash."

He rolled over. He felt her take his wallet and keys. The bitch was robbing him!

She pushed him over the edge of the hill. And, as he toppled over, he heard her say, with a great sense of release, of vindictive triumphant, "Bye, dude. Thanks for this beautiful gun. I love it. You like to quote movies, big shot, well I got one from *The Godfather* for you. Like Michael Corleone said, 'If anything in this life is certain, if history has taught us anything, it is that you can kill anyone.'"

***

Kora North stood holding the Derringer and waiting to see how she would react to having just killed her psychopath partner. She remembered that night when he was unconscious and she'd held the gun to his head and wondered. Now she knew.

What she felt was neither joy nor some form of misery. It was just a kind of curiosity and a little amazement at how easy life could be snuffed out when bringing it into being was such a labor. Just as Booth had killed Lincoln.

She thought of how Leon came into this world and how he'd just left. Nine months after getting screwed by some jerk, a woman had carried this cold-blooded bastard in her womb. Then had to let him suck the milk from her breasts. Had to clean his dirty-diapered ass. And what did she give to the world? A killer.

Wow, Kora thought. *How crazy is this life and death thing?*

Kora walked back to the car, put her CD back on, turned it up high, and was about to drive off to Vegas. But there was something she had to do, and it took her a moment before she realized what it was. One thing Kora's alcoholic mother had taught her, maybe the only thing, was the idea of gratitude. People who take things for granted, who don't show gratitude when you do something for them, are the worst. Always be grateful.

That damn cop had come through for her. She owed Sydney Jesup and that cute badass boyfriend of hers.

She took out her cell phone and texted a message. Then she headed off, hammering down the twisting black ribbon road in her beautiful Mercedes, trunk full of millions, the future looking very bright ahead.

Life, she thought, *is a damn funny thing the way it works out sometimes.* All the shit she'd taken. Men using her like some jackoff toy since she was eight. Making her hate herself.

"I'm rich," she yelled out at the gods of night, holding up the arm with a new diamond bracelet on it, triumphant. "I'm free, rich, and now it's my turn!" Tears of joy came to her eyes.

A smile plastered on her face, she raced on into the fierce, icy effulgence that was the beginning of her new life, her much deserved new life—her first stop, Vegas…

64

When the text message from Kora North came late Sunday evening, Marco and Sydney were in the Shelby cruising around the lake.

The Tahoe basin was as balmy and beautiful under the full moon as any place on the planet.

The guests were all but gone from Thorp's, and the cleanup crews were being supervised by Rouse. He'd made the payout to the poker winners. The death of Thorp wouldn't be reported until Monday, when the body would be discovered.

Sydney stared at the text message, then held the phone over to Marco. "You believe this?"

Scorpion drowned. I swim alone...thanks.

He shifted gears, slowed, and glanced at the smartphone. "Sounds like a short honeymoon."

Sydney shook her head and emitted a dry chuckle, saying, "I thought they'd at least get a day or two. Talk about a nasty honeymoon."

"You think she planned on killing him all along?"

"I don't know."

They rode in silence.

Later that night, they went out on the lake in the Shaws' boat and skinny-dipped under a full moon. They were as quiet as secret Washo Indian lovers a thousand or so years ago on a night just like this.

***

At that moment, four hundred fifty miles to the south in a ravine, Henry Craven Lee, aka Leon, known to himself and a few others— some of them dead—as the Urbanwolf, rolled again. This time, he rolled about halfway down the hill before a piece of flat ground and some bushes stopped him just above the floor of the narrow desert canyon. The bullet had passed through his jacket into his right chest. He didn't know how deep.

He was still amazed that she'd done what she had. But he appreciated it on some level. She was a serious bitch, no doubt.

Then he began to hear the sounds of night in the desert. Small sounds of creatures that come out of their holes, from under their rocks. Predators of the night.

And Leon, a man who'd often wondered how and where and when he'd die, never thought it would be in a place like this.

So he decided he couldn't die here. No way he wanted to be food for the scavengers. He grabbed a handful of dirt and bush and pulled. No. Not here. Not now.

He envisioned the big birds would come and land and squawk and peck his flesh, his eyeballs, clean his bones. Nature being nature.

That bitch. And if he died at the hands of that woman, shot with the second gun to the one that had killed Lincoln, he'd be famous forever if the world knew. But the world wouldn't know. And that aggravated him all the more.

There were plenty of ways the Urbanwolf could die, but as a dog kicked off a hill, that couldn't be. Anger inspired him to crawl, to fight.

Had he the capacity to laugh at his misfortune, and his choice of women, he would have, but it hurt too much and he needed every bit of energy he could muster just to move a few feet at a time...

About the Author

Richter Watkins is the bestselling author of ten crime thrillers including The Murder Option and The Murder Option 2. When not writing, you can find Richter battling politics from his deckchair.

Contact:
http://www.richterwatkins.com/

Other Books By Richter Watkins:

The Murder Option

The Murder Option 2

Lethal Redemption

Betting On Death

Operation Chaos

As Terry Watkins:

The Big Burn

Stacked Deck

Made in the USA
San Bernardino, CA
21 March 2014